The Glow of Death

She shut the door, leaving the morgue with only the dim gray light from the windows . . .

A flat circle of brilliant blue light burst in her palm, then spread to the walls in a shimmering plate. Mother Japh lowered her hand, the plate following, trailing down Liam's chest, then past her own face and down, until it rested a foot or so above the tables.

"What—" he began, and then saw the breath of the first two corpses in the room.

Single flames burned above each corpse's mouth, tiny whirls of fire just by the mouth, straighter jets farther up.

"Their souls," the ghost witch said, and her voice was hushed, almost reverent. "Till they're called— buried, or burned, or fetched by whatever'll take them to the Gray Lands—their souls burn above their mouths. But now turn about again."

He did, and saw immediately that there was no flame above the mouth of the third corpse.

"No flame—no soul. Which is as saying there's a ghost roaming Southwark now."

WIZARD'S HEIR

The spellbinding new adventure from the author of Fanuilh . . .

DANIEL HOOD

Ace Books by Daniel Hood

FANUILH
WIZARD'S HEIR

WIZARD'S HEIR

DANIEL HOOD

ACE BOOKS, NEW YORK

This book is an Ace original edition,
and has never been previously published.

WIZARD'S HEIR

An Ace Book / published by arrangement with
the author

PRINTING HISTORY
Ace edition / August 1995

ISBN: 0-441-00231-5

ACE®
Ace Books are published by The Berkley Publishing Group,
200 Madison Avenue, New York, NY 10016.
ACE and the "A" design are trademarks
belonging to Charter Communications, Inc.

PRINTED IN THE UNITED STATES OF AMERICA

10 9 8 7 6 5 4 3 2 1

CHAPTER 1

THE GODDESS BELLONA had only recently sprung upon Taralon, her worship at first heralded only in the mountain city of Caernarvon, a place well suited to her grim pursuit of the martial arts. But there were wealthy men in Caernarvon, and when they decided to share their goddess with the rest of the kingdom, they spent the money necessary to do it in style.

From the outside, the temple they had purchased in Southwark was undistinguished, a square block of plain masonry at the end of Temple Street, wedged closely between the crenellated home of the old and well-established worship of Strife and the appropriately dark one of Laomedon. The three formed a cul-de-sac, graced by a simple fountain, and the only thing Bellona's temple added to the scene was a modest cupola and a row of small, circular windows.

The inside was different. The decoration of the newly dedicated temple—it had once housed a sect long dispersed, whose name and god few remembered—belied its drab exterior, and revealed the wealth of the goddess's followers. There was no statue of the goddess herself, but there were expensive suits of armor and stands of weapons in the niches between the half-columns that lined the walls. Light from the windows in the cupola glanced off hauberks rendered useless by elaborate gold scrolling, swords encrusted with gems and sheaths of rare silk bound with silver wire.

1

Liam Rhenford, standing in a dark corner by the door, his breath smoking in the cold air, wondered why they had not built an entirely new temple instead of renovating an abandoned one, then shrugged the question away. *Temple Street's crowded as it is,* he thought, and shifted his gaze from the expensive arms to the middle of the large chamber, to the empty fire pit. He pointed discreetly at it and whispered to the man beside him.

"No fire?"

"No burnt offerings for Bellona," his companion, the Aedile Coeccias, answered. "Only that straight from smoking execution, if you take me."

Liam refrained from even smiling. It was all well for Coeccias to make puns—he was the Aedile, and had been invited to view the temple because of his position as the Duke's representative in Southwark—but Liam was only a guest, brought along at his friend's request. He did not want to appear disrespectful, though there were only two acolytes in the temple. They stood to either side of the altar, tall young men in chain mail suitable to battle service, broadbladed spears grounded firmly at their sides. They had not moved since Liam and Coeccias entered the temple.

The altar itself was rather dull, a simple block of stone fit with a shallow bowl and blood gutters for sacrifices. The real heart of Bellona's temple lay behind it, on a shelf cut into the stone of the wall: a war chest of dark oak, bound in iron. It was a plain piece of furniture, as functional as the altar or the mail worn by the acolytes, but rumor in Southwark held that it contained a greater treasury than all the city's temples put together.

Liam studied it for a moment, imagining the wealth supposedly inside. Rumor had elaborated on itself, and mentioned not just gold and jewels, but unsigned notes-of-hand on the great Lowestoft mines in Caernarvon. He thought of the parchment, foot-wide squares representing the labor that dug treasure from the heart of distant mountains.

A passing ray of light played on the surface of the chest but could draw no glimmer; the oak was old, the iron blackened. The light moved on a little, up and behind the chest, and reflected off a chain bolted to the wall. Liam followed the chain up to a staple near the base of the cupola, then at an angle to the center of the cupola, where it slid through another staple and down to a cage.

It was plain, like the chest, the bars set close together, but Liam's eyes were keen enough to make out the figure inside, the lion's body, the broad wings, the eagle's head.

Gods, it's a gryphon! Where did they get a gryphon?

The creature stirred, setting the barred perch swinging. The chain clanked dully. The faint sound of its wings rustling reached the ground, and Liam frowned. He pitied the beast; confined as it was, it could not even stretch its wings. He had seen a gryphon once, free in the air in the far north, and he could still remember the excitement and beauty of it. The gryphon in the cage looked gray in the poor light, like a figure cast in lead. He shook his head, and decided he had looked enough.

"I'll be outside," he whispered to Coeccias, and made to leave.

"Attend a moment," the Aedile whispered back, catching his arm. He gave Liam a stern glance. "We'd do well to show our respects. And I needs must thank that Alastor." He was referring to the priest who had welcomed them to the temple and, after a very brief description of Bellona, had left them alone to inspect the building. Liam was not sure if their being unsupervised was a mark of indifference on Alastor's part, or a sign of tact. He could not tell; he had never understood priests very well.

Liam nodded briefly, and along with Coeccias bent his knee toward the altar. He did not bow his head, though, as the other man did, letting his eyes wander over the temple again, resting at last on the gryphon's cage. After a few long moments, it began to seem as if the Aedile would never break the obeisance.

When Coeccias finally rose, Liam jumped to his feet and went out the large wooden doors, leaving his friend to find and thank the priest for the visit.

It was cold in the cul-de-sac at the end of Temple Street, and stray winds, baffled by the closeness of the buildings, battered themselves back and forth across the square. Liam paused on the steps to pull his cloak close around him.

There was no one in the street, though he could hear voices from Strife's establishment. Someone was shouting orders in the courtyard that lay between the outer wall and the temple proper, which sat like a castle keep at the rear of the compound.

The building to the left was silent, a silence Liam imagined was ominous. Those black walls hid the rites of Laomedon, whose special domain was death and the Gray Lands. Rumor—an older rumor than the one about the wealth of Bellona—said that there was a book inside each of Laomedon's shrines, in which was written the exact time of every man's death. Liam shuddered; though he prayed occasionally, he would never be able to reverence the gods of Taralon the way his friend did—and he was conscious that his seeming lack of respect might have annoyed the Aedile.

When Coeccias came out onto the steps, Liam tore his eyes away from the dark temple and gestured vaguely.

''It'll snow soon,'' he said. The sky was a uniform gray from horizon to horizon.

''Truth,'' Coeccias said. Frowning now, he asked, ''Have you no conceptions of what's proper, Rhenford?''

Stopped on the shallow steps of the new temple, they made a strange pair: Liam tall and thin, clean shaven, his blond hair cropped close, a long weatherproof cloak hanging to his ankles, and the Aedile shorter, much broader in muscle and bulk, for once wearing a clean jacket of quilted gray wool.

Liam gulped, a little surprised at his friend's vehemence, and the strange, appraising look the shorter man was directing at him.

"Are you so careless of your gods in the Midlands, then? As to leave to a temple with no obeisance?"

"I'm sorry," Liam apologized, "I meant no disrespect."

"Here I'm invited to view the temple," Coeccias went on, barely mollified, "invited ere it's even been consecrated, and I cart y'along, as a thing of interest to a scholar, and you want to part without even a glance at the altar!"

"I'm sorry," Liam repeated, meaning it. "I saw the altar. I was impressed. I just . . ."

He could not really explain what he had been thinking. He had long been separated from the gods of his youth in the Midlands, which were mostly similar to those of Southwark. In long travels he had encountered a thousand strange gods, with stranger rites, and had become insensitive to what they meant to those who believed. But he could not say that to the Aedile. There was no way to explain that, to him, one god was much the same as another.

"It was the gryphon," he said finally, by way of a lame excuse. "It shouldn't be caged like that."

Coeccias grunted and offered a wry smile. "It likes you not, eh? Sacrifice? Do Midlanders have no custom of it?"

"No," Liam said slowly, recalling the occasional deer offered to the Black Hunter, or farm animals given up to the Harvest Queen. "No, they do—but nothing like that. Gryphons are . . . special. Not like a steer or a cock. And they shouldn't be caged like that. They can fly, you know. Their wings work."

Starting down the steps, the Aedile barked a laugh. "Truth, Rhenford, y'are passing soft. What is it if their wings work? All the better for them to wing their way to the Gray Lands, and bring message to the gods.''

They strode across the square, Liam shaking his head but making no comment. The fountain was dry, and the trapped wind scoured its stone with a whispering sound. Temple Street was almost deserted as they walked west; one or two acolytes sweeping steps and porticos, and a number of beggars. It was not Godsday and, with winter upon the city, there were no sailors in search of blessings.

Liam was silent until they passed the temple of Uris, at which time he ventured a comment on the plainness of Bellona's treasury.

"Aye," Coeccias said, "a right old war chest. But as I told you, rumor vouchsafes a high stack of drafts, direct to the Lowestoft mines. Old Bothmer Lowestoft is high with the new goddess, they say, a passionate convert.''

"That'll make trouble with the others—a new banker in town. And with drafts on the mine, it won't matter that Bellona hasn't many temples." Ordinary drafts could only be redeemed at a temple of the same god that had originated it, while one from Lowestoft would be honored anywhere in Taralon, or even in the Freeports. The wealth of the Caernarvon mining family was legendary.

Stroking his beard, Coeccias considered this. "That's the right of it. You've nosed it out, Rhenford. It'll make for fierceness in the spring, when the merchants are drawing funds." He chuckled to himself, amused in advance at the competition among temples for the lending business. "Trust you t'ignore the proper ceremonies, but strike the heart of a different matter.''

"I didn't mean to ignore it," Liam protested again, but the Aedile was not listening.

"We'll have snow this night," he said, cocking his head and squinting one eye at the sky. Then he recalled something, and put a hand on Liam's arm, stopping him in the street. "Faith, I forgot! Did see the messenger last night?"

"Messenger?" Over the past few months of living among southerners, Liam had grown more or less used to their dialect, but he missed this word.

"The messenger," Coeccias repeated, "the bearded star!"

"A comet?"

"Aye, a comet! Did see it?"

"No," Liam admitted, "I didn't. When was it?"

Coeccias's face grew childish with wonder, an expression Liam found funny. "Last night, an hour, perhaps two, after dusk. It blazed out of the north, like a rule across the city to the sea. Did you truly not see it?"

"No. I was inside at the time."

For a moment the Aedile frowned, realizing that most people would have been indoors at that hour. "I was posting the Guard, and saw't with these very eyes, like a torch across the sky. I swear, Rhenford, such a thing I've never seen!" He looked again at the sky, as if the trace of the comet still lingered behind the clouds. Liam looked as well, smiling lightly. He had never seen his friend so excited.

"I wonder what news it brings," he said.

"As for that," Coeccias said, walking on again, "for myself I have no faith in that. We term it a messenger, but sure the gods have better ways of revealing their news to us. Why else have temples and all the omen-readers and foretellers?"

"Still," Liam persisted, "what if it did mean something?"

"Pray it doesn't," Coeccias said, crossing his fingers. It was a gesture common in Southwark, and it had taken Liam a while to understand that it was what southerners used to ward off ill fortune. They used a different sign in the Midlands, where he had grown up. "I've no need of new things breeding in Southwark. With a new fane to welcome and the winter, I've enough to worry on. Winter's worst for me, I tell you, Rhenford. I'd rather the summer, even with all the tars ashore, kicking up demons in the wineshops. With the cold and the confinement, people are fractious, like to murder and such. There're three corses already this week cooling their heels for burial. No, it'd little like me to have a new wonder.''

They walked the rest of the way to Coeccias's house without speaking. Liam thought on his friend's position in Southwark, impressed anew by the range of responsibilities entrusted to the rough-seeming man. As the Aedile, he was like the captain of a ship, entrusted with the helm of the city—but he had little of the autocratic power normal at sea.

He worries over it, Liam thought, *like a mother hen*. And yet Southwark ran well, particularly when compared with any number of the larger cities Liam had seen.

The Aedile lived in a small house on the fringes of the Point, the rich section of the city. They stopped outside the door.

''Will you not come in? Burrus'll make a quick cup, hot, something to warm you.''

''No,'' Liam said, looking again at the sky. The clouds had darkened perceptibly. ''I think I'll ride out now, before the snow starts. It looks like it'll come sooner than we thought. Thank you, though.''

''No mention,'' Coeccias assured him. ''Burrus'd be happy to do't.''

''No, thanks. And thanks for taking me to the temple. I really meant no disrespect.''

The Aedile smiled. ''I know't, Rhenford. Y'are just stranger and stranger, the more I know you.''

They parted with a handshake, Coeccias going inside and Liam around to the back to fetch his horse.

•   •   •

He was glad to get out of the city, though it was colder. The wind howled straight off the sea, stinging his cheeks, tearing at his cloak like a clumsy thief. But the countryside, though gray and lifeless, was less oppressive than the narrow streets of Southwark. The cold seemed to leech the color from the buildings, and made the cobbles seem more like metal than stone; Diamond's hooves had rung on them like clashing swords. Beyond the city gates, at least, they thudded normally.

Giving the horse its head, Liam hunched himself against the wind and thought back to the look Coeccias had given him outside Bellona's temple. It had reminded him of something, though exactly what eluded him at the time. The answer came to him as the roan settled into an easy lope, and his body relaxed naturally to the rhythm.

The two men had met only a few months before, in connection with the murder of an acquaintance of Liam's, a wizard named Tarquin Tanaquil. Their friendship had grown out of the search for the murderer, but at first it had been only a partnership, and a not entirely willing one at that. Liam knew the details of the wizard's life, but Coeccias knew Southwark, and had the official standing to pursue the investigation.

The look reminded him of the one Coeccias had given him while they were searching Tarquin's house the day after Liam had discovered the body.

When he thought I'd done it, Liam realized. *He looked at me as if I were guilty of something.*

He brooded on that for a moment, and then shook his head with a laugh at himself.

As I was—guilty of disrespect to his goddess.

Though Bellona could hardly be considered Coeccias's goddess yet. It would be years, Liam knew, before she was fully accepted into the Taralonian pantheon. Years and miracles and a gradual accretion of followers.

There was more, though, of which Liam thought himself guilty. "Soft," the Aedile had called him. Liam was not against sacrifices in principle or in fact, and the blood did not make him squeamish. But he had not corrected the Aedile, as he had not corrected him on the day they looked at Tarquin's corpse, when the officer assumed he had never seen a dead body before. Coeccias entertained a number of misconceptions about him, Liam knew; some he had let flourish because they smoothed the course of the search for Tarquin's murderer, and others he had simply been powerless to stop.

And I never told him about Fanuilh, Liam thought, adding the wizard's familiar to the list. As his ride went on, the list grew longer, things about his past—battles fought, places visited, crimes considered and committed—and even some of the details of the investigation into Tarquin's death. Though he had found the killer, it had happened mostly through luck—but the Aedile believed him to be a kind of human bloodhound.

Diamond's easy lope shifted, and the movement jarred him from his musings. They were on the edge of a high cliff, the sea below them, and a small cove reached by a narrow path.

In the cove was his home, a small villa in the southern style, low and long with white plastered walls and a red tile roof. From the top of the cliff he could not see the front of the house, but light spilled from its many windows, warm and welcoming on the sand and the breakwater and the gray, choppy waves beyond.

He started Diamond down the path, watching the house the whole way, trusting the horse. It was still strange to him, to think of the house as his own. Often, on returning to the cove from the city, he expected to discover that it had vanished in his absence.

It never had, of course, but he was still unaccustomed to the idea of a permanent home.

Sharp wind picked up sand from the beach, and Diamond's hooves flung up more as Liam urged the roan to a quick sprint from the end of the path, and then reined it in sharp in front of the patio.

Smiling at the quick stop, he jumped briskly from the saddle and led the horse to its stall, a small shed to the side of the main house. It was cold inside, but while he unsaddled the roan and brushed it down, the shed grew warmer, magic responding to their presence.

With the horse fed and bedded down, Liam left the shed and walked around the house to the patio, and the front door, a glass-paned affair that slid along wooden grooves.

He paused there, rubbing his hands and blowing on them, and thought, *I'm home.*

He closed his eyes, concentrating on the thought, forming it into a block and pushing it out and away. Suddenly the thought vanished, and a similar block filled his head.

Welcome, master.

He formed another thought, molding it more carefully, crafting the interrogative.

How was that?

Excellent, came the return thought. *It was easy to pick up.*

"Good," Liam said aloud, "then I'm coming in, because it's freezing out here."

The door slid open easily, and a blast of warmth struck him. He stepped in quickly and shut the door, though he knew the magic of the house would keep out the wind, as well as any sand the wind might care to bring with it. His boots, though, were another matter, and he took them off by the door, so as not to track wet sand across the shining wooden floors.

Walking down the corridor to the right of the entrance

hall, Liam hung his cloak on a convenient peg, and reveled in the warmth of the enchanted house. He turned into the second door and smiled down at Fanuilh, his familiar.

The creature lay in a small basket on the floor, underneath the first of the three worktables that filled the room. It was a dragon, complete with leathery wings and a wedge-like snout filled with sharp teeth, but it was tiny, the size of a large cat, or a small dog.

"Like a puppy hound," Liam said aloud, and laughed when the dragon reared back its head.

I am not a puppy, it thought at him.

"You might as well be," Liam joked, indicating the basket, with its padding and blanket. Fanuilh's reaction pleased him; for a long time after their meeting, he had wondered if the dragon had felt any emotions at all. And while there was no emphasis in the thought that followed, there was no way he could avoid thinking of it as indignant:

I have eaten puppies, Fanuilh thought. *And you should practice with your mind.*

"I've told you before," Liam said, squatting down and scratching the dull black scales of the dragon's back, "I think that's silly. There's no point making the effort to think at you when you're right in the room." The dragon rolled over, exposing its dull gold belly for scratching, but its thought seemed reproving.

Master Tanaquil always did.

Before the murder, Fanuilh had been the wizard's familiar. It had joined its current master by a process Liam preferred not to remember—a painful bite and an even more painful splitting of his soul, so that part resided in the tiny form he was scratching.

"Well, I am not him. Get used to it, familiar mine. And while you're at it, think about when you're going to teach me how to keep you out of my head."

One of the drawbacks to having a familiar, Liam had

learned early on, was that it had access to his mind whenever it wanted. The dragon had promised to show him how to cut it off, but they had not yet reached that point in the lessons it was giving him.

You are not ready. You can barely project a thought to me from the top of the cliff. You must practice.

"But if you can read my thoughts, why do I have to project?"

To cut me off, you have to be able to project. And you have not yet seen the silver cord.

Liam frowned, but continued scratching. "You and your silver cord. I'm not sure it exists."

It does, the dragon insisted. *It is the ethereal bond that joins us. You must practice seeing that as well. Master Tanaquil could see it effortlessly.*

"Fanuilh," Liam said sharply, "understand this." He poked the dragon in the belly for emphasis. "Tarquin is not your master anymore. I am—and I am not a wizard. But you promised to teach me this, and you will."

It stared at him for a moment, no readable expression in its cat's pupils, and then ducked its head once, low, in submission.

Of course, master.

Liam nodded severely and stood up. "Now, I'm going to eat. Do you want anything?"

The dragon nodded, bobbing its head on its long neck.

"Something raw again?"

Its head moved rapidly up and down.

"Come along, then. Though you really should be hunting, I think. You're going to get fat, lounging around the house all the time."

I fly every day, the dragon thought, trotting after him, out of the workroom, across the entrance hall, and down another corridor to the kitchen. Its claws clicked on the wood as it walked, the noise shifting slightly as it crossed onto the flagstones of the kitchen.

"Fat," Liam repeated.

There was a large baker's oven set into one wall, and he stood by it with closed eyes, imagining the food he and Fanuilh wanted. From experiment, he knew there was no need to close his eyes. He found it easier, however, to envision a meal that way—and it seemed appropriate, in any case, like he was wishing and having the wish granted.

The oven was magical, a small part of the magic that pervaded the house. It was a strange sort of magic, one Liam had never considered before—a very practical wizardry that took into consideration small things such as keeping sand out of the front hall, or heating Diamond's shed, or preparing meals. It even kept the small privy by the bedroom clean and sweet smelling, an amenity that never ceased to delight Liam.

The house was his, but it had been built by Tarquin. The wizard had left it to him, in a will signed and registered only a few weeks before his death. When Liam thought of it—which he tried not to do—the legacy bothered him. He had known the wizard for only a few months before his death, and only as a passing acquaintance. It was an extravagant legacy, entirely out of proportion to their relationship. But then, Tarquin had been the perfect model of an eccentric old wizard, with his long white beard, his sigyl-sewn robes and impenetrable, often pompous conversation. Liam occasionally missed their meandering talks.

Opening the oven, he removed the two platters he had imagined, and set them on the table. He hooked a stool with his foot and drew it over, while Fanuilh crouched and sprang up, landing lightly in front of its meal.

This had become something of a ritual for the two of them over the past two months, eating dinner together, the dragon crouched over a platter of raw meat and Liam tucking into some dimly remembered dish from his long travels. The oven could produce whatever he could imagine, and he made a practice of calling forth things that had never been made in Taralon. Some, indeed, like the one he ate that night, could not have been made there, because the rice and vegetables in it grew only in lands far to the south.

Where is that from? the dragon inquired, at the same time as it delicately tore a chunk from its cut of meat, and snapped the piece down whole.

"Originally, I'm not sure. I first had it in a place called Mahdi."

A Freeporter colony?

"No, though the Freeporters trade there. It's about two months' sail west of Rushcutters' Bay."

Far.

"Hmm."

What was the new temple like?

Liam described it briefly. It was a polite fiction he had enforced on Fanuilh—the pretense that the dragon could not just search his memory at will.

The gryphon was gray?

"It looked that way, though the light was bad. The cupola is strange; the light angles down and leaves the dome shadowy. Gryphons aren't gray?"

No.

It had finished its meal and, after a quick stretch, clicked across the table to Liam's plate, watching him. When he was done, he pushed the plate away and smiled.

Are you finished?

"Yes. Go ahead."

This, too, was a ritual. The dragon wanted to try whatever he called up from the oven, and now it ducked its head into the stew of rice and vegetables.

"I'm going to read," Liam said, standing.

Do you wish to practice? Fanuilh asked, its head deep in rice.

"No, not tonight. Tomorrow."

Too wet, it commented, as he left the kitchen.

"You wouldn't like it dry," Liam called over his shoulder, with a laugh.

Too cooked.

He did not go to the library, despite his announced intention. He lingered in the entrance hall, looking out at the dark beach, and then entered a room on the same side of the house as the workroom.

Magic, sourceless light swelled up as he came in, revealing a series of waist-high wooden cases with glass tops. Assorted jewelry and wands lay inside, bedded in black velvet. There was a hanging on one wall with a stylized eagle on it, rising powerfully in flight over purple mountains; on another were a sword, a shield and a horn that would have fit in Bellona's temple, as well as a stringless lute hung by its neck.

Fanuilh called this the trophy room, and assured him that all the items were enchanted, though it had yet to explain exactly what each did. Liam had found that he was not particularly interested—they were all Tarquin's, as far as he was concerned.

In fact, most of the things in the house were Tarquin's. Liam owned few personal possessions and had left most of the wizard's things where they were. He had thrown away only the stock in the workroom, which included all things needed for casting magical spells: herbs and roots, countless glass jars and flasks containing stranger things (including the severed head of a dog and a human hand), for which he had no use. They were the "material components" of spells, Fanuilh had told him, and he could not cast spells. As it was, he had felt guilty about throwing them away, and had actually gone and apologized over Tarquin's grave.

He had buried the wizard himself, in the heavier soil where the beach met the cliff.

After a few minutes he grew bored of the trophy room. Until Fanuilh explained them, they were little more than curiosities.

The dragon emerged from the kitchen as he returned from the entrance hall.

I will fly tonight, if you do not mind, master.

"Go right ahead," Liam said, feeling magnanimous, and a little ridiculous. He could not imagine a reason to mind. "Though it's going to snow."

It will not bother me.

"Good. You need the exercise."

I am not fat.

"Yet."

Fanuilh made a little sniffing sound and slid the front door open with its paws. Liam closed the door when the dragon was out, and laughed to himself.

I really shouldn't make fun of him, he thought. *He doesn't understand my humor.*

Which, he realized as he went to the kitchen, was why it was fun to joke with the little dragon.

In the weeks when he first moved into the house, platters and plates and cups from the oven had accumulated around the kitchen, piling up until there was no room to eat. In despair, he had asked Fanuilh what to do with them, and the dragon nonchalantly suggested he put them back in the oven, which was what Tarquin had always done. Since then, dirty dishes had not been a problem—they simply disappeared in the oven between meals—but Liam had been strongly tempted to strangle his familiar for weeks afterward, whenever he cleared the table.

He thought of that as he put the empty dishes into the now-cold oven, and then went to Tarquin's library.

The wizard had been a man of wide interests, and his

library reflected it—an eclectic selection of texts, from convoluted discussions of the esoterica of magic to equally
convoluted philosophical texts, with collections of poetry,
fiction and history in between, as well as a number of volumes of travelers' tales. There were three different bestiaries and, thinking of the sad creature in Bellona's temple,
Liam pulled down the thickest.

The entry on gryphons began with an intricately illuminated capital G and an elaborate picture of a group—*Pride?*
Liam wondered, *Flock?*—of the magical animals. It told
him little he did not already know: that they were rare, most
often found in the north of Taralon, in the King's Range.
That they grew rarer the farther south one went, that they
were unknown in the Freeports. That they were fierce and
proud, that they were beautiful. He had not known that their
hearts were useful in a number of powerful spells, but it
did not interest him and he had already heard that they had
a language of their own.

The last paragraph of the entry, however, was entirely
new to him. Written in red ink, as opposed to the black
used for the rest of the text, it began with the heading:
STONE GRYPHONS.

"Though bearing a distinct physical resemblance to the
creature described above in all particulars except color,"
the paragraph read, "STONE GRYPHONS should not be confused with their earthbound kin. Of a slate gray color, these
beasts are magical creatures of an entirely different com-
plexion. They haunt battlefields and graveyards, and eat the
souls of the dead, as opposed to the fresh meat favored by
the common gryphon. It is also held that they can walk the
Gray Lands, and move freely through the ethereal, astral,
earthly and heavenly planes. Little else is known of them,
though no living man has ever recorded receiving a hurt
from them."

Liam frowned over the page. Could Bellona's acolytes

be holding a stone gryphon for sacrifice? He paged through the other two bestiaries; one had no entry even for normal gryphons, and the third mentioned the normal kind, but not their gray cousins.

With a dissatisfied *hmph* he replaced all the books on the appropriate shelf, and drew out the book of philosophy he had been working on.

While he tried to puzzle out the strange arguments the book presented, it began to snow, softly at first, then harder. He looked up in the middle of a particularly inane digression and noticed that the library's skylight was covered with a light dusting. Putting aside the book, he went out to the entrance hall and slid open the door.

The patio had a dusting of snow on it as well, and the light from the house made it glitter prettily. He breathed deep, enjoying the salt cold in his lungs.

"Fanuilh!" he called. There was no answer. He called again, then bent down, made a snowball, and lobbed it out toward the sea.

He was wearing only stockings, and the snow quickly soaked them. He hopped back in, stripping them off and dropping them on his boots by the door.

He can let himself in, Liam thought, and went to bed.

There was a bedroom down the hall on the right, but he did not sleep there—it was where he had discovered Tarquin's corpse. Though two months had passed, and he had buried the wizard in the bedclothes and bought a new mattress filled with cotton ticking, he could not bring himself to sleep there.

Instead, he went into the library, where there was a divan long enough to hold him. The room darkened as he took off his clothes and wrapped himself in a light sheet, and he fell into blackness quite comfortably.

CHAPTER 2

WAKE, MASTER.

In his dream, Liam was reading a giant bestiary, filled solely with pictures of Fanuilh. He turned the pages one after another; each entry was accompanied by a picture of his familiar. And all began with two illuminated words: *WAKE, MASTER.*

He closed the book and woke up.

A pure white light suffused the library, a combination of the house's magic and the sun shining through the covering of snow on the skylight.

"What is it, Fanuilh?" He groaned and sat up, stretching leisurely.

You must come see. There has been a robber.

Liam checked in midstretch.

Come see.

He threw aside the sheet, jumped into a pair of breeches and ran out into the entrance hall, where he skidded to a stop.

Fanuilh was crouched by the door, its snout close down by the floor, examining a set of sandy footprints. It reminded Liam absurdly of a dog sniffing out a trail, though he knew the dragon's sense of smell was not as keen.

They go into the trophy room, and into the workroom.

"Ahh," Liam groaned. "Robbers. Wonderful, really, wonderful." He cursed, once, with feeling. "All right, let's see what they took." With a resigned expression, he

20

crossed to the trophy room, careful not to step in the sand and puddles of melted snow left by the robber's feet.

The flying rug, Fanuilh noted, *and something from the cases.*

Liam nodded: the hanging with the eagle was gone from the wall, and the lid of one case was open. He looked in— one of the wands, a slim ebony stick, was missing.

"Very particular thieves," he murmured. The dragon leapt up onto the cases; its claws clicked on the glass. "Nothing else missing?" Fanuilh's head swayed from side to side. "All right; the workroom."

He caught his familiar around the middle and hoisted it up to his shoulder; perched there, it rode him into the workroom. The shelves were empty—his own work—and the intricate, perfectly detailed model of Southwark was still on the third worktable, by the window. Tarquin had made it for the last spell he cast before his murder.

The wizard's book of spells, however, which had been chained to a lectern in front of the third table, was gone. The chain was looped neatly on top of the lectern, one link snapped.

Liam and Fanuilh both stared for a moment at the pile of chain.

"Very particular thieves," Liam said again.

Only three things—the wand, the carpet, and the book.

"Go check Diamond," Liam said suddenly.

Without hesitation the dragon sprang from his shoulder, flapping its wings gently, and flew out of the workroom.

When it returned, its master was dressed and back by the lectern, kneeling to examine the footprints.

The horse is there. But with the rug, the robbers would not need the horse.

"Wait," Liam said, touching the sand with one finger. In a strange way, he was not upset by the robbery. Instead, he was excited, in a purposeful way. Without being aware

of it, he was responding to the robbery as if it were a call
to action—and the opening of the sort of mystery the Aedile thought him so good at solving. There were steps to
take, he knew, a logical course of action. First, a set of
questions. "Hold on a moment. One thing at a time. First,
when did you find this?"

*I returned from my flight only a few minutes before I
woke you.*

"Out all night, eh?" He kept back the joke that occurred
to him. "So they could have come anytime after I went to
sleep. Now, what did they take? I mean, besides the spellbook. I know about that—but what's the rug? And what's
the wand?"

*The rug flies. It can carry a person. The wand levitates
objects.*

"Objects?"

Things too heavy to be carried by a man.

"Very good." He stood up, brushing his hands on his
knees. "We have to assume our thief knew what he
wanted."

One of Fanuilh's thoughts began to form in his head, but
Liam held up a hand, and it disappeared. He scratched the
back of his head for a minute, pursing his lips, then caught
what he was after.

"Didn't you say the house was protected?"

Yes. The thought formed instantly, as if it had been
ready. *No one could enter without the owner's permission.*

"And the spell still holds, even though Tarquin's dead?"

You are the owner now.

Liam sucked at his lower lip for a moment.

"Who could break the spell, and get in?"

A wizard of sufficient power.

"So our thief is a wizard."

There are no wizards in Southwark powerful enough.

And I would have noticed the expense of energy necessary to breach the spell.

"But it was done," Liam pointed out reasonably.

Yes, but not with a spell. I would have noticed.

"Are you sure?" He knew little enough about how magic worked, and would have to trust the dragon's judgment, but he wanted it to be sure. "No doubts?"

None.

"All right, then, any other possibilities? A common housebreaker shouldn't have been able to open the door."

A breaching spell could have been laid on the thief, or an amulet or ring or wand.

"And that you wouldn't notice?"

Only at the moment the spell was laid. I would not notice the use of the enchanted item—only the original casting.

The discussion was moving into realms Liam did not understand, and he decided to cut it short. He wanted to move on to his next obvious step.

You are going to report it to the Aedile.

"Of course. As soon as we clear up a few things. The protection on the house could have been broken only by a wizard, but you say there are no wizards in Southwark."

None.

"Or a breaching spell could have been placed on something—almost anything, correct?—which would have let the thief enter."

Anything at all.

"So we have either a careful wizard, or a thief with access to enchantments. And in either case, we have someone with a very limited list of desires—just the wand, the rug and the book. The book argues for a wizard, because a thief would probably be unable to use it. But the lack of a spell used indicates a thief with magical assistance."

There were thieves, he knew, who specialized in stealing enchanted items. Most often they worked on commission.

But he could not imagine such a thief in Southwark—the
city was simply too small to warrant such specialization
and, if Fanuilh were right, there were not enough wizards
around to make it pay.

None at all, the dragon corrected. *No wizards.*

"Well, we'll let Coeccias sort that out. I just want to
have the right information to hand him."

The dragon cocked its head at him, its yellow eyes slitted
in puzzlement.

"Well?" Liam said after a minute of his familiar's scrutiny. "What?"

You are going to report it to the Aedile.

"Yes," he replied, "what else would you have me do?"

You could find the thief yourself. He stole your *things.*

Liam shook his head. The dragon had persuaded him—
forced him, really—to investigate Tarquin's murder, and
although he had eventually found the killer, he could not
say that the process had been pleasant. Not pleasant in the
least.

"No," he said at last, "not this time. This is Coeccias's
work. He's best suited to it—I'd only make a mess of
things again."

The dragon had no shoulders to speak of, so it could not
shrug, but Liam could tell that it would have.

As you will, master.

"Exactly," Liam said. "As I will. I'm not going to get
beaten up or involved with murderous women or go creeping around in the rain again. We'll let Coeccias handle it."

As you will.

Nodding suspiciously, Liam backed out of the room and
took his cloak from the peg.

On the ride into Southwark, Liam had time to compose
his thoughts. Diamond enjoyed the snow, kicking up great

gouts, prancing and blowing. The barren fields were suddenly pretty, mantled in white.

It's not my place to pursue this, Liam decided. Robbery was not murder, of course, not as likely to turn dangerous.

Stop that, he told himself. He would not pursue it. Finding sneak-thieves was Coeccias's responsibility. There was no need for him to go in search of his stolen possessions.

They're not even mine, really. They're Tarquin's.

Sighing, he admitted that this was not true. The wizard was dead; he had named Liam his heir. The book and the rug and the wand were his.

But that doesn't mean I should try to find them. Coeccias can do that.

Then why, he wondered, had he asked Fanuilh those questions? And more important, why was he so keyed up? Why had the little dragon's announcement made him jump from the divan, not in fright or anger, but with excitement?

And why was he letting Diamond amble that way, curvetting about in the newly fallen snow, instead of spurring him hard for the Aedile's offices? Why was he in no hurry to report the crime?

It is not your place, he told himself fiercely. *That's why there's an Aedile.* Pulling his cloak forward to protect his face, he startled the roan by booting it in the ribs. The horse sprang forward, racing for the city.

Fanuilh had woken him only a little after dawn, and their discussion and his ride had taken less than an hour. Liam trotted into the city square, reined in sharply and stared about him.

The square was practically deserted. At that hour, despite the snow, it should have been filled with people, buying and selling, passing the time, crossing the expanse of cobbles to any one of the five major streets that fed into it.

Now there were only a few forlorn hawkers, huddling around a tiny brazier.

Liam clucked his horse on, noting even as it clopped along that the snow was trampled and scattered everywhere.

"A lot of tracks," he muttered to himself, "a lot of milling about."

He dismounted in front of the squat bulk of the city's jail, the headquarters of the Guard, and looped Diamond's reins through an iron ring on the wall. The cold metal stung his hands, and he reminded himself to get gloves.

The Guard at the door, rubbing her bare hands miserably, recognized him as a friend of Coeccias.

"Good morrow, Sir Liam. Come t'attend th'Aedile?"

"Yes. Is he here?"

Her face brightened, a smile spreading across her frost-reddened cheeks. "Nay, but gone over to Temples' Court, for the hurlyburly."

"Hurlyburly?"

"Have you not the word?" She grinned, and Liam knew that she was making up for not being a part of whatever was happening in the nearby neighborhood. He shook his head. "Truly?"

"Truly. What's happened?"

"Uris take me, who could 'scape it? It's bruited all the town over!"

Although Liam had a certain amount of sympathy for the woman, left behind to guard the empty jail while the Aedile—and most of the Guard, guessing from the tracks in the snow—were off at whatever had happened, his hands were cold.

"What happened?" he repeated, enunciating carefully.

"There's been murther!" She slurred the last word, as southerners tended to do. "One's tried to take off the hierarch of the new fane!"

"Murder?" This was news, certainly, worth more than

his mere robbery. And of a priest, as well. He had noticed the tendency of natives to ignore the difference between Temples' Court, the neighborhood, and Temple Street proper, where the homes of the gods were.

"Oh, aye, vicious, too, in the dark of night, a dozen masked men—"

The Guard stopped abruptly, snapping to attention, catching up the halberd she had leaned against the wall. Liam peered over his shoulder and saw Coeccias crossing the square. Thunder stood out on his forehead, and his fists were clenched.

"Rhenford!" he bellowed. "Rhenford, praise all the gods there are, just the wight I've need of!"

Liam froze. While they investigated Tarquin's murder, the Aedile had acquired an exaggerated sense of his skills as a bloodhound. In a flash of intuition, Liam knew his friend was going to ask him to look into whatever had happened over in Temple Street.

Coeccias took his time over it, though. He gave Liam a slap on the shoulder and the Guard a glare as he came up the steps, then stumped on into the jail. Liam followed him in. There were cots along the walls, and weapons piled haphazardly about. Fires roared in twin hearths, set at each end of the room, but the Aedile went straight to an open barrel in the middle of the floor. He dipped a tin cup in and tossed down the contents.

Wincing at the sight, Liam loosened his cloak. The barrel held a local kind of hard liquor that left him gasping and choking. The stout man, though, only sniffed and dipped his cup again.

"Truth, Rhenford," he said, "that's like life. And it scarcely daybreak!" He turned, his thunderous expression slipping away, replaced by a frank look of exhaustion. "I'd swear Old Man Sun dawdled in bed a day, to keep Mistress Night abroad. I'd warrant I've never passed a longer."

"I can imagine," Liam said, settling on his haunches by a fire and warming his hands. "Murder, eh?"

"Murder?"

Liam nodded at the door. "She said there'd been a murder over at the temple of Bellona."

Anger swept away Coeccias's exhaustion, and he took two steps toward the door before stopping himself. "Damn her!" he shouted instead. "Next it'll be the Duke's been taken off and the sea's turned to blood! Rumor! Gods, Rhenford, it likes me less than . . . less than . . ." Words failed him, and he spluttered on for a moment before Liam interrupted.

"No murder, then?" The idea, strangely, did not relieve him much. If the Guard had exaggerated the emergency, then Coeccias might be able to focus on his robbery—and he found that a small part of him wanted just the opposite.

"No! What's passed is bad enough, and I'd not be surprised if there were blood in the end, the way Cloten's carrying on, but no, no murder." His beard wagged as he chewed his lower lip, and Liam had to prod him again.

"Then what?"

The Aedile shook his head, as if remembering the other man's presence. "What? Oh, aye, what. Only that some thief's tried to rob Bellona's treasury, and given Cloten a knock on's head while at it."

Liam gave a startled laugh. Coeccias glared at him. "The treasury? We were just talking about that yesterday!"

"Aye, we were—but while we were talking, another was plotting, and tried to lift it late last night. Cloten caught him at it, but he got away."

Holding back another incredulous laugh—he could not imagine anyone fool enough to break into the temple of a warrior goddess—Liam only shook his head, and caught up a poker. "Who's Cloten?"

"Only the greatest ass ever to grace Temples' Court—

or all of Southwark, for that. Do you know that he actually tried to challenge the Hierarch of Strife, to his face? Old Guiderius came in to wish him well, had heard the news, and Cloten, that ass, gave the man the lie outright! In his teeth! Can you imagine?''

Liam could not, because he knew neither man. But he qualified his earlier thought—he had known a thief years before who might have broken into Bellona's temple. He smiled briefly at the memory.

''My Guards had to pull the old man out,'' Coeccias went on, pacing the stone-flagged floor. ''He was that enraged! I've posted most of my men down there to keep the peace, but Cloten only laughed!''

''Who,'' Liam asked patiently, ''is Cloten? And who is Guiderius?''

Coeccias whirled on him, astonished for a moment, then relaxed. ''Aye, aye, I forget. Truth, Rhenford, it's as if I were speaking to myself.'' He took a deep breath, marshaling his thoughts and his calm. ''Cloten's Hierarch of Bellona, and Guiderius of Strife, an old and regular fixture in Temples' Court.''

''Wait—who was the priest we met yesterday? Alastor— I thought he was hierarch.''

''No, no,'' the Aedile said, waving away the question. ''He's but second; 'Keeper of Arms,' they title him. Cloten's hierarch.''

''All right, then, why would Guiderius want to rob Cloten?''

Coeccias rolled his eyes. ''Truth, I could warrant no reason, though Cloten's fixed on it. And thinks it more an attack on his self than a robbery—as if any'd worry themselves with his worthless life, and it weren't clear the thief was after the treasury!''

Liam stirred the fire, thinking. There was an obvious reason, of course: Strife was a war god, and there would be no love lost between competing sects. Still, feuds among churches were few and far between in Taralon, and Coeccias seemed sure it was just a robbery.

"So," he said, "why am I just the wight you're looking for?"

Coeccias stopped pacing, a guilty smile twitching on his lips. "Truth," he faltered, "I was hoping you'd, ah, that you'd . . ."

"Help you? Help you find the thief?"

"Rhenford," he said, opening his hands and speaking frankly, "I'd not ask if it weren't trickish. It's as much this Cloten I need a hand with as the thief. He's difficult."

"Difficult?"

"Prickly, a headstrong horse with his own mind and the bit between his teeth. I fear me he'll pursue this with Guiderius."

"Well, all you have to do is find the thief. Then he can't blame Guiderius."

Coeccias rolled his eyes. "Oh, aye, just find the thief. I'll snap my fingers and make the rounds of the usual cutpurses, and one'll confess, eh? This is no ordinary thief, as well you know, Rhenford. This is a passing job, and called for a passing thief."

"I suppose that's true," Liam said, recalling his own thought on the thief brave enough to try a temple dedicated to war.

"Truer than true—and the reason I ask your help. You've a penetrating eye, and a head for this. Come, will you?"

There was hope in the Aedile's eye as he looked at his friend, and Liam knew he would have to put it out. The man had put too much stock in his success in finding Tarquin's murderer.

"I can't," Liam said simply. "I've got my own robbery to worry about."

He gave a quick account of the burglary, mentioning both the wards the thief had passed and the things he had taken. When he was done, Coeccias was wincing.

"Passed through the house while you were abed, did he?"

"Yes."

"And took only magical things?"

"Yes. That's why I came in this morning—to tell you about it. I'd hoped for your help."

Coeccias ran a thick hand through his unruly hair, frowning. "It likes me not to have things magical in the hands of a thief. But with this in Temples' Court . . ."

During his ride into town and his discussion with the Aedile, Liam had realized an important thing about himself. He was bored. Not the boredom of an hour, or of an afternoon. It was deeper, a dissatisfaction with the placidity of his life over the past two months. For over ten years, his life had been constant movement, a whirlwind progress that had led him halfway around the world, only to drop him in Southwark. In Southwark, where, except for the brief week when he sought Tarquin's murderer, he had done exactly nothing.

Not true, he told himself at the fire. *I've had my work with Fanuilh, and Coeccias and I are now friends. That's worth something.* He was not sure, however, how much, and he was now sure that it was not enough.

"With this in Temples' Court," Coeccias finally said, picking up his earlier statement, "my cup's full."

There was one thing to check before committing himself. "Well, are there any thieftakers in Southwark?"

"Thieftakers?"

"Yes, men who catch thieves for a living," Liam explained, though he could tell from his friend's puzzled look that there were none. Southwark was undoubtedly too small to need them.

"There's me," Coeccias said, "and the Guard."

"I know, but in some cities—Torquay, for instance, and Harcourt and most of the Freeports—there are men who do it for money. They're hired to solve a particular crime, usually small things like housebreaking."

Coeccias sniffed at the idea, and Liam turned his head so that his smile fell into the fire. If there were no thieftakers, and Coeccias had his hands full dealing with the trouble in Temple Street, then . . .

"In that case, I imagine I should try to find the thief myself."

"Truth, Rhenford, that'd be grand," the Aedile said, as if he had forgotten his earlier request for help. "If you'll track your thief, I'll track Cloten's."

Liam paused. "Agreed." After all, he told himself, tracking a thief could not lead to as many complications as tracking Tarquin's murderer had. And it would certainly be easier than placating an irate hierarch. "Can you give me the names of some pawnbrokers—ones who are used to handling expensive items?"

With a pleased smile, Coeccias bustled about, finding pen, ink and paper in a cupboard, laying the sheet out on top of the liquor keg. "There's not so many as fit," he said as he wrote, "only two, when all's said, if y'are thinking of fences. Y'are?" Liam nodded. "There're others who'll take lesser items, but only these two for things the like of yours." He blew on the sheet of paper to dry the ink, then handed it to Liam. "And while you're conning your thief, keep your ears pricked for word of mine, eh?"

"My pleasure," Liam said, taking the paper and noting the two names and addresses in the Aedile's unruly handwriting. He did not really think his thief would be fencing his goods; he needed the names for something else entirely. "I trust you'll do the same?"

Coeccias offered him a mock bow. "What say we meet on a schedule and exchange information?"

They decided on dinner the next day, at a familiar inn, and Liam pulled his cloak close around his shoulders, preparing to go.

"There's something else," he said, standing by the door. "Where can I find Mother Japh?"

The Aedile considered for a moment. "I'd think her in her morgue now. Why?"

"I need to ask her a little about magic. Where's her . . . morgue, did you call it?"

"Aye, that's her word for it—a place we keep unclaimed bodies. Next door, beneath the courts. Though I'd not seek her there, 'less corses like you."

Liam took in the Aedile's warning with a sober nod; sooner or later he would have to disabuse his friend of the notion that he was blood shy.

"Right. Perhaps I can send in a message."

"That'd be best," Coeccias said solicitously.

Once again hiding a smile, Liam stepped out of the Guard barracks and into the cold morning. There was an oddly familiar itch between his shoulder blades, and his hands flexed on their own. He recognized the feeling.

He had something to do that was worth doing.

CHAPTER 3

A BRIEF WORD with the Guard on the steps assured him that she would watch over Diamond, and
Liam walked over to the building next door.

The Duke's courts were large for a city as small as
Southwark, filling most of the western side of the square.
The squat Guard barracks looked like a poor relation huddled up against their side, their rude stone clashing with
the neatly dressed blocks of the courts, rising in three massive stories pierced by rows of narrow, widely spaced windows. A thin, square tower rose another two stories from
the middle of the building, housing the bells that tolled the
city's hours. Torch brackets had been riveted into the stone
front, and Liam knew from experience that at night the
courts flickered with firelight, its long shadows stretching
and dancing across the facade and up to the bell tower.

There were no torches now and the courts looked deserted. Liam went up a broad staircase to the wooden doors
and pulled at the heavy knocker. Rubbing his hands to keep
off the cold, he examined the coat of arms hung above the
doors: three red foxes on a gray field, without subdivisions
or signs of intermarriage. The Dukes of the Southern Tier
kept their line apart from the general nobility of Taralon,
marrying among the petty landowners and merchants of
their duchy. It had done little to endear them to their peers,
but it had kept their interests firmly rooted in their own
lands and left their coat simple.

A withered old porter eventually cracked the door and demanded his business.

"I'd like to see Mother Japh," Liam told him, and was rewarded with a sour grunt and a slight widening of the crack. He slipped inside, blinking at the sudden darkness. However brilliantly illuminated they were on the outside, the Duke's courts were ill lit inside. The grumpy porter held up a lantern and grumbled.

"Come along, then," he said after squinting at Liam's face for a moment. "She's below."

They went along a broad hallway in the heart of the building, the porter's lantern throwing distended shadows on the chilly stones. Thin lines of orange light stood out beneath the doors that lined the empty hall, and Liam barely made out the words painted on them: Wills and Deeds, Shipping Registrar, Ducal Imposts, Births and Deaths. He shuddered a little at the last word, and picked up his pace to catch the porter, who had gone on without stopping.

Liam found him by his light and his misshapen, monstrous shadow, several steps down a narrow circular staircase. They descended, Liam growing colder as they passed below street level. The courts themselves, he guessed, were on the higher floors—and he further imagined each, as well as the tightly shut offices on the first floor, with its own roaring hearth and a snug official warming his toes by it. The porter's breath steamed as he led the way from the bottom of the staircase.

There was a long, low-ceilinged corridor, with solid-looking doors on either side. No light escaped from under them, including the last one, at which the porter left him without a word.

Bemused, Liam knocked once, then twice more, quickly, as the porter's light dwindled, then disappeared.

"Who's it?" he heard, from the other side of the door.

"It's Liam Rhenford, Mother Japh. Aedile Coeccias sent me."

He heard a light laugh and the door scraped open, revealing a wizened old woman in a light shift, a rug in one hand.

"In, in, Rhenford, let not the cold in!"

He jumped into the room and she slammed the door, tucking the rug around the bottom of the jamb. It was stifling in the small space, so hot he could remove his cloak, so hot the windows were unshuttered, mists of condensation across them.

"It's warm," he said, draping his cloak over his arm and tugging at his collar.

"And so it should be," the old woman chuckled, gesturing at the huge fireplace that filled one end of the room. It was easily the largest Liam had ever seen, suited to a foundry or a large smithy. Only a fraction of the hearth was used, but it was enough to set him sweating. "It was supposed to be the base of a . . . oh, the word goes from me—you'll know it—it was to heat the whole pile, through chimneys in the floors and such."

"A hypocaust?" He looked with new appreciation on the huge stove, noting the breadth of the flue.

"Aye, that's the very word, only it doesn't work as it should. The masons mistook the plans, and laid the whole awry, so that," she said, with a wink and mischievous grin, "it only serves to warm me, and the rest make do with braziers and the very smallest of hearths."

Liam smiled back. A hypocaust was no mean trick of architecture; he was not surprised that it did not work, only that it had been attempted. "But how is it," he asked, turning his gaze from the fire to the foggy glass, "that you have windows here, in the basement?"

Mother Japh cackled and, taking his arm, led him over to one of the windows. She rubbed a spot clear of condensation and bade him look through it. "That's Narrow Lane," she said, pointing down at a snow-filled road that earned its name, barely ten feet from side to side. "Behind the building, you see? On the front there's the square, but behind, there's Narrow Lane, and a much lower thing it is. So there's my windows, that I had them unshutter and glass when I came here. And how they carped! But they're there, and give good light toward the end of the day."

With another smile, Liam turned from the window and surveyed the room. He had met Mother Japh only once, really, on the morning he discovered Tarquin's body. She had seemed friendly then, once she had made certain that he was not the murderer. They had exchanged a few words on the rare occasions since then, whenever they passed each other in the street, but had never gone beyond that.

Now he looked at her room, noting the numerous pots by the furnace of the would-be hypocaust, the jars and bins, the worktables with tops battered and scarred and burned. Mother Japh, he knew, was a ghost witch, but he had no real idea what that meant: he knew even less about witches than he did about wizards, which was precious little.

"Do you live here?" he asked, careful to keep any tone of judgment out of his voice. He had not noticed a place to sleep among the clutter of items, though there was a door in one wall that might lead to a bedroom.

"Faith, no," she laughed, a happy, amiable chuckle that screwed up her already-wrinkled features. "Only work, and stay when's cold, for that the wood and coal are free, grace of the Duke." She laughed again. "Faith, living in the morgue!"

"What is that, exactly, a morgue? Coeccias mentioned it as well."

"Why, it's where we keep corses, do you see, those un-claimed, tars, thieves, beggars, and so on. When the Guard finds them, eh?" His questioning look around the room provoked her to a stormy laugh. "So he looks for 'em! Oh, that's strong, it is! They're not *here*, Rhenford, they're *there*"—she pointed at the second door—"and precious few at the moment, so there's no worry."

"No worry," he agreed, wondering if Coeccias had communicated his misconception about Liam's squeamishness to the ghost witch.

"But now, you've not come to see my corses, nor to repair the hypo-thing, have you? You've a question, eh? Or two?"

He had more than two, and those that came first to his mind—*What exactly is a ghost witch?* was prominent among them—he put aside, remembering the real purpose of his visit.

"I do, and I hope you can answer them."

"With a will, if I can," she interrupted, "though mind, I'm no scholar."

As briefly as possible, he explained the theft of Tarquin's things and the magical wards the thief had overcome, and she clucked in sympathy.

"What I want to ask you is, whether you know anyone in Southwark who could do that. Anyone who could break one of Tarquin's spells."

"Don't you know?"

"Me? No, that's why I'm asking you."

"But I'm a witch—you're the wizard!"

He looked at her, stunned. "I'm not a wizard!"

"Go to," Mother Japh said, waving a hand at him. "In course y'are. You live in a wizard's house, don't you?"

"Yes," he admitted.

"And you've befriended his familiar, haven't you?"

"Yes, but . . ."

"And now you want to search out a spellbook and a magic wand and carpet. And you say y'are no wizard! Pshaw!"

"But I'm not," Liam insisted. "I don't know anything about magic." While this was not exactly true, it was far closer to the truth than the idea that he was a wizard.

"Truth? Nothing?"

"Nothing."

She accepted his avowal grudgingly, as if she did not wish to believe it. "The whole city's sure of it. It's bruited about everywhere."

Swallowing an angry impulse, he reflected that it made a certain amount of sense. If they followed Mother Japh's logic, then the rest of Southwark would have come to the conclusion that he was a wizard.

"Not a very forward wizard," the old woman amended, "but a wizard for all that."

"Well, I can assure you I'm not," he said reasonably. "And that's why I came to you. I know witchery and wizardry aren't the same—"

"More than most can say," she interrupted.

". . . but I was hoping you could tell me if there were any other wizards around."

"As it happens," she said, "I can. Can tell you that there aren't, that is. Apart from you, that is. And since you say you're not, there aren't any."

"Are you sure?"

"As sure as I can be," she said, with no trace of affront. 'Wizards don't come to Southwark, see you. Tarquin Tanaquil was the only one as did, and see how he was served! No, wizards don't come here. There's no Guild branch— Southwark is too small—and the Duke's court is deemed unfriendly to 'em."

"Unfriendly?"

"It's not, but's seen that way. He only follows certain old rules and ways, that curb wizards in ways that like them not."

Liam was aware of the Duke's penchant for the ancient

laws of Taralon, and vaguely remembered an old set of regulations that prescribed the activities of wizards—those "engaged in the arcane arts," the code said, "or pursuing said knowledges and applications."

"Apart from Tanaquil, no wizard's visited Southwark since I was born, though I know they're thick as flies by a bilge to the north—in Torquay and Harcourt. If one were to come, I'd warrant, even disguised, the word'd go out."

"So there's no wizard in Southwark?"

"I can't say it for fact, but so I'd guess. Wizards have a . . . smell about them, eh? A feel, like a great lord or lady, eh? They can't help but seem like wizards."

"Do I smell like a wizard?" He asked only in jest.

She stared at him for a moment. "Aye, you do, or something strange, at the least."

"That's nice to know," he said, and the irony was not lost on her.

"Don't take it so, Rhenford. It means only that you don't resemble the common run—and for that, I'll show you something."

She bustled over to the second door, touching his arm. He followed, frowning heavily over her comments. The first time they met, she told him his face was too innocent to be believed; now she was telling him he smelled like a wizard, and that the entire city thought that was what he was. He had not liked being told he was too innocent—he liked it even less to be thought of as a wizard.

The room beyond was larger by far than the one they had left. Its end was shadowy, the windows stopping half-way down, with the light from the door barely reaching that far. But what Liam saw was enough.

There were a dozen tables in view, and more in the dark part of the room. The tables were stone slabs raised on squat blocks, barely waist-high, and there were corpses on three of them.

"This is your morgue?" he asked, bothered not in the least by the sight of the bodies but by the fact that Mother Japh spent so much time near them.

Like living in a graveyard, he thought, and must have grimaced, because she laughed.

"Oh, it's not so bad, Rhenford. There're not always so many, and they come and go with frequency; never here more than a se'ennight. And I needs must be near, to keep the spells going."

"Spells?" He walked to the nearest body, a naked man with bluish skin under a coating of tattoos, and a bloated face. The morgue was cold, but not cold enough to keep corpses from rotting; some of the heat from the hypocaust's furnace had to seep through the intervening wall.

"For to keep them fresh, see you? It'd fair clear the whole square if they was to rot." The notion set her laughing again, and he noted the little bundle lying between the feet of the corpse. He pointed at it, and she nodded. "Aye, that's my work. It'll keep the body from rot for almost a month, with attention. A simple witchery, but I didn't bring you here for to show you that. See you that last?"

She pointed at the third corpse, separated by a few tables from the others, and he walked over. It was a man, small and lightly built; a weak man, it would seem, judging from the thinness of his arms and the general paucity of muscle. There was a look of vast surprise on his face, his mouth agape in a silent shout; a gash in his chest showed where a knife had gone in.

"What do you make him?"

Liam looked at the face, the thin arms. Then, to prove to himself that the atmosphere of the morgue was not getting to him, he reached out and rubbed one of the man's hands. A chill reached him from the dead skin. "A clerk?"

Her face lit up. "Why?"

"No calluses except on the pads of his fingers, no mus-

cle, no scars. Not like the sailor over there.'' He gestured
to the tattooed blue corpse.

Mother Japh nodded happily. ''Aye, y'are as sharp as
Coeccias says, and more.'' He ducked his head, both
pleased and displeased with the praise. ''But that's not what
I wish to show. There's more beyond. Now watch this.''

She shut the door, leaving the morgue with only the dim
gray light from the windows. Her thin brown shift rustled
over the floor as she paced to the center of the room and
raised one hand. A flat circle of brilliant blue light burst in
her palm, then spread to the walls in a shimmering plate.
Liam was considerably taller than the ghost witch, so the
plane of light broke around his neck—and for all the world
he could have sworn that he was treading water in a cobalt
blue sea, coruscating with little phosphorescences.

Mother Japh lowered her hand, the plate following, trailing down Liam's chest, then past her own face and down,
until it rested a foot or so above the tables.

''Face about,'' she told him, and he turned, dazzled by
the way the blue light played around his waist, flashing and
sparkling.

''What—'' he began, and then saw the breath of the first
two corpses in the room.

Single flames burned above each corpse's mouth, tiny
whirls of fire just by the mouth, straighter jets farther up.
No more than a foot tall, they reminded Liam of the breath
of dragons.

An irrelevant thought came to Liam: that Fanuilh could
not breath fire.

''Their souls,'' the ghost witch said, and her voice was
hushed, almost reverent. ''Till they're called—buried, or
burned, or fetched by whatever'll take them to the Gray
Lands—their souls burn above their mouths. But now turn
about again.''

He did, and saw immediately that there was no flame above the mouth of the third corpse.

"See you?"

"No flame."

"No flame—no soul. Which is as saying there's a ghost roaming Southwark now."

She suddenly closed her fist and the blue field shredded in an instant. Liam started, then rubbed his eyes for a moment. Blue sparks swam in his vision.

"The spirit can't find its body, and so it'll wander, until it comes upon it. This corse was found in Narrow Lane," Mother Japh went on, pointing out the window, "just a few yards from here, and I've been hoping the spirit'd find the body, but it hasn't." She heaved a deep sigh, clearly touched by the plight of the lost spirit.

"Does this happen often?" Liam asked, staring in wonder at the surprised face.

"It's rare enough—true ghosts are, see you—but's a murder, eh? The wound in the chest, most like a theft, and Narrow Lane's dark and dangerous at night, for all of Coeccias's work and that it's right by the Duke's courts. With a strong taking off like that, losing the spirit's possible."

Liam breathed hard and backed away from the spiritless corpse, leaning against an empty table.

"It seems winter is the time for strange events in Southwark. Two major thefts—or a major theft and an attempted major theft—a spiritless body, the comet . . ."

The ghost witch's gray head bobbed up and down. "And a new goddess, mind you." Her nod took on a judicial quality, and she pointed one gnarled finger at him. "A new goddess. There's something there, I'll tell you. More than the messenger, or your thieveries, or this corpse. There's something there."

A brief silence fell on the morgue, and Liam suddenly found that he wanted to leave.

The ghost witch accompanied him up the stairs with a shielded candle, a shawl thrown over her shoulders. She opened the main door of the court, but blocked his way for a moment.

"Thank you, Mother Japh," Liam said. "At some point, if you would, I'd like to talk to you about witchcraft."

He expected a pleasantry or, more likely, a joke. Instead, the old woman's face creased worriedly.

"Be you careful searching out your thief, Liam Rhenford. There's more at work here than meets the eye."

A chill wind cut through her thin shift and she ducked suddenly down the corridor, clutching her shawl tight, headed for her furnace room.

Mother Japh's warning in his ears, Liam remembered the way Coeccias had winced when he heard that the thief had been wandering around the house while he slept. He had planned to head straight back to the beach; instead, he asked a question of the shivering Guard in front of the barracks, and guided Diamond north, to the section of the artisans' quarter known as Auric's Park.

In a narrow alley begrimed with smoke and ash he found a swordsmith, and bought a matched hanger and dirk. There were few armed men in Southwark's streets—it was a small city, too small for the political rivalries that sent swordsmen roaming Harcourt or the Freeports—and he had not felt the need of weapons before. But he had been a soldier on occasion, and the feel of the hanger's hilt in his hand was oddly comfortable.

With his purchases tied to his saddle, he set off, out of the city.

The snow had settled over the fields outside Southwark, and though the sky was uniformly leaden, the empty expanse and the open country lifted Liam's heart. After the closeness of the Duke's courts and of the city in general, he threw back the hood of his cloak and was pleased to let the cold wind bite at his face.

A certain, undefinable thrill ran through him; the nearest he came to it was a sense of purpose. Finding the man who had robbed him was no earthshaking enterprise, he knew, but it gave him something to do, and he discovered for the first time that he did not like having nothing to do.

It was something he had never had a chance to learn before. Born the only son of a minor Midlands nobleman, he had grown up amid the constant chores and duties of his position—and the battles and rumors of war that swept that turbulent region. He escaped them only briefly, to study in the great city of Torquay—and was then called back urgently, only to see his father killed and his home burned in one of the Midlands' pointless feuds. From that point on he had traveled, never stopping in one place for more than a few months, seeing the world as soldier, clerk, sailor, scholar and merchant captain. His residence in Southwark was due only to the fact that he had been shipwrecked on a voyage out of the Freeports, and the ship that rescued him hailed from the small city. Why he had stayed so long— almost six months—was sometimes a mystery to him, and while he did not want to leave Southwark, he knew now that inactivity was not his natural element.

He reined Diamond in above the cove, the lonely sail of a fishing smack just visible at the extremity of vision. There was a strong breeze up out to sea, and the small boat scudded westward, toward the roadstead at Southwark.

Too strong for him, Liam reflected, noting the power of the wind and the height of the waves. *Hope he makes port*.

The thought sat in his mind for a long moment, and then he formed another, and pushed at it.

I'm home.

The dragon's thought came almost instantly.

I hear you. You are projecting very well.

Liam allowed himself a self-congratulatory smile.

There is a man here to see you. He is waiting on the patio.

He turned his eyes to the beach, but the house cut off his view, and he started Diamond down the path warily.

What is he like?

He wears a long cape, the dragon reported, *and a hood, and he carries a sword. But he is not hiding.*

His own sword was not hung from his saddle properly, but he loosened it in the sheath and laid it across his legs anyway. The trail switchbacked, and it was not until he reached the sand that he saw his visitor, a tall, ominous figure in a long black traveling robe. He was pacing back and forth rapidly as Liam urged his roan across the beach.

At Liam's cough, the stranger whirled, apparently startled, dropping into a fighter's crouch with one hand on the sword at his waist. Liam found his own hilt, but did not draw. It would have been awkward, anyway, and he was glad when the other relaxed. The stranger's speed was disconcerting.

"Pray, sir, are you Liam Rhenford?" The voice was low and polite, but with a wet burble to it, as if the stranger were sick. The dark hood covered his face, and Liam saw that there was a piece of cloth sewn across the neck of the cloak to fully hide the wearer's face.

"I am," he answered, keeping his face calm. He did not like the professionalism of the crouch he had seen, nor the way the other's hands clenched rhythmically at his sides.

"The wizard?"

Something in the way the stranger's voice cracked when he asked the question made Liam cock his head.

"No," he said, carefully. "That's my name, but I'm not a wizard."

"But you have a familiar," the stranger said, and Liam

recognized the crack in the man's voice: he wanted a wizard. "And only wizards have familiars, and they said in the town you were."

The wind was strong on the beach, plastering the stranger's thin robes around him. His whole body was quivering, like a spring wound too tightly, and his hands continued to make fists in rhythm. The skin looked slightly scaly. Liam saw, but kept his face clear and his voice even.

"What do you want a wizard for?"

The stranger's hood tipped up, and Liam knew he was being examined. Then, with a ritual slowness, the scaly hands came up and pulled the hood back.

Liam blinked once. Diamond skipped suddenly, and he quieted the horse with a low word and the pressure of his knees.

It might have been a mask, sewn from the imperfectly cured skin of some albino snake. Fine cracks laced the scales around the man's eyes and mouth, larger ones on his neck and brow. His eyes were surprisingly deep, blue wells in the desert landscape of his face. It was not a mask, though, and Liam could even remember the name of the disease.

"Low-root," he whispered. "That's low-root fever, right?"

The mask tightened only a little; the stranger's eyes did not move.

"Yes."

"You're from Caernarvon?" Low-root, he had been taught, appeared around that city only, and was named after a plant that grew there whose roots looked like the skin of the stricken.

"Yes."

"Oh, gods," Liam said slowly, eyes widening. "Did you come all the way here for a wizard?"

The sick man shrugged, a jerky motion. "I serve Bellona.

When the opportunity came to travel here, I took it. I had heard there was a wizard here who could help me.''

"I'm sorry," he said, meaning it. "There was, but he's dead. He died only two months ago. This was his house." He looked away from the ravaged face to Tarquin's house, and understood the crouch and the sword, and the service to Bellona. Sufferers of low-root were notoriously fast; the disease gave them speed and reflexes that were the envy of the healthy. To compensate, the affliction killed them early—and made them look like monsters.

"I see," the stranger said stiffly, shrugging again. "Then I will go."

"Please," Liam blurted, sliding from his saddle and taking a quick step forward, "please, I'm sorry. You must be cold—it's cold here—come inside and have something warm."

The other man only shook his head, a bitter smile cracking his cheeks. "I have waited too long. We are on double watches today."

"Look, I mean it. Something warm. You must be cold."

"I am not cold."

With an insight that chilled his heart, Liam realized that the man was young. It was impossible to tell from the disfigured face, but he was sure the other was no more than eighteen. Too young to accept death so easily. Liam felt a wild urge to do something, anything, for this sick man.

"Something to eat, then. I can fix something quickly. I can't imagine they feed you well in the temple. And it must have been cold. I hope you haven't been waiting long."

He was babbling, and knew it, but he felt the other's disappointment keenly, as if he had failed in some ill-defined responsibility. Tarquin had once told him that people were forever pestering him for spells: spells for love, spells for revenge, everything from small cures to full-blown miracles. Now, Liam realized, they might look to him for those spells—and he would have nothing for them.

"I would have something to eat," the other said.

"Good! Just let me put my horse away. It won't take a moment."

Liam ran Diamond to the shed and sped back, sure the stranger would be gone. He was waiting by the door, however, staring out at the sea with a bleak look. He blocked the entrance for a moment.

"I never thought the sea was so big."

Liam laughed, a little too heartily. "Big? This isn't big. Why, there's land less than eighty leagues away on the other side. The Cauliff's big, and Rushcutters' Bay—not this."

Caernarvon was landlocked, though, a mountain city, and the stranger only nodded gravely.

He waited in the entrance hall while Liam ducked into the kitchen, reappearing a moment later with a typical Southwark pie and some plates. He led the way into the parlor at the front of the house, and set the dish down.

He felt the sick man's eyes on him as he cut out two pieces and laid them on the plates, and the weight of the stare made him hesitate as he handed the stranger one.

"Low-root is not catching," the other said, hesitating himself from taking the plate.

"I know," Liam answered, holding the plate out with a firmer hand. "You're born with it, aren't you?"

The other man nodded once, and took his meal.

He ate with surprising appetite, well more than half the rich pie, laden with fish and vegetables. He spoke sparingly, but Liam learned a little. His name was Scaevola, and though he was born with the fever, his very poor parents had not strangled him, as most did. Not that that was any great kindness, Liam gathered, as life was not easy in Caernarvon, even for the healthy. The rise of Bellona's temple had literally been a godsend for him—they accepted anyone, at the insistence of Bothmer Lowestoft, to whom the goddess had revealed herself. He had learned swordcraft, and though he was only a low acolyte, the temple had treated him well.

When he was done eating, Scaevola stood and bowed, the motion graceful and fluid, with none of the jerkiness that had marked his eating.

"Grace you, Liam Rhenford, for the food. I must go now."

His host could find nothing to say, and settled lamely for: "Double watches, eh?"

"Since the attack on Hierarch Cloten, yes."

Liam walked him to the door, and when Scaevola shyly put out a scaled hand, pleased himself by taking it instantly. It was warm, almost hot, and he felt a heat rising off the acolyte, but he held the grip for long enough, and it was Scaevola who broke it.

"Grace you."

"And you," Liam said, then cleared his throat. "Tarquin left many books here. I could look through them; perhaps there is something there."

A pained grimace rippled across Scaevola's face. "Perhaps. Perhaps not. I doubt it."

"I do, too," Liam admitted, blushing, "but it doesn't hurt to look, does it?"

Scaevola considered this, a furrow running across the scales of his forehead. "Sometimes it does," he said, and before Liam could respond, he slipped out the door.

He was a swift black shadow on the gray sand, and he flew up the path in a smooth run.

It was still early afternoon when Scaevola left, but Liam wasted the rest of the daylight in wandering moodily about the house. He had checked Tarquin's books thoroughly— he was already familiar with most of them—and found nothing about low-root fever that he did not already know.

The visit had depressed him, and Fanuilh kept out of its master's way. It approached him only later, after the sun had set, when he lay on the divan in the library.

Master? it thought. *Did you speak with the Aedile about the robbery?*

"You know I did, Fanuilh," Liam said glumly, "and you know what happened. I'm in no mood for pretending that you can't ransack my head at will tonight."

I do try not to look. But it would be easier if you knew how to block me out.

"Yes, yes, yes," Liam said, dragging himself to a sitting position on the divan and focusing on the dragon. "You're right, of course. We'll practice."

It was a surprisingly successful session. Liam almost caught the hazy outline of the silver cord Fanuilh said bound them, and he managed to project his thoughts to his familiar for almost half an hour.

Later, the dragon sent a thought from deep within a bowl of rice and red beans usually served two oceans away from Taralon.

You have a plan for finding the thief.

"Yes," Liam said. He was massaging his temples. The practice had given him a headache. "I do."

Are you sure that is the best way to find thieves?

"If there is a guild in Southwark, yes. Much the best way."

But as he stretched himself out in the library a few minutes later, he found he could not muster much enthusiasm for the idea he had come up with in Coeccias's office. Scaevola's parting words echoed in his head, and he lost them only when he finally fell asleep.

CHAPTER 4

LIAM FELT BETTER about his plan in the morning. The sky was still gray, the waves outside his windows short and choppy, but the depression he had felt after Scaevola's visit had lifted, and he was able to eat his breakfast with something approaching high spirits.

Fanuilh came into the kitchen, talons clicking on the stone floor, and hopped onto the table.

"Good morning," Liam said around a mouthful of bread.

Good morning, master, the dragon replied.

"Breakfast?"

Yes. You will look at pawnshops today?

"Indeed I will." He went to the oven and imagined his familiar's usual breakfast of raw mutton.

And this will help you find thieves?

"I hope so. I'll need your help."

What will I do?

Liam explained. He found he did not mind the dragon's resumption of the pretense of separated minds, and detailing the plan helped him clarify it in his own head.

It seems a circuitous way to find them.

"It is," he admitted, going back to the oven and pulling out a wooden platter heavy with mutton. "But is there really another way? I can't very well go into town and start calling out for thieves." He smiled a little at the idea. "And it should work."

It should, the dragon thought, tearing off a small piece of mutton with its needlelike teeth and swallowing it whole. *But what if it wasn't a thief? What if it was a wizard?*

"If it's a wizard," Liam said with a frown, "we're sunk. But neither you nor Mother Japh thinks there's one in Southwark right now—and if there was, how would I find him? I suppose you can keep your eye out for any flashes of power, but if our hypothetical wizard didn't use any magic to get into the house, then why would he use it afterward? Which means we can only hope it's a thief."

What will you do if you catch him?

"I'm not sure. The big guilds actually forbid stealing from other thieves, and punish offenders quite harshly. But a small one—who knows? If I can convince them I'm a thief, I may be able to buy the things back."

And how will you explain that to Coeccias?

The dragon had finished most of its mutton before Liam answered. "I don't know. I don't think he'll like what I'm proposing."

Then do not tell him.

Liam chuckled. "I may not, at that. Now, tell me, do you think you can do what I asked?"

It raised its head from the last of the mutton and licked the tuft of hair on its chin. *Certainly*, it thought, and Liam imagined a hint of affronted pride. Imagined it, because he had never known the dragon to display any emotion, beyond curiosity—and he was not sure that was an emotion.

"I never doubted it," he told his familiar. "I think we should go."

The riding does you good, Fanuilh thought at Liam. *You do not look so fat.*

At the edge of Southwark, by the worn pair of pillars that were called the city gates, Liam checked his horse and frowned up at the sky. He could barely make out the thin dot against the clouds that was his familiar.

What are you talking about? he projected. *You're the one who is fat.*

That was good.

I mean it, Liam thought. *I am not fat.*

Very good, was the only response; Liam snorted and gave Diamond a thump on the ribs to get him going.

"Fat," he muttered to himself. He had never been fat, and even the two months of plentiful food from Tarquin's magic oven had not put any weight on his thin frame. The muscles in his arms, he had to admit, were not as dense as they once had been, but what did he need muscular arms for?

"Nothing," he said under his breath, but he touched the hilt of his hanger and offered a quick prayer to his Luck, to make sure of it. He personified it that way—his Luck; it was the only god he ever specified in his prayers, and it almost always repaid his faith.

Coeccias had given him the names of two fences and, after he had stabled Diamond at a convenient hostler's, he walked leisurely to the shop of the first. The sun had made the streets clearer, though there was still snow in the gutters and slush in the deeper ruts. He was glad for his thick boots and his warm cloak, and the sword at his side hung comfortably. His pace acquired a little swagger, and he was whistling by the time he came into Auric's Park.

The first pawnshop was in a cramped alley near the smithy where he had bought his weapons. It was wedged between a wineshop and a grungy stall that sold hot sausages and what looked like moldy bread. There was nothing written over the shop, but there was a board with a symbol painted on it: two squarish pieces of wood with jagged edges clearly meant to mesh. A ticket.

Liam kicked some of the snow and slush from his boots

and went in. Once his eyes adjusted to the dim light, he took in the crowded shop and its proprietor.

A jumble of goods filled every available inch of space, piles of seabags and faded clothing, furniture broken or merely old, a barrel of rusty swords and spears, a glass case filled with a riot of jewelry. Unguessable shapes hung from the ceiling, one of which Liam tentatively identified as a loom, and one other as a section of ship's railing, complete with belaying pins and dangling rope ends. There were tapestries on the walls, layers and layers of them, of unguessable value. What might have been intricately woven cloth-of-gold peeped from behind a crude thing of wool. Tied to each piece were claim tags, the broken halves of wooden lozenges marked with numbers. A thick layer of dust cast a gray pall over everything—goods, floor, and owner. The last stood behind a stack of three sea chests, approached by a narrow lane through the stacks of pawned items.

The dust seemed thickest on him, and Liam could have sworn there were cobwebs in his hair. He was old and stooped, with an expression of vague bewilderment which only grew vaguer when he recognized his customer's fine clothes.

"Hail,.milord," he mumbled, "welcome to my humble shop."

"Good day, my friend. I wonder if I can help you."

The pawnbroker raised his arms helplessly.

"Help *me*, I mean," Liam corrected himself with a smile. "I'm looking for some goods."

The old man looked around his shop, as if noticing the clutter for the first time. "I hope so, milord." He paused, clearly daunted. "What did you wish?"

"Some of this one's things have gone free," Liam said carefully, "and this one wants them back. They're green

things, and this one believes they may have been enslaved.''

He received only a wide-eyed goggling in response; the
pawnbroker shuffled behind his counter of sea chests.

"They're green," Liam repeated, emphasizing the second word.

"Milord?" the old man said, gumming his upper lip and
looking absently at a pile of clothes to his right. "I . . . I'm
afraid I don't have any green things. There are some passing pretty colors among these, I think." He began to pick
through the clothes.

Liam touched the pawnbroker on the arm and gave him
a gentle smile. "It's all right, my friend. I'll try somewhere
else."

"There were some pretty colors here," the old man said.
"I was sure of it. . . ."

He was still poking through the pile when Liam left,
breathing deep to get the dust out of his lungs.

Did he say anything, master?

Liam jumped; he had forgotten Fanuilh, and now he
scanned the sky, noticing that the dragon was perched on
the roof of the sausage stand only when the creature flapped
its wings. A quick glance showed him that no one was near;
the sausage seller's back was turned.

No, Liam projected. *I think he may be too old. Stay near,
though. Follow him if he goes out. And don't let anyone
see you!* He was proud of the way he managed to give the
last sentence an imperative accent in his head.

Very well, Fanuilh thought back. *You will go to the other
fence now?*

Liam nodded. He could feel a prick of pain at his temples; he had projected too much. Risking a wave at Fanuilh,
he walked out of the alley, in the direction of the second
address Coeccias had given him.

On first viewing it from the deck of a small coastal

trader, he had decided that Southwark looked like an amphitheater. From the placid roadstead, the city spread up in a semicircular fan of buildings. The highest seats, though, were the best: the Point, Temples' Court, Northfield and Auric's Park all sat on a high ridge of ground, looking down on the rest. The city square and the homes of the large class who dealt with shipping needs—chandlers, clerks, small shopkeepers, trade agents and factors—were in the middle and steepest part of the amphitheater; while the lowest part held the Warren, as well as the manufactories and warehouses that fronted the harbor.

Liam left Auric's Park, heading down the progressively narrower streets, passing the city square by a wide margin and eventually reaching the blurry high border of the Warren. Shrill, piercing winds shrieked through lanes that were made into tunnels by overbuilt upper stories. More than once his cloak flared about behind him, caught by a mischievous wind and flapping like the wings of a crippled bird.

The snow in the gutters was turning black, and he carefully kicked the filthy slush off his boots outside the second pawnshop. It was on one of the area's wider streets, which led down to the harbor. A sign similar to the first hung over the door, the ticket halves painted white this time.

Inside there was the same clutter of goods, but there was less dust, and the woman who owned it stopped her vigorous sweeping, sizing him up immediately.

"Good day, milord! Have you come for something special?" She reminded him of a fox; her red hair encroached on her face in pointed sideburns, and her long nose twitched as she faked a curtsy.

"Actually, I was. Some of this one's things have gone free, and this one wants them back. They were green. I thought they might have been enslaved." The phrasing was not perfect, he knew, but he wanted to be able to deny the words, if necessary.

The pawnbroker's long nose twitched furiously, and he saw her pupils draw into tiny beads and then expand, along with her smile.

"Green things, milord? I fear me I do not catch you."

She did, though, and he saw it.

"Now I come to think of it, I doubt you would have these things. I'm sorry to bother you."

He offered her a slight bow and she nodded back primly. Her nose twitched once again, as she walked him to the door.

"If there is aught else I can do, milord?"

"No, thank you."

He walked more than twenty feet before he heard her close the door.

There was a corner only a hundred feet farther up the street, with a rain barrel under a low-hanging gutter. The cobbles ran relatively straight; he took up his post by the barrel, and found he could look down on her door easily.

Slipping his cold hands through the slits of his cloak and into his breeches pockets, Liam made a mental note to buy gloves, and began his wait.

The fox, he was sure, would go to ground soon. The old fence in Auric's Park would probably amount to nothing—he was so old, Liam figured, that he probably would not notice the sky dropping on his head, much less the hints scattered in his shop. He had left Fanuilh there for the sake of thoroughness, but he laid his hopes on the fox.

The red-haired pawnbroker did not disappoint him. Liam's feet were beginning to ache from the cold and his back was hurting before she came out, but come out she did, bundled up in a long scarf and a ragged fur. There were more people in the street now, but he had chosen his spot well. The street descended so steeply that he had no trouble picking her head out in the crowd. She was heading down toward the harbor.

Twice he was sure he had lost her—at a corner, blocked by a pair of recalcitrant oxen with plumes of steam rising from their nostrils, and in a cramped lane nearly choked with stalls selling charms and fortunes—but both times her coppery hair gave her away.

It was only a short trip, despite the anxiety he felt each time he lost sight of her, and her final destination disappointed him. She stopped in front of a stall where hot food was sold, and received a heavy pot over the counter from a woman who, judging from her red hair and long nose, might have been the pawnbroker's sister.

Liam stood with his back to the stall, pretending to examine a collection of sailor's scarves and listening to their conversation. They shared a barked laugh about a man named Raker—and that was all. The pawnbroker did not mention his visit, and left the stall with the pot.

Disappointed, Liam trailed along behind the fox, following the smell of stew from her pot. *Rabbit*, he noted. *Of course it would be rabbit*. He did not lose her on the way back, but she only went to her shop. He trudged up the street, glancing sourly at the door as he passed, and resumed his position by the rain barrel.

There had been no guarantee the plan would work immediately, he told himself, or at all, for that matter. She would not necessarily run right out and tell the Guild. He had hoped, however, that she would, guessing that Southwark was small enough that a stranger dropping chant around would be picked up immediately.

The pawnbroker is leaving his shop.

Liam had so far dismissed the old man that Fanuilh's thought came as a surprise.

Where? he projected, ignoring the instant throb in his temples.

He is heading out of Auric's Park.

Follow him. Show me when he stops.

Yes, master.

He had not expected the old man to do anything—but then, he reminded himself, he might only be going out for rabbit stew. Nonetheless, Liam quickly grew impatient with his watch. The red-haired woman did not emerge from her shop, and no one went in. Again the cold was seeping into his boots.

In his mind's eye, he saw the dusty pawnbroker shuffling slowly along, and willed him to hurry.

He is going to the Point, Fanuilh reported at last, but Liam only nodded, forcing himself to concentrate on the woman's door. The Point made a certain amount of sense, he realized, though exactly where the man would end up would certainly be interesting.

He is going into a house, Fanuilh thought.

Show me, Liam projected back.

Are you sure, master? Liam had never enjoyed using Fanuilh's eyes—he found the experience disturbing. But this time he nodded, and closed his eyes quickly. There was a flicker in the darkness, and when he opened his eyes again, he was looking down on an entirely different street, apparently from the roof of a building. The old pawnbroker was just approaching a run-down town house. He checked to the left and right, then opened the door and ducked inside.

If that isn't it, Liam projected, *I don't know what is*. The town house's windows were all shuttered, and its general air of disrepair made it look like a rotten tooth among the healthy, occupied homes to either side.

He closed his eyes—Fanuilh's eyes—and when he opened them, he was looking into the concerned face of a beggar.

"Pray, master, is all well?"

Liam smiled with delight, and dug into his pocket.

"All is perfect, my friend," he said, and set off for the city square, leaving the astounded beggar behind with a handful of coins.

Coeccias was in the barracks when Liam stopped by, though he said he was going out immediately.

"Truth, Rhenford, that Cloten'll be the death of me, if I'm not his first. Now he's given the lie to the Death herself, in front of Laomedon's own fane!"

Liam knew that Laomedon's highest priests had no names of their own, but were referred to simply as Deaths; he had not known, though, that Laomedon's Death in Southwark was female.

"It's a she? The Death is a woman?"

The Aedile waved away the interruption. "To her very face, I say! Can believe it? I've to go there now and calm him, before he tasks the Duke with it." He was wearing a clean black tunic with the Duke's foxes on it, proper for an official visit.

"Calm him? I thought it was a she."

"Not the Death," Coeccias explained, "she took it all in course. Very cool, she is. She did not even deign to answer him, and that liked Cloten not. He vowed that if I do not find the thief soon enough, he'ld start looking on his own."

"Can't have people looking for thieves on their own," Liam muttered, but the Aedile caught it, and laughed.

"Truth, not often, Rhenford! But tell me, how goes your search? You'll have conned and caught yours by now, eh?"

Once again, the display of unwarranted confidence made Liam wince. He hastened to correct his friend. "Not at all. I have an idea or two, but very hazy ones. In fact, that's why I came—I need a little information."

"Ask then, but quick. Only the gods know what Cloten'll do next."

"Is there a thieves' guild in Southwark?" If there was no guild, then he had just wasted his morning. It was a question he should have asked the day before, but it had never occurred to him that there would not be one.

Coeccias's head jerked up and he stopped the pacing that had taken him from one end of the long barracks to the other ten times in as many minutes.

"Why ever would you ask? Y'are not thinking of contacting them?"

"No," Liam lied blandly, thinking of his earlier conversation with Fanuilh. If he could buy back his things, he did not want the Aedile to know about it. "But it would give me some help in figuring out how to approach the thing. Guild thieves have different ways than rogues—they spend more time together, for one thing, and they often frequent the same wineshops and taverns."

Coeccias thought for a moment, stroking his beard. "There is," he said at last, and slowly, "but how t'approach them is beyond me. They're a close band, and I have heard they're short with outsiders."

That was no surprise to Liam; all guild thieves were short with outsiders. "Do you know anything else?"

The look Coeccias gave him was composed equally of uncertainty over telling him more and curiosity at what he already knew. In the end, he covered both, and added a warning. "Here's all: they name their princeps—that's how they style the guild leader—they name him the Werewolf. I know not if it's the man's name or a general title. They are a close group, all said, and lay low, unlike one of your big-city guilds. I catch the individual thief from time to time, but have never tied them to the whole. And I don't try, Rhenford. However much of a hound y'are, they're wolves. The princeps's name says it."

Liam nodded, accepting the information and the warning. "I'll be careful," he promised.

"As you were with Ancus Marcius and's toughs, eh?" Ancus Marcius was a merchant Liam had wrongly suspected of murdering Tarquin; the suspicion had cost him a beating from the man's bodyguards.

"More so. Much more so."

Coeccias smiled briefly at the memory, then heaved a sigh, recalled to his duty. "Now I needs must go. Waiting will not like Cloten in the least."

The two men crossed the square together. The normal crowds were back: hawkers and street performers, customers and beggars. The snow was gone, trampled beneath hundreds of feet, leaving only a dark, wet sheen on the cobbles. They parted at the far corner, Liam heading north to the stables where he had left Diamond, Coeccias heading east for Temple Street.

Once on his horse, clattering toward the city gate, Liam remembered Fanuilh. He formed the dragon's name in his head and projected carefully, ready to stop at the first hint of a headache. To his relief—and pleasure—there was none, and the dragon responded immediately.

Yes, master?

Return to the house. I'm finished in the city. Until tonight.

Yes, master.

No stab of pain in his temples yet; he projected again.

I'm getting better at this.

Yes, master. I will see you at the house, and we can practice more.

Liam nodded happily to himself and spurred Diamond to a trot. He was getting better at communicating with his familiar, and he had a plan.

Once beyond the pillars at Southwark's eastern edge, he urged the roan into a flat-out gallop.

• • •

Scaevola was waiting on the patio; Liam saw him from the path, and eased back the wild grin etched on his face by his cold gallop to a smile of greeting. In the back of his head, though, he scolded himself. The sick man had been right; there was nothing in Tarquin's books to help him.

"Hail, Liam Rhenford," Scaevola said, his disfigured face expressionless.

"Hello," Liam replied, dismounting and putting out his hand. He was happy—and a little ashamed—to see that the other man was wearing gloves. "I'm afraid I do not have anything for you. There was nothing in the library."

Scaevola grasped his hand firmly, waving away the apology with his other. "I expected nothing," he said, and a shy smile cracked the scales on his cheeks. "There never has been anything."

Liam nodded, unsure what to say. He pitied the younger man, but did not think it right to express his sympathy. After an awkward pause, Scaevola pointed to the bundle at his feet.

"I saw—yesterday, you were wearing a sword—I thought . . . All of the other acolytes at the temple are exhausted, and there has been no practice. . . ."

He flushed, the blood lining the edges of scales; the whites of his eyes stood out brightly. Kneeling fluidly, he unwrapped the bundle and stood, holding two wooden practice swords.

"You want to spar?"

"I thought, perhaps . . ." Scaevola let the sentence trail away, put off by Liam's unfeigned astonishment.

There was another heavy pause, which Liam struggled to fill.

"I don't—I'm not much of a swordsman, I'm afraid."

"Of course," Scaevola blurted, kneeling again to put the practice swords away. "I understand."

"No," Liam said quickly, "don't put them away. I'll go a round with you. It's just that I really am not much of a swordsman. Just let me put Diamond away."

He led the horse to the shed behind the house, leaving the acolyte on the patio, kneeling by his bundle. He was being honest when he said he was not good with a sword; while he had often been a soldier, his experience in combat was small, and he had never developed much skill. Most soldiers did not, he knew. War was more a matter of having enough men in the right place at the right time, of feeding armies and keeping them paid and healthy, than of the individual warrior's prowess. The battles he had been in were all crude things, where victory came from brute force and sheer numbers, not the finesse of single swordsmen. Only a very few experts—some warrior monks, members of the Society of Heralds, and, of course, devotees of war gods— ever became masters of swordsmanship. The average soldier was more concerned with being fed and keeping his footing on a field made slippery with blood.

So when he returned to the patio, he repeated his warning, even as he picked up a practice sword and made a few tentative cuts in the air.

"As I said, I'm not very good."

"No matter," Scaevola said, taking the other sword. "You'll want to remove your cloak."

The cold bit through his tunic, but he brought his sword up and saluted.

They fought four brief matches—not as brief as they might have been, but Liam saw after the first few passes that Scaevola was holding back. Even so, he was amazed at the other's speed. The wooden sword flickered practically unseen, dodging past his rather feeble guard, whispering around his ears or flicking at his legs. He jumped and twisted as well as he could, but Scaevola was everywhere, gracefully pushing him around the patio as if he were a child. He never came off the defensive, desperately putting up his blade to try to ward off Scaevola's lightning blows. Soon—far too soon, he thought—he had no thought but for the clatter of sword on sword and the next pointless attempt to parry. At the end of the fourth match, he breathlessly called a halt.

"Enough," he said, dropping the sword. He had forgotten the cold; sweat ran down his face and soaked his tunic, but the other man looked unruffled, his breath coming easily. He looked at Liam with concern.

"I'm sorry. Are you not well?"

"No," Liam wheezed, "just out of practice."

Fat. The echo of Fanuilh's words rang in his head, a counterpoint to the pounding of blood. He was not fat, he insisted to himself, only out of practice.

He caught his breath. "It's too cold. Let's go inside."

Scaevola bundled up the swords and followed him into the house.

Liam was exhausted; he slumped at the kitchen table, wiping sweat from his face and breathing hoarsely. "Are you hungry? There's something in the oven." He managed to focus for a moment, imagining a pie.

The sick man hesitated, looking at him with something close to pity. Liam shook himself and straightened in his chair.

I can't be that *tired*, he thought. "Go ahead," he said aloud. "And get me a glass from that jug, would you?"

Scaevola hastened to pour a cup of wine from the jug by the oven, and placed it solicitously in front of Liam, then retrieved the pie. He sat opposite his tired host, picking uncomfortably at the food.

"I am sorry, Liam Rhenford," he said at last. "I should not have asked you to spar."

Liam shook his head. Three greedy swallows of wine had given him a little strength, and his hands had stopped shaking. "I am out of practice, that's all. I have not worn a sword in some time. And when I did wear one," he added, "that was really all I did. Wear it. I can count on the fingers of one hand the number of times I have drawn a sword."

Neither was true: he had drawn more times than he could count—he had simply never gotten good at it. But the excuses seemed to make Scaevola more comfortable, and he began eating with a will.

After a few minutes, when he was completely sure of himself—that his hands would not shake, or his breath whistle in his throat—he put his thoughts to the man across the table. The symptoms of the fever did not bother him much, though he had to admit that they were awful. Instead of revulsion, he felt curiosity at the strange mix of benefits and disadvantages conferred by the disease. Scaevola was practically a monster to look at, but without a doubt he was the fastest swordsman Liam had ever seen.

The sick man felt his scrutiny and looked up from his pie expectantly.

"Are you the best in the temple?"

"Yes," Scaevola admitted, without a trace of modesty— a simple fact. "I teach the others. Though now, with the double watches and all the excitement, there is not much time for practice."

"Ah," Liam said, "the excitement. The robbery. I understand Hierarch Cloten is greatly . . . agitated by it."

Scaevola rolled his eyes, the leathery scales around them not moving at all. "Agitated is no word for it. He has accused everyone of the crime. I cannot imagine why he would make trouble with our dear goddess's father, but he does."

"Father? Bellona's father?"

The acolyte put his spoon down. "Some of us believe," he said thoughtfully, "that Strife is Bellona's father, his get by . . . well, we differ on Her mother. It is a cause of discord in the temple. Alastor, the Keeper of Arms, says Uris is her mother, though I am not sure of that. Cloten says she has no mother or father. That she merely is.'' His tone indicated what he thought of that.

"I had no idea.''

"Her worship is but young,'' Scaevola explained. "Many details are to be determined, though most are coming to believe Her divine parenthood.''

"But Cloten does not?''

"No. He has arguments, sometimes heated, with Alastor, and I have heard that he has ignored certain instructions from Caernarvon. But he is Grand Hierarch Lowestoft's nephew, and cannot be naysayed.''

Liam listened carefully. Temple politics had never caught his interest much, the gods of the Midlands being old, well-established and placid, but the information might be of some use to Coeccias in his investigation. And there was something he was interested in himself.

"Tell me about the gryphon.''

"A sacrifice,'' Scaevola said diffidently. "Hierarch Cloten says we will offer it up when we open the temple officially.''

"Where did you get it?''

"We caught it on our way here from Caernarvon. There was a fight, just as we were coming out of the mountains. Some brigands.'' His eyes lit up at the memory, and for a moment he was silent, as if reliving it. "When it was over, and we were dedicating the combat to Bellona, we found it at the edge of the field, among the dead. It was strange, though, it was scavenging, only looking at the fallen, and it made no effort to flee.''

Liam frowned; the gryphons he had seen and read about were fierce fighters, jealous of their freedom.

"We chained it easily," Scaevola went on, "and it has not given us any trouble since."

"How do you feed it?"

"We do not," Scaevola said, avoiding Liam's eyes. "On our way here we tried to, but it refused all we supplied. Keeper of Arms Alastor would bring it something different every day, but it would have none of it. By the time we got here, Hierarch Cloten forbade him to try anymore."

"Let me guess," Liam half joked, "Alastor didn't listen, so Cloten hung it from the ceiling so he couldn't get at it."

Scaevola did not share the joke. "There was a great argument over that. Those who built the temple before us had hung something from the dome. I do not know what it was—Keeper of Arms Alastor says a large image of their god—but the chain was there when we moved in. Hierarch Cloten decided it immediately. Many of us do not like the idea."

"Really," Liam said, for lack of anything else. Bellona's worshipers seemed to have quite a few points of contention.

They were quiet, brooding for a while. Finally, Scaevola pushed away his plate and stood up.

"I must return now. Thank you for the meal—and the practice."

"Not at all," Liam replied. "I only wish I could have been more of a match for you." He got up and led the way to the door.

"You are untrained, that is all. You could be quite a warrior if you tried."

Liam laughed at the comment. "I don't think so."

They shook hands, and once again Liam watched the acolyte run across the beach and up the path.

He stretched leisurely and went back to the kitchen, where a thought at the oven soon produced a bucket of warm water. He stripped and washed the dried sweat from his body, thinking about what he had learned.

At first glance the theological differences among Bellona's followers did not seem like much, but as he thought about it he saw a potential hint or two. If Cloten was Bothmer Lowestoft's nephew, he would be doubly interested in protecting the notes on the Lowestoft mines, particularly if his orthodoxy was in question. That might explain his extreme reaction to the attempted robbery, as well as his wild accusations of Guiderius.

A string of questions gradually occurred to him, things he would ask of Cloten, of the Keeper of Arms, Alastor, of Guiderius and the lower followers of Bellona.

As he put on a clean tunic and breeches, he stopped the ideas.

"Tell Coeccias," he muttered to himself. "You've got your own thief to catch." He turned his thoughts to his own search and what little headway he had made.

The abandoned house in the Point was a good starting place, and the plan he had made the day before still seemed the best way to approach it. He would take care of that later that evening, after his dinner with the Aedile. But apart from that, he had done little. If his thief were not a thief at all, but a wizard, he still had no way of proceeding.

How do you find a wizard? he wondered. Fanuilh could find one, if he performed a magical act, and Mother Japh had assured him that if there was one in Southwark, word would spread quickly. But those were hardly sufficient; he needed a more concrete way.

With a heavy sigh, he went into the library and began picking books off the shelves.

CHAPTER 5

AN HOUR LATER, with fifteen tomes on magic
piled at his feet, Liam was no further along toward
a method for finding wizards than when he had begun. The
books dealt with the details of working magic or the the-
ories behind magic or reports of magics that had worked
and some that had rather spectacularly *not* worked, but
never with the people who worked, theorized or reported.
There were no biographies of wizards or descriptions of
their habits, no quick and easy list of characteristics to look
for, and after leafing through the last book that even
vaguely mentioned wizardry, Liam set it down on a teeter-
ing stack, leaned back and closed his eyes.

He did not sleep, though; only slipped into a pleasant
torpor, tired from the sparring with Scaevola and an hour
of reviewing books he did not understand.

Some wizard I am, Liam thought, a frown settling onto
his face. *I don't even know half the words.* He knew he
was better educated than most people, and had some skill
with languages, but the jargon of magic had often proved
far beyond him.

With a sour grunt he rolled over, wincing at a bruise
from Scaevola's wooden sword, and began reviewing his
plans for the evening. He was to meet Coeccias for dinner,
and after that he would be free to follow up on the house
the old pawnbroker had visited. The prospect excited him,
not least because it was his only idea. If it did not lead to

his thief, then he would be forced to start over, and he guessed that would mean giving up.

The problem was that he knew too little. When he had looked for Tarquin's murderer, Fanuilh had been able to give him names and, to a certain extent, motives, concrete starting points. With this robbery, he had only questions: why had the thief taken only the rug, the wand and the book? A proper thief would have taken everything that was not nailed down, even if he had been commissioned to take only those three items. And what if it hadn't been a thief? The breaching of the house's magical wards suggested a wizard, but both Fanuilh and Mother Japh were convinced there were none in Southwark.

Except me, he noted, rolling over with another grunt. There were simply too many questions and only one place he could imagine to find answers.

Liam forced himself to sit up and open his eyes. A weariness was settling over his limbs, and he stretched to be rid of it. *No sense walking into the local guild sleepy*, he told himself, and went to the kitchen to splash cold water on his face. Coeccias had made the thieves sound extremely dangerous, and he wondered for a moment whether he ought to bring his sword.

Bring it, came Fanuilh's thought, a heavy imperative in his head.

"They might take that the wrong way," Liam said out loud.

Project, the dragon ordered.

He sighed heavily, but found that it was not as difficult as before. *They might take offense if I go armed.*

Bring the sword.

The dirk, he suggested. *Just the dirk.*

I will come, too.

"Oh no," Liam said, leaving the kitchen and walking toward the workroom. "They'll definitely take you the wrong way." Fanuilh lay in its basket, curled up nose to tail, and offered him a brief glance. "They'll think I'm a wizard."

And if they do?

"Thieves aren't terribly fond of wizards, and these don't sound like the kind you want angry at you. The big-city guilds have strict rules about violence, but from what Coeccias says, the southerners may have their own ideas."

Then I will hide nearby—on the roof or in the street.

Liam considered the suggestion. "All right. That would make sense. But you're not to interfere, unless I'm clearly in danger. Understand?"

Yes, master. Will you practice now?

"I don't think so," he said, looking out the window at the rear of the workroom. The narrow space between the back of the villa and the cliffs was already filled with dark shadows. "I think it's time for me to meet Coeccias."

They had chosen to meet at the White Grape, a small inn on the border of the Point and the middle section of Southwark, not far from the city square. It had no stables, and Liam was forced to find a hostler some distance away, but the walk to the inn and the ride into the city, not to mention his earlier exercise, only served to sharpen his appetite. Coeccias was not there when he arrived; he chose a table and drank a beer, patting his rumbling stomach every few moments.

The serving girls knew the two of them, and when Coeccias finally threw open the door and stumped in, one of them jerked her thumb at where Liam sat. The Aedile threaded his way through the crowded tables.

"You're late," Liam noted, a little sharply. "I ordered two of their sea pies."

"Truth, I'm lucky to get away at all. I needs must've done something very ill, to be saddled with that Cloten, but for my life I know not what.'' He fumbled off his padded wool coat and dropped heavily into his seat. A serving girl brought him a mug before he could ask, and he drank half of it in one gulp. ''Rhenford,'' he went on, wiping foam from his beard, ''that's the best of a bad day.''

''So Cloten is still making trouble for you?''

''Aye. He has set a day, by which if I don't have his thief in hand, he'll—I quote here—'see to the matter himself.' See to the matter himself! He'll to war, he means, and lay siege to both Strife and Laomedon, the fool.''

''I take it you've made no progress, then?''

''None,'' the Aedile admitted with a rueful grin. ''Not the least. And how to? Cloten swears it was a dozen men, if not more, all armed and armored, but his guards say they heard nothing.''

''You've spoken to them all?''

''Aye, though Cloten seemed to think that a waste of time. 'Why do you ask them?' he says. 'I was there. I was the one who was attacked. Ask me, ask me. I've told you all you need to know.' '' The Aedile's impression of the Hierarch made him sound like an angry fishwife, and Liam smiled. ''It's not so funny, I warrant, when he's in your face. And he spits when he talks, as well.'' He swiped a large hand across his beard, and then laughed. ''I spoke to the guards, though, in the end, and only one heard aught. A queer fellow, all muffled and jerky, as if he crawled with fleas, but said he'd heard something like spurs in the street outside.''

''Muffled? Hooded, you mean?'' Coeccias nodded. ''I think I've met him, too. His name is Scaevola, and he has low-root fever.''

''Low-root? The Caernarvon plague?'' The Aedile groaned and covered his eyes with his hands. ''Bad enough they send me Cloten, but the plague as well!''

''It's not catching, you know. You're born with it.''

Coeccias slowly drew his hands away from his eyes. "Y'are? Y'are sure?"

"Yes. No one's ever caught low-root fever, that I know of."

"Hm. Well, if you say it, I'll warrant it, but it likes me not, all the same. Bellona's brought more trouble to Southwark than I'd like, goddess though She is."

Liam studied the worried expression on his friend's face for a moment, then spoke hesitantly. "I think she may have brought something else." He described Scaevola's two visits to his house, and the theological dispute about Bellona's parentage. "He didn't seem to think it was terribly important, more of a minor disagreement, but if Cloten is arguing with his second in command, and ignoring orders from the main temple in Caernarvon . . ."

"It might go far to explaining his strong reaction," Coeccias mused, picking up the thread of Liam's thoughts. "But what does it tell us about the attempted robbery? Precious little, as I see it."

"Well," Liam answered slowly, "this is only a thought, but what if your thief wasn't after the treasury? That is, what if he wasn't a thief at all?"

Coeccias's mug paused halfway to his mouth, and his jaw worked soundlessly for a second. Then he put his mug down softly. "I take it," he said carefully, "that you're suggesting an assassin."

Liam shrugged. "Not a real assassin, in the sense of money for a life taken. But a disaffected believer, someone who disagrees with Cloten, or thinks he's promoting blasphemy. After all, he did say it was a group of men, not just one thief. And you say Scaevola heard spurs in the street."

"Aye, aye," the Aedile murmured, tugging now at his beard, his food forgotten. "But then, why in the street? Why not in the temple? Bellona has no real worshipers in Southwark yet. All Her acolytes are in the temple—so why the street, outside? And I have my doubts about Cloten's 'armed band.' More likely one or two, given the time it took them to get away before his own guards arrived. A dozen couldn't escape in a minute.''

''All right, but would a thief go armed? Most don't. And they certainly don't wear spurs. Though you are right about the noise being outside. It doesn't make any sense.''

The same thought occurred to both men at the same time; it made Coeccias rock back in his seat, while Liam whistled.

''Guiderius,'' the Aedile suggested.

''Or the Death.''

''It could be, though more likely Guiderius. Bellona threats Strife more than Laomedon.''

''For that matter, She threatens every temple on the street, given that treasury. I must say, though, that I can't see anyone trying murder over moneylending.''

Coeccias snorted. ''Y'are new in Southwark, Rhenford. It's been done. But you've the right of it—most likely Strife or Laomedon.'' He heaved a deep sigh. ''Which means now I needs must start a whole new line of questions, and very trickish ones at that. Truth, trickish isn't in it. 'Pardon, Keeper of Arms Alastor, but do you disagree with Hierarch Cloten enough to take him off?'''

''It does seem a little complicated,'' Liam admitted.

''Complicated? Like crossing a room full of black cats under a new moon without a candle, Rhenford. 'Pardon, Hierarch Guiderius, but did you try to kill Hierarch Cloten, for that his goddess also practices war?' A little complicated!''

''Don't forget that some of Her acolytes think she's Strife's daughter. I don't know how Guiderius would feel about that.''

Coeccias sipped at his beer, frowning miserably. ''Truth, Rhenford, this goes from bad to worst. One thief was bad

enough, given Cloten . . . but now you make a religious war
of it!''

"I didn't make a war of it! Somebody else did; I'm just
giving you ideas."

"In future," Coeccias grumbled unhappily, "keep them
to yourself."

It was strange, Liam reflected in the lull that followed,
how much they both disliked asking questions. Both were
good at formulating questions, and knew it—though Liam
thought the Aedile placed entirely too much faith in him
on that score, as on many others—but they hated the process of asking. Perhaps, he decided, the problem was not the
questions, but that the answers were all too often the ones
they did not want to hear.

Coeccias had resumed his interrupted meal. When he
shoved his empty plate away he settled back in his chair
and gave Liam a long stare.

"So. Now that y'have muddied the search for my thief,
pray tell me about yours. In hopes that I can make it difficult, see you."

They both smiled a little. "It's not good," Liam said. "I
checked on those two fences, and neither had any idea what
I was talking about. And I've looked through all of Tarquin's books, but there was nothing there about how to find
a wizard."

"Mother Japh said she'd told you there were no wizards
in Southwark."

"Yes, she did, but she might have been wrong. And if
there are no wizards, how would a thief get the spells necessary to break the wards on the house?"

"She also said she showed you her morgue."

Liam nodded, and then realized what he had admitted.
Coeccias thought he was squeamish around the dead.
"Yes," he said noncommittally, and felt the color rising to
his face. "It was helpful."

"She said," the Aedile went on, a little smile playing on his lips, "that you warranted her one of the corses had probably been a clerk, for that you felt his hands."

Liam stammered out that he had, his face burning red. He had not thought that Mother Japh would talk to Coeccias, nor that he would ever be caught in his lie. It had merely been something about which he felt vaguely guilty, a small secret that he hid from his friend for the sake of convenience. Now Coeccias's smile was growing.

"I've a theory, Rhenford, and I would that you'd help me with it. Do you recall asking me about thieftakers? Was that the word? Thieftakers?"

"Yes," he answered, wondering where Coeccias was going. He felt like blurting out the truth—that he had seen a thousand corpses, been in a dozen battles, seen and heard and been things the Aedile would never believe—but the confident expression on his friend's face held him back.

"Y'have always presented yourself a scholar, Rhenford, but I think not. Know you what I think?" Liam shook his head and waited. Coeccias smiled with satisfaction, and leveled a finger across the table as he pronounced: "I think you were one of these thieftakers."

Liam laughed harder than he had for months. He liked the Aedile, and had more respect for his ability as an investigator than the man did himself, but he could not imagine a more outlandish conclusion. A thief, yes, and a spy once or twice, but a thieftaker? His laughter annoyed Coeccias.

"It fits, does it not? With your nose for a villain, and what you know of thieves? Come, tell me how a man would know such things if he weren't one of your thieftakers?"

"It could be," Liam managed, wiping tears from his eyes, "and I admit that it would seem to make sense. But I can assure you that I wasn't."

"Then how do you know all the things you do?" his friend demanded.

"By listening," Liam explained, "and asking questions. Sooner or later, if you listen enough and ask enough questions, you learn a little about everything. For instance, from listening to you I know a great deal about being the Duke's man in Southwark, but that doesn't make me the Aedile, does it?"

Coeccias grudgingly admitted that this was true, and for just a moment Liam worried that his friend was truly angry with him. Then he realized that the Aedile's frustration came from disappointment: he had hoped that Liam was a thieftaker, because it would explain him. Most people had a rightful place and position in Taralon—sailor or merchant, soldier or priest, what it was did not matter—and that place made it clear who they were. Liam, on the other hand, had no place. He lived in a wizard's house and had a wizard's familiar, but he was not a wizard; he called himself a scholar, but he neither wrote books nor took pupils; he hunted thieves, but was neither thieftaker nor Guard. He defied understanding to a certain extent. It was a sobering thought.

"In any case, if I were a thieftaker," he said, "I'd be a rather poor one. It's already two days, and I haven't found my man."

"But y'have an idea, I warrant." The Aedile seemed resigned to the fact that his guess at Liam's past was a failure, but his old faith in Liam's skill was still showing in full force. "What will you next?"

"I'm not sure. I have to give up the idea of wizards for a bit, and follow up on thieves. The fences weren't much help, but I think I may know a way to get in touch with some thieves."

With a wave of his hand, Coeccias indicated that this was as much as he had expected. "In course, but what then? Are these thieves yours, or will they only know yours?''

"Again, I'm not sure," Liam said, though he was. If the Southwark Guild was as vicious as Coeccias claimed, they would not stand for an unlicensed thief in the city, which meant they would have to know his thief. The question was, what would happen from there? "I'll have to see. And as far as what I do then, I think that will be up to you," he hedged.

"How so?"

"It may happen that these thieves won't tell me who my thief is, but they may take him a message."

"Ah, I see you now. The message will say you'd be willing to buy back your goods." Sometimes Coeccias surprised him with the quickness of his perceptions.

"Well, yes, it would—if that does not bother you."

"Bother me? Why should it?" The Aedile seemed genuinely puzzled, and Liam breathed a mental sigh of relief.

"I thought you might object to my dealing with them."

"I have no objections. If it's the only way to recover your goods, then so be it. Look you," he said seriously, leaning over the table and ticking off his points on blunt fingers, "I tell you this in confidence, Rhenford, though I guess you already know it. There are things in Southwark I can do. I can patrol the streets, and prevent or sound out the grossest murders. I can break up riots and bar brawls. I can see that the taverns on the waterfront do not vend paint for wine and poison the tars. I can keep tabs on the brothels and close the theaters and bear-baiters. I can keep the scales in the markets honest and, as a rule, I can keep the number of cutpurses down to a few. But there is much I cannot do. I cannot question the great merchants or the gentry, I cannot interfere with the temples, and—most to the point—I cannot break the Guild. I have not men nor time, nor inclination.''

It was a long speech for Coeccias, and he sat back when he was done, vaguely embarrassed at having made it. Liam nodded, though; he had known or guessed at most of it.

"Then that is what I'll try to do—buy them back."

"Fair as fair can be. Though mind you, if y'have the chance to clap your thief, do it. It'd like me to take in a housebreaker. Who knows where he'd lead me?"

They finished their beers, each wondering where it would.

By the time they left the White Grape, a cold, clear night had covered Southwark with a dark sky, punctuated only by the hard, brilliant points the stars made, and their breath trailed away in white plumes. They parted outside the door of the inn, Coeccias back to the barracks in the city square and Liam ostensibly for the hostler where his horse was stabled.

He had not been honest with the Aedile when he told him he would be going back to the beach. His intention was to visit the abandoned house on the Point, but he judged it too early, and he wanted a little time to go over the finer details of his plan.

After walking a few blocks, he discovered that these were not many, and that the finest point he had to go over was whether he would carry out the plan at all. If Southwark's Guild was as dangerous as Coeccias said, it might prove foolish. They might not be bound by the rules that held in other guilds—they might not be bound by any rules at all. And they might look askance at an uninvited visitor. An unpleasant image occurred to him: his own body laid out in Mother Japh's morgue, one of her preservation bags between his feet and a little blue flame dancing over his mouth.

Unless my soul goes wandering off, and there is no flame, he thought, and pulled his cloak closer. Could his soul go wandering off? Part of it rested with Fanuilh, he knew. Would that keep it in place? He could have asked the little dragon, but refrained. He did not really want to know.

Instead, he wandered through the city, out of the middle district, north of the square and into the artisans' districts. The streets were dark, illuminated only occasionally by candlelight from windows and irregularly placed torches on the walls; he imagined himself a shadow, gliding through the city outside the warm pockets of life. The feeling disturbed him even more than his earlier image of Mother Japh's morgue, and he began to cast about for something to occupy his time.

His feet took him of their own accord to the Uncommon Player, but he stopped at the door of the rowdy tavern. The Player was his favorite in the city, a meeting place for minstrels, actors, the more adventurous artisans and a general crowd of interesting types that never failed to entertain him. He chose, however, not to go in that night; he wanted his head clear for his work later on, and the Player had a rule about the minimum number of drinks ordered.

As he stood at the door wondering what to do, he saw a bright pool of light from around a distant corner, where the entrance of the Golden Orb was. It was Southwark's only theater; he had been introduced to both the Orb and the Player while looking for Tarquin's murderer. There should have been no lights there; by the Duke's law, it had been closed since the beginning of winter, as a precaution against the spread of disease.

Hoping for something of interest, Liam left the light and noise of the Player behind and turned the corner. The gold-painted wooden globe that usually hung over the theater's doors was gone, replaced by a series of boards painted with various fantastic animals; the cheap smoky links beneath each tended more to obscure than reveal the paintings, but

Liam recognized a lion and a giant boar. The others he gave up on.

A forlorn-looking boy hopped from foot to foot by the one open door, clutching a sheaf of pamphlets. His cheeks were bright red with cold; a ragged scarf hung around his neck and trailed down to his knees.

"What's inside, boy?" Liam asked, looking at the painted signs.

"Animals," the boy said sarcastically, indicating the boards. "Pictures of 'em, aren't there?"

"I thought the theater was closed."

The boy looked at the open door, frowned in concentration for a moment, then looked up at Liam with a sneer. "Doesn't seem that way now, does it? Seems passing open to me."

"Right. How much to go in?"

"Ask the keeper," the boy said, jerking a thumb at the open door and resuming his hopping.

Smiling, Liam entered the Golden Orb, and behind him he heard the boy mumble at the empty street: "Come see the animals. Come see the menagerie. Come see the blasted animals, you idiots."

The lobby was empty, so he opened one of the doors to the groundlings' area and poked his head in.

"Hello?" he called.

A voice answered him from the far side of the theater: "Get back out there and get me some customers, you little bastard!"

Liam cleared his throat. "I am a customer."

The Orb was octagon shaped, with galleries and private boxes on seven sides and the stage on the eighth, and longer side; from the roof, high above where the groundlings stood, hung an enormous chandelier. Normally it held hundreds of candles, but only a dozen or so now flickered, so that Liam could only hear and not see the voice's owner jump up, trip over something and then come running over to the doors.

"Your pardon," the woman said breathlessly, stopping with a rushed curtsy. "I thought you were that wretched boy, come to complain of the cold. You're here to see the menagerie!"

"Yes," Liam said, smiling. The woman wore a strange mix of clothes: a long skirt so broad and shapeless that it had to hide a few more skirts underneath it, a man's boiled leather vest with metal studs on it and a hawking glove on one hand. Her steel gray hair was pulled back tightly from her pocked face, which was covered with vividly colored, inexpertly applied makeup. In her ungloved hand she held the skinned carcass of a rabbit.

"Well, first is first, sir," she said cheerily, "and I needs must ask you th'entrance, which is a silver crown or its equal—though not its better, for I've no change—and well worth it, you'll see, I'm sure."

Liam produced the coin, but the woman, realizing her hands were full, laughed. "Oh, you'll have to hold it for now, sir, 'til I'm rid of this coney. Now just do me the favor of lighting one of those lanterns, and I'll show you the greatest menagerie to grace Southwark since . . . well, since last I was here with it, and it's better now by far!"

There were two rusty lanterns by the door, and flint and tinder, and when he had one lit, the woman led him across the theater floor, talking all the while.

"I'm wont to be closed now, sir, you see, but with the snow and the cold, the trade is down, and I need to be here at all hours, on the off chance of someone like yourself— mind that cage"—of which there were several, large and small, scattered across the groundlings' area, all covered with patched tarpaulins of sailcloth—"seeing the wisdom and stopping in." She led him up to the stage, climbing nimbly with her skirts bunched up in the hawking glove.

He followed, and they stopped in front of the largest cage, where a bucket with the bloody rabbit skin inside stood.

"I'll show you this last," the woman went on. "I shouldn't show it first, for that it's the main attraction of the menagerie, and the true claim to greatness. But I've this coney, and it to be fed, and it must be fresh or it'll not eat. So." With a deft twist of her wrist, the woman flipped up the edge of the tarp and tossed the meat inside. A slow rustling issued inside the cage, and as the sound of powerful jaws crunching through bone filled the area, the woman smiled happily.

"Now," she said, taking off the hawking glove and proffering her clean hand, "we can be introduced. I'm Madame Rhunrath, proprietor and keeper of Taralon's Greatest Menagerie."

Liam started to take her hand, then, realizing she was holding it palm up, pulled a silver crown from his pocket and handed it over. She bit it quickly and smiled again. "No offense meant, sir, none at all. Mere precaution."

"None taken, I assure you."

"Good! Then we'll see Taralon's Greatest Menagerie!"

It did not take long to see the whole thing. Madame Rhunrath led him from cage to cage, pulling off the tarps and displaying her animals, most of which were not pleased with the idea. She had three wolves, a bear cub that could balance a ball on its nose, a very large and very sleepy snake, a mountain goat with enormous, doubled-curved horns, four long-tailed monkeys that wore matching vests and could juggle, and three large hawks. It was not an impressive collection, but Liam enjoyed the woman's patter; once she realized that he knew something about animals, she cut out most of the obvious fictions and displayed a remarkable knowledge of the habits and characteristics of her stock.

"The monkeys, now, poor things," she said, "are too

cold. They're from the distant jungles, south of the Freeports, and the weather here likes them not. In the summer, they chatter and juggle like little demons—I taught them myself—but just now they're rather useless.''

There was a cage of sparrows near the rack on which the hooded hawks stood perched. ''But I'll warrant an educated gentleman like yourself has seen hawks hunt, eh? I let a sparrow and one hawk loose at a time, and it gives the city folk no end of a thrill to see the hunt . . . but I imagine you wouldn't care for it.''

''I've hawked,'' Liam said politely, ''though I can imagine it must be interesting to see it in a building. Still, no need to waste a sparrow for just me.''

Madame Rhunrath breathed an open sigh of relief. ''Sparrows are expensive.''

There was only the cage on the stage left, but she mentioned it somewhat diffidently. ''I'm afraid you'll think it rather poor now, knowing all you know of animals, but there it is—it's the best I've got.'' She led the way up to the stage and pulled back the tarp. ''Just a lion, I'm afraid.''

Though not natural to Taralon, the lion had taken on a certain mythical status in the kingdom; they featured regularly in heraldic devices and in stories, and for the average Taralonian, seeing a live one would be a once-in-a-lifetime event. For Liam, who had traveled more than most and seen a number of the creatures, it was still a pleasure. He had seen enough to know that Madame Rhunrath's was a fine specimen, in good condition, and he told her so.

''I take good care of him,'' she said proudly as the lion stalked back and forth in its cage, lashing its tail against the bars. ''A big cage, plenty of fresh meat. He's the best in Taralon, even better than the ones in Torquay. If I could get but one other passing attraction, I could leave the Southern Tier and head north.''

''What sort?''

"Sorry?"

"What kind of animal? What would you prefer?"

Madame Rhunrath shrugged, as if the possibility were remote. "Oh, a unicorn, or a salamander—though keeping the fires high would be a problem, so no, no salamander— and manticores are too dangerous, with their spikes. Wyrms, as well. A sphinx would pass. I heard tell once of a menagerie that had a demon, but it got loose one night and ate them all. In the south, they say, there are animals bigger than houses with noses like tails that can do tricks. One of those would be nice."

"Elephants," Liam said. "They're called elephants."

The menagerie keeper's jaw dropped. "Have you seen them?"

Liam was not paying attention, though. He was watching the lion pad around its cage, a half-snarl on its face. "They have a gryphon in Bellona's temple."

"A gryphon," Madame Rhunrath sighed. "What I wouldn't give for a gryphon. That'd bring them in."

Thinking of the gryphon reminded Liam of his business, and he turned from the cage. "Thank you, madame. It was well worth the crown."

She walked him to the door, apologizing for her meager display and asking him to tell all his friends to come. "None of those who know as much as you do about animals; it's sure to disappoint. But those who're ignorant or city bred—and your servants! Sure, your servants would enjoy it!"

Liam, reflecting on his staff of personal attendants, smiled and said he would mention it to them.

CHAPTER 6

THE SURLY BOY was still hopping from foot to
foot and muttering to himself, but Liam ignored
him and strolled down the street. The musky smell of the
animals hung about him for a moment, and he breathed
deeply of it before the cold wind tore it away. When he
was far enough from the theater that the boy could not see
him, he formed a thought and projected it.

*Well, servant? Would you like to go to Madame Rhun-
rath's menagerie?*

Fanuilh answered almost immediately, *I do not have a
crown for entrance.*

Perhaps you could be an exhibit, Liam thought.

Fanuilh did not respond.

Liam walked slowly; it was not quite late enough for
what he intended. Despite having been reminded of the
gryphon in the temple, he had enjoyed the menagerie. Madame Rhunrath clearly liked her animals, and treated them
as well as they could hope for in a cage. He wondered how
she managed—it had to be difficult to keep her stock in
food if the crowds were as thin as they seemed. He was
also curious about her location—the Orb was supposed to
be closed to prevent large gatherings, where disease could
spread. Coeccias had been strangely inconsistent in enforc-
ing the Duke's law.

There was no one in the street; the windows of most of
the houses he passed were dark and the rare torches had

almost all burned out. He wished he had borrowed one of Madame Rhunrath's lanterns.

Look up.

He glanced skyward immediately, more in search of Fanuilh than in response to its command.

"Where are you?"

Look south.

He could see only the diamond-hard stars at first, but then, as he swept the southern sky, he saw the moving flicker and the hairy white tail.

"A comet!"

There was a perceptible lightening, the sky shading from black to deep royal blue, as the comet moved. Liam stared at it with childlike awe; he understood now why Coeccias had been so excited. It was like the first long mark on a blank slate, a splash of white paint on black velvet. He had seen falling stars, but none compared to this.

"If it isn't a message from the gods, then it ought to be," he said to himself, then tore his gaze from the heavenly sign with regret and resumed his walk. The glow from the comet cast an eerie half-light on the streets, catching on the snow that had not been swept away, turning blacks to grays and whites brilliant. He found his eyes jumping to left and right constantly; doorways and alleys and sidestreets that were earlier invisible were suddenly filled with vaguely threatening shapes.

Fanuilh? he projected.

I am at the house.

Good, he answered, not meaning it. He wanted the dragon with him in the disquieting streets, not perched at his destination. Steeling himself, however, he picked up his pace and stopped looking from side to side, focusing himself on the quickest route to the Point.

The streets there were wider, and there were more lights in the houses. He realized that he was practically jogging,

and forced himself to slow down when he came to within
a block of the abandoned house. Having seen it only
through Fanuilh's eyes, and that from above, it took him a
moment to recognize it at street level.

A leathery rustle drifted down to the street, and Liam
saw Fanuilh briefly fan its wings from the rooftop.

I am here. I will wait.

*Good. Follow my thoughts—don't interfere unless I ask
you to.*

I will not, master.

Liam nodded his approval to himself, but made no move
for the door of the abandoned house. He distracted himself
from his task by thinking of how easy his communications
with the dragon were becoming, and how wonderful and
strange the comet was.

What finally stirred him to approach was an unbidden
image of himself standing in the middle of the street in the
dead of night, staring like an idiot at an empty house.

Get moving, he told himself, stepping off the cobblestones onto the stoop. *It doesn't matter if it looks like it's
haunted.*

In the faint light of the comet, with snow dusting the
windowsills and the tops of the shutters and the steps to
the door, it did look haunted. There was nothing in the
architecture—plain stone, well cut and neatly laid, though
unadorned—that would inspire fear, and when he had
looked through Fanuilh's eyes the place had been merely a
little sad, something discarded. It was different at night.

Which is what they want, Liam scolded himself. *Why
would thieves choose a place that looked inviting?* He
gripped the hilt of his dirk, went up the rest of the stairs in
three quick steps, and pushed at the door. It did not give,
and for a moment he felt a wave of relief wash over him,
quickly quelled by a firmer grip on his dirk.

The knob, idiot.

It turned easily under his hand, as if it had recently been oiled, and swung open without a sound. A dark corridor lay before him, at the end of which he could just make out a black curtain. Liam took a deep breath and walked quietly down the hall, his hands spread out to touch either wall, conscious of the thick carpet beneath his feet and, strangely, beneath his fingertips. By the time he guessed that they were there both to muffle sound and warm a house that could not allow smoke to appear from its chimney, he had reached the end of the corridor.

He listened for a moment, but heard nothing, so he pushed aside the heavy curtain and blinked in the light of a single candle.

Then he was falling, shoved violently from behind, being picked up and slammed against the wall. There was a knee in his stomach, a grimy hand over his mouth and a cold steel point against his throat. Two bright, feverish eyes caught and held his glance; the wickedly smiling mouth, inches from his, spoke.

"Hello! Coming in the middle of the night! All unannounced! Bad manners!"

"Hey," said someone else from the corridor, a woman, "he's left the door open!"

"Well, then, close it, you stupid whore!" said the man who was holding Liam.

Master?

Liam shook his head once, but could not project. The knife at his throat pressed a little closer, and the man clamped his hand harder on Liam's jaw.

"Leaving the door open! Bad, bad, bad!" With each "bad" he banged Liam's head against the wall and dug a little with the knife. When the man had finished, he screwed up one eye and examined his prisoner. "Now I wonder," he said, "will it talk? Will it shout? If I take my hand away—though not my knife, no, no, not that—will it make a noise?''

Liam shook his head steadily, as steadily as he could manage with the pressure on his stomach and the man's hand on his jaw.

"I closed the door," said the woman somewhere to Liam's left, "and I'm no whore!"

"Shut up, slut," the man said, and jabbed a little with his knife. "Now, ere I kill you, I'm going to take my hand away, and ask what your business is here. And you'll not make a noise, eh?"

Liam nodded slowly. The thief withdrew his knee and took his hand away, but kept the knife in place.

"Well—your business?"

"This one wants to drink the *princeps*," Liam said and, with a confidence he did not feel, added: "So hie the *gladia* from this one's breather."

"Uris!" the woman exclaimed, and Liam's eyes flashed to her for a second. She was only a girl, no more than twelve, dirty and dressed in a ragged smock. "He chants!"

"Shut up!" the thief hissed. When he returned his attention to Liam his eyes squinted meanly. "Where'd you learn that, eh? Eh?" He dug again with his knife, and a warm trickle went down Liam's throat, beneath his collar and further down his chest.

Forcing nonchalance, Liam ignored the cut and tried to look bored. "This one chants for this one's a chanter. *Momenta* hie the gladia. This one would drink the Werewolf."

The chant was little more than a slang, more a set of parallel words and archaic phrases than its own language, but just the few words he had used had a great effect on the man holding him. His gleaming eyes screwed up, then widened.

"Japer," the girl whispered.

"Go tell the Werewolf," Japer ordered.

"But, Japer—"

"*Go!*"

The girl scampered out, ducking beneath another black curtain. Japer eyed Liam nervously.

"Where'd you learn that?" he asked again, this time with a degree of uncertainty.

"A far *carad*," Liam replied, which was not true. He had not learned his chant in a far carad, another guild, but from a solitary thief who had once belonged to a guild. There was no need to reveal that; he could provide enough details to get away with the lie. With a slight frown, he peered down at the knife. "The gladia?"

"Not yet," Japer growled, and then the girl returned, breathless.

"He says bring him."

In a series of swift motions, Japer pulled Liam's dirk from the scabbard and tossed it to the girl, who fumbled with it, then jerked his prisoner forward by the front of his tunic.

"Watch the door," he told the girl, who was searching for the dirk on the floor.

"But, Japer—" she protested, standing up.

"Watch the door, bitch!" he said, then spun Liam around and jabbed the knife at his back. "Through the curtain."

Beyond the curtain a set of stone steps led down to the cellar of the abandoned house, and Liam went down them with an approximation of a saunter.

Master? Fanuilh asked. *Is this wise?*

Of course, Liam projected. *Perfectly wise.*

There was light at the bottom of the stairs, an uneven orange glow, and when he left the last step Liam saw that it was coming from a small brazier, banked with nuggets of coal. Around the brazier were four men, each holding a skewer, cooking chunks of meat over the coals. They all looked up when he entered.

"*Avé*, brothers," Liam began, but was interrupted by a kick from Japer that sent him to his knees.

"So this is the stranger who chants," said one of the men, handing his skewer to another and standing up. He wiped his hands on his dirty breeches and walked over to Liam.

"This one is the princeps," he said, and offered Liam a hand up. It was easy to see why he was nicknamed the Werewolf: grizzled salt-and-pepper hair welled up from his chest and over his face, up his cheeks around his eyes, which were a luminous green. And his incisors were disproportionately long.

Liam hesitated before taking the Werewolf's hand, then allowed himself to be drawn up. He did not know why, but he was grateful to see that he was taller than the head of the Southwark Guild. The shorter man smiled, a deliberately feral smile, but Liam refused to let it shake him.

The teeth and the eyes must take him far, he thought.

"Avé, princeps." Liam waited.

"Avé," the Werewolf responded at last. He should have called Liam "brother"; the omission was not good. "Carad Southwark plays no rogues."

That was all right. Liam had anticipated that the Guild would not allow thieves who were not members to practice in the city.

"This one is not operanding," he said. "*Sola* larking." He was not working, only visiting.

"What carad?"

"Badham Wood." This drew the attention of the men around the brazier, and a curse from Japer, behind him. The Werewolf smiled.

"Badham, eh?"

"*Doh*." Yes.

"This one has drunk the princeps of Carad Badham."

"Stick," Liam supplied, the name of the thief he had known, and waited patiently for the next question. He knew roughly what it would be.

"Wings tell this one Carad Badham liberates much momenta." Gossip told him that Badham Wood was doing well now.

Liam shook his head and smiled, feeling the expectant gazes of the other thieves in the cellar, and the heavy gaze of the Werewolf. "Carad Badham is long broken." The Badham Wood Guild had disbanded a decade before. It had been more a loose association of bandits and highwaymen than a proper guild, but it was accorded that status out of respect for its princeps, Stick. A legend in the Harcourt Guild in his youth, Stick was exiled for an unknown offense and took up with the brigands in and around Badham Wood, a vast stretch of forest near the King's Range, far to the north. "Stick is long no princeps. Last this one heard, he chanted in the Freeports."

There was a distinct change in mood in the cellar. Japer took his knife away from Liam's back, and the thieves by the brazier resumed their cooking. The Werewolf's smile grew less feral, became almost friendly—almost. There was still an edge of wariness to his voice.

"Doh," he said. "Wings told this one that, too. So, a chanter, eh?"

"Sola larking," Liam answered. The word could mean many things, from visiting to loafing to being retired—anything but actively stealing.

"No chanting?"

"None," Liam assured him. "Sola larking."

The Werewolf was silent for a while, studying him, undoubtedly trying to unnerve him with his fierce green stare and the way he rubbed at his cheeks, pulling his lips back to reveal his abnormally long teeth. Liam guessed that he was out of danger; the question now was whether the visit would be of any use.

After a minute of unbroken quiet, during which Liam became aware of a slight draft through the cellar carrying a sewer stink, the Werewolf spoke again.

"*Peir* drink the slavers momenta? Peir drink the carad momenta? An not chanting, peir?" Why had he gone to the fences? Why did he want to meet the Guild? If he was not stealing, why?

Of course they had been waiting for him, Liam realized. Ever since the old pawnbroker had come that morning, they had been expecting the stranger who chanted to appear. That explained why three men who were eating seemed to ignore him with such calm—though he could see that they were paying keen attention to his conversation with the princeps. He wondered why Japer had not known about him.

"Some of this one's portables have gone free, and this one would reslave them."

The Werewolf shrugged. "Portables, eh? Open window. Drink the slavers."

"Closed window. They're green."

"Ah." The princeps nodded sagely and pulled at his cheeks again. The glow from the brazier caught on his teeth. Green things were enchanted; few fences even in large cities would handle stolen magic. "Locked window. This one can't abet." He could not help. Liam sighed. If they would not help him simply because they thought he was a fellow thief, he would have to call on something higher. He sighed again, for effect, and crossed his arms.

"Does Carad Southwark not *connit* the *Legium*? Does the Werewolf not connit the Legium?"

Liam had met Stick just as the Badham Wood Guild was breaking up, and despite the fact that there was a good twenty years between them, the two had traveled together for almost a year. During that time the legendary thief had, for no good reason that Liam could understand, made it his duty to teach the younger man everything he knew about thievery. It had been a considerable amount, not much of which Liam had ever had a chance to practice. The basics—picking locks, moving and climbing quickly and silently—had been useful, and he had even picked a pocket or two when desperate, but he had never thought he would need to know about the Legium.

A body of law created centuries before, the Legium was an oral code for thieves to follow, rigidly enforced by guild disciplinarians in the larger cities of Taralon and the Freeports. The code varied slightly from city to city, but was generally based on that maintained in Harcourt, where it was supposed to have originated. The Southwark Guild looked fairly rudimentary, but he hoped they held to it.

The Werewolf looked offended, drawing up his chin and sniffing haughtily. "This one connits the Legium."

"Then connit the *pre legio*." The first rule of the Legium was that thieves did not steal from other thieves—at least, not when they would be caught.

"The carad did not connit a larking chanter in Southwark."

"*Unum*," Liam said, agreeing. It was a fair argument—the Guild had not known he was a thief, and thus stealing from him did not break the pre legio. He began to smile, though, thinking that the Werewolf had as much as admitted that one of his thieves had robbed Liam. The princeps, however, spoke on.

"And how connit it the portables were freed by a carad chanter?" How did Liam know he had been robbed by a Guild thief?

"Carad Southwark plays no rogues," he answered with a smile, which brought a laugh from one of the eating men.

The Werewolf had just said there were no non-Guild thieves in the city.

The princeps smiled grimly; a point for Liam.

"An the portables were freed by one of this one's chanters, this one does not connit it." If Liam's things were stolen by a Guild thief, the Werewolf did not know of it. "But Carad Southwark is *magnum*; this one can drink the chanters, and spy."

If your Guild is so great, Liam wondered, *why are you all dressed in rags and hiding in an abandoned building?* But he did not say this; instead he shrugged.

"This one will not splinter the pre legio. The legio slaver is a fair split." He would not insist on the pre legio, which would require the offending thief to return the goods and make some reparation. The fence's rule meant that a thief had preference over fences in buying things stolen by another.

The Werewolf tugged at his lower lip thoughtfully. "A fair split, *vertas*." "Vertas" was a modifier, like "indeed" or "truly." "An this one can spy the chanter with the freed portables, can part *lux*?" If he could find the thief who had the goods, could Liam pay cash?

"Doh," Liam assured him.

"Unum," the Werewolf said. It was done. "This one will spy the chanter, and make the split. What portables, and when liberated?" He would find the thief, and arrange the deal; he needed to know what had been stolen.

"A book, a wand and a rug, all green," Liam said. The chant had no words for these. "Two *ombers* past." Two nights. He held up a finger, forestalling the Werewolf's smile. "Bar this one wants to drink the chanter's soul." He wanted to meet the thief himself.

The princeps's incipient grin faded, leaving a crestfallen look behind. He had obviously been thinking of what he would skim off the top of the deal; he would tell the thief one price and Liam a higher one, then take the difference. Liam thought of this, but that was not really why he wanted to meet the thief who had robbed him. More important to him was knowing how the thief had gotten past the wards on the house, and what he planned to do with the magical things he had taken.

Still, he wanted to laugh at the hurt look on the Werewolf's face. "An will wing this one the chanter's *cognom* and *caster*, this one'll part a gift for the carad." If the Werewolf would tell him the thief's name and where he lived, Liam would make a donation to the Guild. The grizzled princeps's smile returned, and one of the men around the brazier tipped Liam a wink. They had finished eating, and were passing around a clay jug of wine with a jagged shard broken out of the rim.

He was suddenly aware that the sewer stink had grown stronger, and was mixing most unpleasantly with the lingering smell of cooked meat.

"Unum?" he said quickly.

"Unum," the Werewolf said. "What's the gift?"

Liam considered only for a second. "Not momenta. An this one drinks the thief and reslaves the portables, then the gift. It'll be magnum." How great, he did not know, but from the way the Werewolf's eyes gleamed, he could tell the man was hoping it would be vertas magnum. Magic was expensive and unique; the Legium had a number of specific rules about it, none of which, Liam was grateful, applied in this case.

"Unum," the princeps said, sticking out his hand. "This one will spy it out and wing it to the caster. The caster?"

Liam took the man's hand, but shook his head. He did not want to tell the Werewolf where he lived, even though the man could probably find it out easily. "Not this one's caster. We will drink in the *iter*, in the glare." He wanted to meet in the street, during the day.

The Werewolf shook his head and laughed, a little nastily. "This one is the princeps. This one does not travel in the iter, sola on the iter. In the ombers." As princeps, he did not go out *in* the iter, the streets, only *on* the iter, the rooftops. Iter meant both, *in* or *on* made the difference. And he only went out in the ombers, at night.

"Then another chanter," Liam suggested, and a little maliciously jerked his thumb behind him. "Japer."

Laughter from the three men drinking wine, and a curse from Japer.

"No," the Werewolf said, "not Japer, bar Mopsa. Japer, hie Mopsa."

Grumbling, Japer clumped up the steps and returned a minute later with the young girl from the entrance.

"Pickit," the Werewolf said, "drink this chanter." A pickit was a small tool for opening doors; it also meant an apprentice thief, someone inexperienced. "That one's cognom is Liam Rhenford. Drink that one. Will drink him again."

Liam nodded at the girl, who stared sullenly back at him. "Avé, Mopsa."

"Avé," she replied, and then burst out: "But, Wolf, do I have to? I'm—this one—is no frog!"

All the men laughed, Liam, too. She was clearly a very new pickit, and her chant was weak. She was being told to bring him a message, which made her in chant a croaker, a kind of bird that was supposed to have its own language. She had used the word for informant.

The Werewolf cuffed her lightly on the side of the head. "As told, pickit. Drink the chanter when told, and where." He looked at Liam. "When and where?"

"Next middle glare, in Narrow Lane, behind the Duke's courts." Noon the next day should give him plenty of time to find the thief; the place had popped into his head unbidden.

The Werewolf seemed to think neither strange.

"Unum," he said, and shook Liam's hand again. "Then the magnum gift."

Liam nodded. "Avé, princeps. Till the middle glare." He took one last look around the cellar, received a nod or two from the other thieves, and headed for the stairs. Japer blocked his way for a moment, then stepped surlily aside.

Walking slowly up the stairs, he did not allow himself to think; he concentrated only on getting past the two curtains, past the street door, down the stairs and into the cold street. Then he took a deep breath, cleaning the sewer smell out of his nostrils and noticing suddenly the patches of sweat beneath his armpits and down his back.

Perfectly wise, he told himself, and, shuddering, began jogging away from the Point.

A block away, Liam made to pull his cloak close around his neck, and brought his hand away tacky. Japer's blade had not cut deep, but there was a thin trail of dried blood from his throat down beneath the front of his shirt. He cursed, licked his fingers, and tried to scrub it away, all the while continuing to put distance between himself and the Southwark Guild.

Thousands of thoughts crowded through his head at once, a situation Fanuilh, who could see his thoughts, had once described as watching a flock of startled birds leap into the air and mill violently about.

His plan had worked; the pawnbroker had led him to the Guild. His chant had held up, his knowledge—and the Guild's application—of the Legium had been sufficient. Carad Southwark struck him as a singularly poor affair; the guilds Stick had described to him had led him to expect a sort of underground court. Of course, he had been talking about the truly big guilds, in Torquay and Harcourt and the Freeports and even Caer Urdoch, where membership could number in the hundreds. Even so, the Southwark Guild seemed pitiful. The Werewolf, for instance, had seemed a little stupid, for all his cunning, no match for the godlike pictures of the princepses Stick had talked about.

The one in Torquay, for instance, always called the Banker, regardless of whether it was his real name or nickname, was supposed to have a pleasure barge the size of a grain ship. And the princeps in Harcourt, whose name Liam could not remember, was rumored to be in regular consultation with that city's ruling council. Liam could not imagine the Werewolf doing anything more than the occasional housebreaking.

Straw in his hair, the night boy at the hostler's made it more than clear that he resented being awakened to perform his duties, and Liam, with the difficulties entailed by holding his cloak closed with his fingers to hide the blood at his throat and trying to keep the cloak from touching that blood, forgot to give the tip which he would normally have felt the boy deserved. The boy's grumble reminded him of the tip, but also made him decide to forgo it.

Liam was already past the city gate when Fanuilh made its presence known by dropping lightly onto Diamond's neck. Though at first the horse had been frightened of the dragon, it had come to accept it, and only showed that it recognized the extra rider by rippling the muscles of its neck and snorting once.

Fanuilh sat staring at him, and Liam slowed Diamond to a walk.

"So, you see . . . perfectly wise," he said.

Your throat is cut, the dragon thought.

"Only slightly—a nick. I've done worse shaving."

He could have killed you.

"Yes," Liam admitted readily; the thought had not been far from his own mind throughout the whole visit. "But I did not think it likely. They are thieves, not assassins.''

There was no hint in Fanuilh's next thought to show what it felt, no indication of why it changed the subject, but Liam imagined it might have followed a *hmpph* of exasperation. His father had often made abrupt changes in subject when, as a boy, he had insisted on following a line of conversation that was inappropriate—and he had always preceded them with a *hmpph*.

There is no word for "you."

"Eh?"

In the chant, there is no word for "you."

After a moment, Liam confirmed this. "No, no word at all. More than that, thieves don't use "you" at all. When there is no chant word for something, they usually use the regular word, but they just drop the pronoun altogether. And that's strange, because almost the first word you learn in any language is 'you,' as opposed to 'me' or 'I.' ''

They discussed the chant for the rest of the ride home, Liam trying to explain it and Fanuilh asking a series of alternately pointed and pointless questions. As Diamond ambled down the cliff path, Liam summed the language up: "It's not really a language, you have to understand. There are all sorts of things for which it has no words. It is more of convention, a secret sign, a way for thieves to recognize and communicate with one another to the exclusion of others. They can talk about all the various aspects of a job, but not how to cook a meal, or mend a shirt. There are sixteen different words for locks—sixteen!—but no word for pot or horse.''

I have only one more question, the dragon thought, clearly realizing that its master was tiring of the discussion.

"What?"

Diamond broke into a jog, sensing home. To the east,

the black of the sky was shading to blue, as the day approached. The evening had lasted far longer than Liam expected.

How did the Werewolf know your name?

CHAPTER 7

THE QUESTION WAS still in his head a few hours later, when Fanuilh woke him from a deep sleep. The dragon was still sending the image of a bestiary into his dreams, the illuminated W of WAKE growing more and more elaborate each time, twisting intricate traceries of vines in vivid colors.

He had tried to puzzle out how the Werewolf had known who he was, but without success. He knew he had not mentioned his name, and Fanuilh agreed. He could not remember telling the old pawnbroker his name, either. There was no way the princeps could have known it. Sleep had overcome him a little after dawn, while he was still wrestling with the question.

Yawning and bleary eyed, he slumped at the kitchen table with a mug of hot coffee, a drink he had encountered in a land far to the south. Fanuilh sat on the table opposite him, eating raw mutton with gusto. It hated the taste of coffee but enjoyed the smell, so there was a steaming bowl in front of its platter; after every few bites it would raise its head and sniff deeply. The sound made Liam smile, and the coffee was helping to wake him up.

"There's no way he can know my name, no way that I can imagine. . . ." He let the sentence trail off, watching the thin slits of his familiar's nostrils expand and its eyes close in appreciation of the rich scent. An idea struck him, and it seemed obvious. "Unless . . . unless what Mother

Japh says is true, that everyone thinks I'm a wizard."

Fanuilh cocked its head. *Everyone knew Master Tarquin.*

"Exactly! Because with only one wizard in the whole city, everyone would at least have heard of him. And thieves, particularly guild thieves, would be particularly interested in local gossip. And they had almost half a day after the pawnbroker told them about me to figure out who I was."

You are somewhat distinctive.

"No I'm not."

You are taller than most, and your nose is long and thin, and your hair is blond and you dress better than most. You are distinctive.

Liam did not agree, but he let the point go. It did not matter much, anyway; Southwark was small enough that any competent group of thieves should have been able to figure out who he was from a description. With the simple riddle solved, he felt able to start his day, but there was a little coffee left.

"The Werewolf," he mused, cupping his hands around his mug, "was probably trying to impress me, do you see? To show that he was clever, that he knew my name even though I hadn't offered it."

If so, you disappointed him.

"That I did," Liam said with a chuckle, "that I did." Then, a little nervously, he touched the base of his throat and stopped laughing. The cut there had scabbed over completely. He touched it once more, then forced his hand away.

And even if you had reacted with astonishment, the dragon thought on, *would he really have been being clever? How difficult could it be to identify the only wizard in Southwark?*

"I'm not a wizard," Liam began heatedly, and then stopped himself. "Oh. I see what you mean. It doesn't matter if I am or not, because people think I'm a wizard. That's annoying.''

Why?

The last of his coffee disappeared in a long gulp. ''I don't know. I don't like being taken for what I am not. I don't want people to expect more or less from me than I can offer. And before you say that I allow Coeccias to do just that, you can stop and reflect that that's a different situation entirely.''

Is it?

''Not at all, but I want it to be, so it is, at least as far as you're concerned. Now, it's time for me to go meet the girl.''

On the ride into Southwark, he thought about what he had said to the dragon. Whether or not people in the city believed he was a wizard, it was different from what Coeccias believed him to be, but only in degree, not kind. Just as there was no feasible way to disabuse the entire city of the notion that he was a wizard, there was no way he could see to show Coeccias that he was neither a blood-shy weakling nor a brilliant thieftaker. Or at least no way to prove it without revealing that he had, to a certain extent, lied to his only friend. He could simply tell the truth, of course, but he feared his friend's reaction.

How the Aedile managed to hold two such contradictory opinions about him was another riddle he could not even begin to fathom.

As he rode into town there was more activity in the city than on the previous two days: the sun was shining and the worst of the snow was gone, trampled to a thin black slush underfoot. People filled the streets, busy on errands neglected; carts from the countryside thronged the city gate and blocked countless intersections; children threw sloppy handfuls of snow from rooftops and the mouths of alley-

ways. It took him longer than it should have to reach Narrow Lane, in part because of the crowded streets and in part
because he did not really know how to get there.

With Diamond safely stabled, he crossed the city square
just before noon. He had assumed that Narrow Lane could
be entered by way of Chandlers' Street, which entered the
square just south of the Guards' barracks, but when he went
around that corner, there was no sign of other streets. He
went back into the square, up past the Duke's courts and
turned into Butchers' Road, but there did not seem to be
an opening there, either. As he came back to the square,
the bells in the tower began ringing noon, and he hurried
over to the barracks and asked the Guard on duty how to
find Narrow Lane.

The Guard looked at him as if he had grown another
head, and practically refused to give him directions.

"You don't want to go there, Master Rhenford. It's not
fit for you, sir, I swear it's not."

"Look," Liam fumed, "I do want to go there, and I want
you to tell me. Now."

At last he prevailed, and the Guard explained the rather
complicated route he would have to follow. Narrow Lane
was a horseshoe whose apex touched the back of the courts
and the barracks: he had to go down Butchers' Road,
through Tripe Court, make a left into the alley at the first
bath house, pass three dead-end alleys, then turn left again
at Narrow Lane. Noon was almost half an hour gone by
the time he reached that section of the lane that touched
the Duke's courts, and he bitterly regretted the choice of
meeting place.

Narrow Lane was more an alley than a lane, and more a
tunnel than an alley. Overhanging balconies and overbuilt
stories cut out the sunlight, leaving only chill shadows; in
a number of places the buildings on either side of the lane
actually met. A few obscure shops were scattered along its

length, but for the most part it was residential, with doorways leading to interior courtyards or steep, dark flights of stairs. It was only slightly less dirty than the Warren, the slum area by the waterfront, but it felt more oppressive. The few people in the road eyed him suspiciously, and once he dodged a stream of liquid that arced down from the sky, looking up to see a laughing boy doing up his breeches in a window four stories above.

He could not help shaking a fist at the boy, but he also could not help laughing a little himself. He did not belong there.

If he'd hit me, Liam thought, *that would be different.*

Mopsa was waiting for him at the very top of the lane, where the cellars of the Duke's courts formed a blank wall of stone, at the foot of which had accumulated a talus slope of refuse, thrown out at the curve of Narrow Lane. He recalled from his childhood a bend in a river, where improbable things had washed ashore while the current hurried on in a different direction. Mother Japh's windows were a good fifteen feet above his head.

"Avé, brother," Mopsa said, as though doubting whether he were really a brother at all. "Y'are late." She was squatting by the blank wall, up to her ankles in slush and dirt, and looked even more ragged in the daylight. Her hair hung limply down to her shoulders, cut unevenly and clotted with mud, and he could not tell what color it was. A blanket was thrown around her shoulders, but she clutched herself beneath it.

Liam hated being late, and because he felt foolish for suggesting a rendezvous he did not know how to get to, her reprimand stung him. But he did not like being scolded by a twelve-year-old, particularly a foolish one.

"First off, *pickit*," he said, emphasizing the word heavily and leveling a long finger at her, "you never talk like that in the street, understand?"

"Like what?" she said defiantly, thrusting out her chin.

"In chant," he said quietly. "It's a good way to draw down the Guard on you. Do you think they don't know what the chant is, or can't recognize a few words of it?"

Mopsa's eyes narrowed skeptically, and she stood up, crossing her arms. "Not the Guards here, brother. They're fools."

He closed his eyes for a moment, summoning patience. He did not get along well with children. "Pickit," he said quietly, "don't chant in the streets. And don't call me 'brother.' "

"Why not?"

"Because you're just a pickit, not a full chanter. You should call me 'uncle.' And besides, no one would believe you were my sister anyway, if they should happen to overhear you being so foolish as to chant in public."

Mopsa grudgingly accepted this. "All right, Uncle. Now, do you want to hear Wolf's news?"

"Yes."

As she spoke, Liam began to regret what he saw as his rather harsh correction. She was thin, too thin, and he wondered about the Southwark Guild. Stick had always told him that apprentices in Harcourt were fed and fussed over so much that they often turned out fat and useless. He recalled the way Japer and the Werewolf had treated the girl, and his regret grew.

"He says it could only be Duplin, for that my other uncles"—she weighted the word with disdain—"were all otherwise occupied. More, he's the only one of my uncles that would treat with green things. And none have seen Duplin in two days."

"Since he robbed me," Liam figured. "Do you know where I can find him?"

"He has many hidey-holes, and might be in any of them." She paused, balancing the advantages and disadvantages of her next sentence. "Wolf said I was to help you find him. I know most of his places."

Liam began to smile, and then a gust of wind swept down Narrow Lane, setting Mopsa shivering and bringing her smell to his nose. She reeked of the sewers, and he thought of the smell in the cellar the night before. He angled his head away.

"Tell me, Mopsa, when you leave the Point by the sewers, do you never wash after?"

The girl's teeth stopped chattering, and she looked at him in stark amazement. "How did you know about the sewers?"

"Because—oh gods"—another whiff reached him—"because you stink of them, just like that miserable cellar."

She took an exploratory sniff, and shook her head. "But that doesn't mean . . . I mean, we could use the roofs."

"There's not a lot of shit on the rooftops, Mopsa. How many places does this Duplin have?"

"Six or seven," she said, still puzzled both by his assertion that she smelled and his knowledge of the sewers.

"Close together, or far apart?"

"Passing scattered. Duplin ranges the whole city. A great one for artisans' homes, he is—he can pick a lock anywhere from here to Auric's Park."

The wind died down, and the smell fell away, but Liam made a quick decision. "Come on," he said, turning back down Narrow Lane, "if I have to go anywhere with you, you're going to have a bath."

"A bath?" she said, then hurried after him. "I can't have a bath."

"Why not?" Liam asked, busy checking the upper stories for mischievous boys.

"I've no coin to pay for one, to start."

"I'll pay," he said absently, still on the alert. "Any other reason why you should stink?"

She could think of none, and trotted after him in silence, trying to keep up with his long-legged pace. He led her to the bath house he had passed earlier. It was an unpretentious building, long and low with tiny, grilled windows billowing steam. The foyer was a small room; two doors led to the interior, with two wooden counters flanking them. The floor was cold tile, wet and slippery, and he stepped carefully up to the counter by the door marked with a figure wearing a dress.

"My niece would like a bath," he said to the woman there, who looked over his shoulder and blanched at the site of Mopsa, cringing a little by the door.

"Mother Uris," the woman exclaimed, "she's filthy!"

Mopsa snarled a ferocious curse at the woman, and Liam had to bite back a grin.

"She's been playing in the street, I'm afraid, and my sister is coming for her today—she's been visiting—and I can't let her see her like this."

Color was disappearing rapidly from the counterwoman's face as she wilted beneath Mopsa's baleful stare.

"I can't let her in the baths like that," the woman stammered, then blinked and took control of herself, turning her attention to Liam.

"A private bath, then," Liam suggested, pulling a handful of coins from his purse for effect. "She really does need to wash."

The counterwoman weighed Mopsa's language, state of disrepair and angry glance against Liam's polite tone, expensive clothes and obvious resources.

"Private baths are dear," she warned him.

"Nothing's too dear for my dear niece," he assured the woman, and in a matter of moments she was herding Mopsa—careful not to touch her—through the door to the women's baths. A minute or so later, she was back.

"Her clothes," the counterwoman said, "should be burned."

"Burn them," Liam said cheerily. "Do you know where I can buy some others quickly? Nothing showy, though, just a plain frock and a warm coat."

The woman did know a place, and after he had paid her the exorbitant fee for a private bath, he went to the shop, a few streets away. He returned a half an hour later with some decent clothes and a pair of shoes, and handed them over to the counterwoman. Then he waited. And waited. And waited. He chatted a little with the men's attendant— there were apparently a number of excellent clubs that met at the bath, one of philosophers, one of ships' captains, one of chandlers—and he waited some more.

It was over an hour before Mopsa returned, bundled in her new coat and shining clean. Her hair, Liam saw, was mouse brown.

"Good bath?" he asked, opening the door.

"Three of them," the apprentice thief said with some satisfaction. "I got the water in the first two so dirty they had to change it. Said they were going to melt down the tubs."

Liam waved good-bye to the counterwoman and closed the door.

"I would think, though," Mopsa was saying, "that you could have gotten some better clothes."

"Want to stand out, do you? Good practice for your line of work."

The sarcasm was not lost on the girl, who looked up at him from where her head was sunk in the collar of her new coat. "I guess they're warm enough. But don't you mean *our* line of work?"

"No," Liam said, "I'm retired."

"Just larking?"

"Retired," he insisted. "Watch your mouth. And now, where do we find this Duplin?"

Of the six places Duplin usually frequented, two were in the Warren. Liam wanted to visit those first because the afternoon was growing old, and he did not want to get stuck in the area after dark. Mopsa, surprisingly agreeable, led the way down to the waterfront. Being warm and clean seemed to have taken much of the edge off her, and Liam guessed that it had been some time since anyone had done anything nice for her. He thought to ask her about it, then decided not to. Instead, he asked her to tell him more about Duplin, the man who had robbed his house.

"No one said he did it," she reminded him. "Only that all the others were busy, and he hasn't been seen since the night your things were set free."

He nodded; the point was moot. It had to be Duplin; everyone swore there were no wizards in Southwark, and everyone swore there were no thieves but Guild thieves, and he was the only one unaccounted for on the night Liam was robbed. And he had not been seen since.

Probably drinking himself silly with the money he got from my things, Liam thought sourly, realizing that it was entirely possible that Duplin would already have sold them.

Never mind, he told himself. *Duplin will tell us who he sold them to, and we can follow them from there.*

The more Mopsa told him, the more he was sure Duplin had done it.

"An overweening type, a passing grandee, he is. Full of himself. Rightfully, though, to some thinking—a great one for locks and windows and chests, and smooth on the roofs. He taught me how to climb a sheer one, says I'm good at it for that I'm a girl, and small."

"It helps," Liam said, remembering a roof that had collapsed under him. It had been foolish to try to climb on thatching, but nothing much had come of it.

"I should say," Mopsa boasted. "I'm the fastest on the iter in all of Southwark!"

"Mouth," Liam said, and she clapped her hand over hers.

"Sorry," she mumbled.

"Go on."

"He's always freeing—taking—big things. Jewelry or plate, unique things. He had a silver teapot, a time, that was shaped like a swan. It was a monster, and no slaver— fence—would take it, so he had to melt it down. And he likes to plan. Plan, plan, plan. He does half as many jobs as anyone else, he spends so much time planning, but his jobs always give more, much more, because he thinks big and he thinks ahead."

By then they were in the Warren, with its crowds thinner and poorer, its buildings and streets dirtier, dirtier even than those in Narrow Lane, and its layout far more confusing. Mopsa threaded her way through the alleys with ease, though, and Liam simply tagged along. She spoke to a number of people on the way, mostly urchins as dirty as she had been. Her new smock and coat were plain, and a little too big for her—she had to hold a fold of the smock in her hand to keep it from dragging in the slush—but she conspicuously stroked the material whenever she met a child she knew, and they reacted appropriately, eyeing the clothes with envy.

"My uncle," she said to one of them, nodding her chin at Liam with a smug expression.

"Yes, dear," Liam said the second time she tried this, "and uncle grows tired. Let's hurry."

The friend darted off and Mopsa resumed their walk with a sniff. "You might at least let me show a little. Do you know how long it's been since I've had a new coat?" She began calculating, counting time on her fingers.

"Never mind that," Liam said. "I don't want to know.

And besides, didn't I tell you? I'm taking those back once we find Duplin."

She froze in the street, shocked. "You're not!"

"No, I'm joking, now come on."

"You're not!" she repeated, this time a warning.

"I said I was joking. Now come on!"

"You'd better be," the girl said, "because they burned my other clothes."

Wishing he had not made the joke, Liam gestured down the street. "Can we, please?"

"Swear you were joking."

"I swear."

In the end, they got to Duplin's hideouts only in the Warren that afternoon. The first was just a wineshop, where messages were often left for him. The barkeep knew Duplin, but had not seen him in over a week.

"Gone up the hill," he said, jerking a thumb toward the Point. "Vowed never to come here again. Wish he'd come back, if just to keep his punk from coming in and weeping and shouting every night."

The "punk" lived at his real hideout in the Warren, a single room off a dark courtyard. She was in her forties, and long faded; the wattles of her neck wobbled as she bemoaned her fate and Duplin's inconstancy.

"Said he was off on a big job," she whined, "the biggest. His last, he said, sure to set him up for good, and he'd be gone a week and then be back for me and we could set up a carriage and live like lords and ladies."

When it was clear that that was all she knew, Liam beat a hasty retreat, as the woman appeared to be working up to a good strong cry—one, he suspected, that might put the whole rickety house in danger of collapsing.

In the street, Mopsa giggled and tugged at Liam's arm.

"If Duplin was going to set up a carriage with one, it

wouldn't be her. He's got another up in the Point, and a better one than that in between. He's probably holed up with one of them.''

Duplin's informal polygamy amused her to no end, and as they walked back up the slope from the Warren, she regaled him with stories of the amours of various thieves in the Guild. Her commentary was often interrupted by yawns, and Liam realized that she could not have had much more sleep than he had the night before. Furthermore, he had not eaten anything all day, and his stomach rumbled a warning as they neared the city square.

''Are you hungry?'' he asked suddenly, cutting her off in the middle of a meandering story about a thief and three prostitutes.

''Hungry isn't in it,'' Mopsa replied immediately. ''You paying?''

He was, after extracting a promise from her that they would visit Duplin's other hideouts early the next day.

They found a small eatery near the square, and the girl had ordered a broiled sole, a bowl of fish chowder, a sea pie, a jug of wine and a loaf of bread before he could stop her.

''And mind you the bread's fresh,'' she told the astonished serving girl.

''You can't eat all that,'' Liam told her.

''If you can pay for it, I can eat it. You just watch.''

Shaking his head, Liam told the serving girl to water the wine and bring him a sea pie.

Mopsa was almost as good as her word, stowing away the vast majority of her meal in starving gulps, complaining between mouthfuls at the watered wine and working in bits of thief stories during her brief moments on the surface.

''How many are there in the Guild?'' Liam asked at one point.

"I don't know," she replied offhandedly. "Maybe twenty, maybe thirty."

"And are you the only girl?"

"Me? No, there's another. But she's a real chanter," Mopsa paused to debone a strip of sole and eat it, "the best, after Duplin and the Wolf. And she can read, too, whole words and books and things."

"Can't you read?" Stick had told him that all apprentices were taught how, as one of their first lessons. It came in handy, he had said, in all sorts of situations.

"Me? Read? Ha! Not hardly. And who would teach me? I don't think the Wolf can read, and I know Japer can't, or Vellus or Lightfingers or Dancer."

Liam had finished his pie, and sat back to nurse the rest of his wine, leaving the girl to gorge herself in silence. He was surprised once again at how disorganized the Southwark Guild was, how far below Stick's high standards it fell. Small but relatively rich, the crumbs from Southwark's tables ought to be able to support a prosperous group of thieves, but these were hardly better than beggars. Of course, the city had no branch of the Wizards' Guild, either, a fact to which he had never given much thought. Torquay and Harcourt had one, as well as Caernarvon and Caer Urdoch and even Carad Llan—and all had decent thieves' guilds. There might be some connection, not obvious, a combination of age and wealth and population that gave those cities the base for a well-established set of guilds. Perhaps in a hundred years, the Werewolf's ragtag group might come to resemble its better-developed counterparts in the other cities.

Or perhaps not, Liam thought, unsure if that would be good or bad. Certainly it would be better for apprentices like Mopsa.

The girl had by then eaten as much as she possibly could, which was more than Liam would have believed. She lolled in her chair, breathing heavily and clasping her stomach as if she were pregnant.

"Gods," she exclaimed heavily, "but that was good!"

"Are you sure you couldn't eat a little more? A whale, perhaps? A roast ox?"

"A sweet, maybe," the girl suggested, then rejected the idea. "No. Might throw up."

"And we don't want that," Liam said, dropping some coins on the table. "When you're ready, starveling, we'll go."

She was ready remarkably quickly, though she walked slowly and groaned from time to time as they headed for the square. They parted there, Mopsa waddling off into the crowd and Liam pacing aimlessly. When he could no longer see her, he strolled over to the Guard barracks and asked if Coeccias was in.

He was, and invited Liam to sit with him by one of the hearths in the long, low room.

"Truth, Rhenford, it likes me to see you," the Aedile said, warming a cup of liquor over the fire. "Things grow from worse to worst, and I've little idea what to do."

People were piling problems on Coeccias's plate: rumors of a ghost in the Warren, complaints from a group of chandlers about a ship called the *Heart of Oak* that had left harbor without paying several large bills, and concerns, ranging from the curious to the hysterical, about the meaning of the two comets—all of which he was supposed to address.

"Though no one suggests *how*," he said, shaking his head in bemusement.

His biggest problem, however, was still the affair in Temple Street, and Liam winced when he heard of the trouble that had sprung from his suggestions. The Aedile had put questions about the banking business to both Cloten and Guiderius; the first had refused to talk about it, declaring that it was a poor excuse for an investigation into attempted murder, and any fool could see that they were dealing with assassins, not thieves, let alone bankers. Guiderius had grown equally heated, asking if Cloten had raised the question, and what business was it of the Aedile's in any case, did he not have more important things to do. Keeper of Arms Alastor, Cloten's second in command, had vehemently refused to discuss any matters of doctrine, and rather rudely terminated their conversation. Coeccias actually looked woeful while reporting this, and Liam sensed several times that he was on the verge of asking for direct help again.

"And the worst, Rhenford, the worst is yet to come, in two parts: the first, that a gang of Cloten's men clashed with a gang of Guiderius's. Nothing serious, mind, a broken bone or two—but fighting! Fighting in Temples' Court! Can imagine? The second, though, is what likes me least." He beckoned Liam closer, dropping his voice to the sort of hush most people reserved for naming the Dark Gods, for fear that naming them would invoke their presence. "The second: you know of the messengers, eh? The comets?"

Liam did, and mentioned the one he saw.

"Exactly! Two! And has Mother Japh told of her friends' two-headed calf?"

Liam did not remember a two-headed calf, but he understood the significance ascribed to such a monstrous birth, so he nodded.

"Now, look you, I tell you this in confidence, and y'are not to mention it to a soul, but last night, just after the second messenger appeared, all the candles in Temples' Court—all!—blew out. No wind, the priests said, just winked out, like a snuffer put over all at once."

Liam rubbed at the bridge of his nose, trying to fathom the meaning behind the signs. As a rule he did not much believe in omens and portents, but he remembered Mother Japh's words, and wondered.

"And more on it," the Aedile went on, and Liam heard with some surprise a genuine note of fear in his friend's voice, "I spoke with the priests of Uris today. They're the best at hieromancy and scapulomancy and all the other 'mancies, and had been casting and reading entrails and throwing runes all day—and they absolutely refused to say a word about what they'd seen. Refused me outright and sounded frighted about it. What do you make of that?"

Ordinarily he would not have made much of it, but Mother Japh's warning stuck in his head, and he could not help but give it some weight. Coeccias fell silent, brooding over the fire and his cup of wine. After a minute Liam shivered and stood up, pulling his cloak around his shoulders and saying he had to go.

"Must you?" the Aedile asked, a little desperately. "Have you eaten? I'd hoped to talk a little more with you. How goes your search?"

"Well enough," Liam said briefly, knowing that he had not thought enough about what he could tell his friend. He could not come out and admit that he had penetrated Southwark's Guild, and though he was fairly sure Duplin was his thief, he felt an obscure desire not to speak too soon. There was his Luck to consider, and it did not care to be taken for granted. "And I'm afraid I have eaten. I have to get some sleep. It was a late night last night."

Coeccias smiled wanly, a sorry excuse for his normal broad grin. "I'll warrant it was. Y'are close to your man, eh?"

Liam tipped his hand back and forth, temporizing. "I'm not sure. Tomorrow, I hope, will tell. I'll be in the city all day. Do you want to have lunch?"

By lunchtime he could figure out what to tell the Aedile and what not.

"Aye, that'd like me. Noon, then, here?"

Liam agreed, and left his friend in the barracks, staring moodily at the fire.

Liam was uneasy on the ride home, looking about him first in the city, searching for signs of strangeness in the streets, the people, the air. It seemed the same, the same thinning crowds as the night drew on, the same torches and candlelit windows, the same patrols of Guards. But it felt different, smelled different, like the smell just before lightning strikes. It was expectant.

He breathed easier in the fields, with Diamond galloping smoothly beneath him and the wind cutting at his face and hands, but his thoughts slipped to more personal matters, and became confused.

What to tell Coeccias about his search loomed large, a question he was now not sure he could answer. If he told him about the Guild, he might be obliged to help Coeccias break it, and that would not necessarily be a bad thing. There was a part of him, though, that rebelled at the idea, a part that did not like having gained the thieves' trust only to betray it. If he had only found their hideout in the Point, and turned the knowledge over to the Aedile, it might have been acceptable, but he had met them, and used them for his own narrow purpose. He would not feel right now in turning them over to arrest.

That led him to the fact that he had not even thought to ask them if they had had any part in the assault on Bellona's temple. The same problem applied as earlier: if he asked them about it, they would tell him because they thought he was a thief, and telling Coeccias would make him an informant. Apart from the possible danger of reprisals, the idea was distasteful to him. He could draw a fine line between spying and informing, and had done so in the past.

A very fine line, he reminded himself, *but still a line.*

Gods, how do I get myself into these things?

He cheered himself, though: his Luck seemed to be holding. Luck capitalized, personified, Liam Rhenford's Luck, as he thought of it. The mixed fortune that threw him into the frying pan and brought him out only slightly singed, with a meal in his hand. It was a strange image, but that was how he saw it.

In this case, his Luck had brought him close to Duplin, whom he strongly believed to be his thief, but left him with nearly insoluble questions about his friendship with the Aedile and his loyalty, however tenuous and misguided, to the Southwark Guild.

The house on the beach beckoned like a refuge, and he entered it happily.

I'm home, he projected, almost without thinking.

Welcome, Fanuilh thought back.

I'm going to sleep. Wake me an hour after dawn.

An hour after dawn, the dragon echoed, but Liam was already halfway undressed and did not respond. More tired than he had known, he crawled onto the divan in the library and was asleep before the lights had dimmed.

CHAPTER 8

AN HOUR AFTER dawn, Fanuilh dipped into Liam's sleep and brought him out, leaving him to stretch luxuriously on the divan for almost fifteen minutes before:

You really should get up now.

"Why?" Liam asked loudly, then jumped when the dragon thought: *I am right here*, and he saw the creature crouched at the foot of his makeshift bed.

"Why?" he repeated, a little more calmly.

Because you have things to do.

"All right," Liam grumbled, and swung himself upright. His sleep had been long and deep, and he felt good. A short, bone-cracking stretch, then he stood up and made for the kitchen.

Will you have coffee? Fanuilh asked, trailing after him like a hungry dog.

"No, but you may have a bowl if you like."

The dragon ducked ahead of him and jumped up on the table; he did not need to repeat the offer. Steam rose from the jug in the oven as he imagined coffee, and he filled a bowl with it, picturing meat for Fanuilh and sausage and bread for himself in the oven.

They ate in silence, but Liam wondered what a stranger would make of the scene: a man and a miniature dragon seated opposite each other, breakfasting (one on raw meat and an aroma) with perfect composure.

You will find the thief today, Fanuilh predicted when it had finished its meat, and was sniffing in the last of the chilling coffee's scent.

"I hope so."

You are sure this Duplin is the thief?

"If he's not, then we're sunk, aren't we? I have no way of finding a wizard and, if he's not of the Guild, no way of tracking a rogue. It has to be."

Because you want it does not make it so.

"Who said I wanted it?" Liam retorted, without anger. The dragon was only giving voice to his own worries. "And anyway, what does it matter? If it's not Duplin, then what do I lose? A book, a wand and a rug that I don't know how to use. I'm more concerned about what to tell Coeccias."

Tell him nothing.

"That's easy for you to say. He's my friend, and he's the Aedile. Here I've gone and found the Southwark Guild, a thing he said was impossible, but I can't tell him. And I can't tell him because the only reason I found them was because I was once a thief, and now I feel a stupid obligation not to turn them over."

He will understand. He knows his limitations, and accepts them. He will understand—or at least accept it—if you say there are things you cannot tell him.

"I know that," Liam said. "That's the problem. He'll take it as another sign that I'm an expert thieftaker, and a man of 'deep parts,' or something else ridiculous, when all I'm really doing is protecting a bunch of thieves who ought to be locked up."

You were a thief once.

"Only for a little while," Liam protested, "and certainly not dirty and disorganized like these." It sounded stupid even as he said it, and he knew that the well-being he had felt on waking up had been false. There were, as usual, too many questions to answer, too many dilemmas to solve. Life was never easy, particularly when he had things to do.

He pursed his lips and blew, a gesture of resignation. "Right. Forget that. I'll figure out something to tell Coeccias."

You are leaving now?

"Yes. As you said, I have things to do."

I will follow you, his familiar thought, then added, a quick block forming in his head before he could answer: *To guard your back.*

Liam did not refuse the offer.

The ride into Southwark, he realized that morning, was becoming something of a respite for him, a chance to think things out, to resolve thorny issues, to plan his day or, on the return, to mull it over.

Between the top of the cliff path and the city gate he decided what he would tell Coeccias, and what he would do if Duplin was a false lead. First, he would be open with his friend. He would explain what he had done, even how he had done it, and simply say that he could not give Coeccias any information that might be damaging to the Guild. On the other side, he decided that he could tell Mopsa to ask the Werewolf if any of his thieves had taken a hand in the attempted robbery of Bellona's temple. It did not strike him as the handiwork of a set of chanters as disorganized as the Southwark Guild, but he would ask. And if by chance one or more of them were involved, he would insist that Coeccias use the information only to placate Hierarch Cloten. After all, nothing had actually been stolen, and if Coeccias said that he knew who the thief was, but that he had fled Southwark, that surely ought to assuage the priest.

As for Duplin, if he turned out not to be Liam's thief, then that was all there was to it. It would mark the end of his investigation, and he would consider himself no worse off for his trouble. The book, the wand and the rug were useless to him, and though he did not like the idea of having lost some of Tarquin's things, there was little else he could do about it.

Sorry, he told Tarquin's shade, *but there really is nothing else I can do about it. If Duplin is not our man, then we both lose.*

He had meant it as a joke, a small thing to lift his own spirits, but even as the thought trailed away in his mind, he remembered the grave on the beach with a shudder, and apologized to the wizard's spirit for the disrespect.

The shudder followed him into Southwark, though, and colored the way he saw the city. To the north of him lay Temple Street. A pregnant silence hung over the area, and the streets nearby were unnaturally quiet. People seemed to whisper, scurrying on their errands and avoiding the eyes of those they passed. Even the beggars looked apprehensive.

Cities, Liam knew, were like that, especially small cities, and most especially small port cities. People thought country folk were superstitious and easily frightened, but in reality it was city dwellers who became agitated at the slightest provocation. A base of common sense and healthy skepticism ran through the countryside of Taralon, while her cities were hotbeds of rumors, faceless fears and sourceless worries. Here, in Southwark, everyone would have seen or heard of the comets, most would have gotten wind of the attempted robbery of Bellona's temple, some few would know of the tensions in Temple Street, and almost none would have learned of the priests' disturbing discoveries there. Nothing but gossip, yet the townsfolk acted as if Southwark were under siege.

A cold winter, Liam thought, *and nothing to do but sit and shiver*. The trading season was over, only a few coast-huggers were still sailing, and the small manufactories that supplied Southwark's goods were on half-time. The theater was closed, the menagerie that replaced it hardly worth the time. It was no wonder winter was Coeccias's busy time.

Liam was in a gloomy frame of mind when he finally met Mopsa, this time on the corner by the bath house they had visited the day before. As he approached, the girl produced two apples from the pocket of her coat and, with no small amount of ostentation, threw him one. He caught it one-handed.

"Breakfast," she announced with pride, the apples obviously stolen.

"Thanks," he said, his gloom lifting a little. "Not from a stand near here, are they?"

"No, up the hill a ways. The grocer'll never miss it."

"Where to, then?"

"Duplin had four more haunts; three quite near—one in Narrow Lane, as happens—and one up the hill. Can't go there till we've finished the apples."

"The nearest, then."

They walked unhurriedly through the streets toward the first two of Duplin's hideouts, munching on their apples. The sun was out and, though not warm, gave the pleasant illusion of warmth. Closer to the harbor, further from Temple Street, the city lost some of its furtive aspect, seemed almost normal. People bustled a little more, hurried less, dallied in the streets to exchange greetings.

Duplin liked women, Liam decided after they had seen two more of the thief's hideouts, but they did not seem pleased with him. In the first hideout—two small rooms looking out on a dirty courtyard near the Storm King's temple—a girl of no more than eighteen years was installed. She pounced on them as soon as they had entered, demanding information about Duplin. The rent was coming due, and she was running out of pocket money.

"Actually," Liam said, "we were hoping you could help us find him."

"Find him?" the girl shouted. "How could I find him? I've lost him—or he's lost me, the bastard, more to the point—and haven't seen him in over a se'ennight. He's off on one of his jobs, he is, and's probably spending all the coin elsewhere ere coming back to me!"

"Did he say what the job was?"

"To me? Not likely," the girl said with scorn. "I'm just a toss for him—no talking, no loving, just a toss and a snore, that's Duplin."

Liam frowned at the girl's coarseness, and shot a glance at Mopsa. The two were no more than five years apart in age, and while he knew the young thief was no innocent, he was not comfortable having her hear such things. He could have spared himself the worry; she was leaning idly against the doorjamb, hardly listening.

"Nothing at all?"

"Not a word," Duplin's girl assured him.

"And when did you last see him?"

"A se'ennight, I told you, and look you, if you see him, you can tell him not to come bothering me without he's got coin in his pocket." She seemed prepared to go on, but he thanked her quickly, and ushered Mopsa out.

The second hideout was a few blocks away and much like the first, only the woman there was older and knew more.

"Aye, he told me of his job," she said suspiciously, "what's it to you?"

"We were supposed to work something together this week," Liam lied smoothly, having prepared on the walk over, "and I haven't been able to find him."

The lie paid off, far more than he had expected it to.

"So y'are the one, eh?" The woman snorted her disbelief. "Funny, you don't look like a tar."

"Well . . ."

"I know, I know, you're in disguise. Right. Look, if he's ducking you, it's no more than he's doing to me. You were supposed to do that job, what, three days ago? He's probably gone and done it without you, and left us both in the lurch."

"Gods, I hope not," Liam said, feigning worry and trying to be as vague as possible. "It's pretty dangerous."

The woman laughed loudly. "Dangerous, he says! A little ride in a boat and a simple break-in! Dangerous! Y'are just worried about your share!"

He smiled sheepishly. "I suppose I am, yes."

"Well I'm afraid you've lost it, tar, because Duplin must have gone and done it without you."

Liam tried to prolong the conversation, but there was little he could do without admitting that he knew nothing of the job Duplin had planned. He and Mopsa left then, promising to let the woman know if they ran into the thief.

In the street, Mopsa nodded at him with judicious approval. "Well lied, uncle."

He bowed. "Next."

"His next is in Narrow Lane," she said, and began leading the way there, rhapsodizing on the various great lies she had heard in her time. Liam, however, was not listening: he was struggling with the information he had just learned.

Duplin had planned a big job for the night his house was robbed, which made perfect sense to him, but he was puzzled at the inclusion of a sailor and a "little boat ride." The break-in was obvious, but how did the boat ride fit in? And where was Duplin?

Celebrating, Liam thought, answering his second question. *Sitting somewhere and drinking up the money he got from selling my things.* That in and of itself was problematic—he had resigned himself to Duplin having already fenced the book, the rug and the wand, but he wanted them back. Having tracked Duplin, he would then have to track down the fence, or the client for whom the robbery had been committed. The idea of a client raised a number of issues, but he put them aside for the moment; his first question interested him much more than either the hypothetical client or the more probable fence.

Why had the boat been necessary?

The answer, when it came to him, was so plain it was painful. Duplin had decided not to brave the cliff path at night and had left Southwark by sea, rowing or perhaps sailing out of the harbor, past the Teeth, and down the coast to Liam's cove. That explained the sailor—someone to handle the boat.

Mopsa was still rattling on about a huge lie she had told to get out of some punishment or other, but he interrupted her.

"Did Duplin ever accept commissions?"

The girl stopped in midsentence, confused. "What?"

"Commissions. Did people ever pay him to steal things for them?" It was a question he should have asked much earlier, because even though he had convinced himself that Duplin had been the thief, and even imagined he knew how he had gotten to the cove, he still did not know how he had gotten past Tarquin's wards. A client—almost certainly a wizard—was required. More, it would explain why Duplin had restricted himself to just the three things. Without specific instructions, the thief would probably have emptied the whole house.

Mopsa's answer was not quite what he hoped.

"No," she said firmly, "the Wolf won't allow it. See, there was a time a long whiles ago, when some merchant or other—some say it was Ancus Marcius, and some Master Goddard, still others some Freeporter—hired one of the Guild to steal the account books of another, and it led to all sorts of troubles. The Addle came close to breaking us, it's said, so the Wolf's hard against taking jobs from outsiders.

"Duplin, though," she went on, as if considering an idea new to her, "he just might. He and the Wolf are always arguing about the Legium and what's in it and what's not. He's got all sorts of fancy ideas."

"Who's 'the Addle'?"

She looked at him to see if he were joking. "Who's the Addle?"

"Yes."

"The Addle is . . . the Addle. The Ladle. The Big Dog, the head of the pack."

Dog was chant for thieftaker, the Big Dog. . . . "The Aedile? Aedile Coeccias?"

"Who else?" she snorted, then pursed her lips disdainfully. "As if you didn't know who the Addle was."

There was something strange in the way she said the last that made him frown, wondering what she meant. Aedile was not a common title in Taralon, and neither Addle nor Ladle, though they made sense for Southwark, were part of the chant. How was he supposed to know who 'the Addle' was?

They had reached Narrow Lane, and the second to last of the places Duplin frequented. Liam looked skeptically at the run-down wineshop Mopsa indicated, just beyond the bend where the road touched the back of the Duke's courts. It was a cramped little place, barely two yards wide at the street but delving deep into the heart of the building. Shards of glass and clay from shattered bottles and jugs crunched underfoot as he and Mopsa entered, and the air was thick with the smell of smoke, sour wine and other, less pleasant things. Liam picked his way carefully across the open floor, to where a thickset man slept in a chair, his feet propped up on another. A dog, a dimly seen shadow with flashing teeth, snarled from behind the man's chair, and he jerked awake, bellowing: "Get out! Get out, you bastards!"

Then he saw Liam and Mopsa, frozen stock still, the daylight at their backs. He spat, ran a hand over his completely bald head. "Sorry. Who are you?" His second greeting was only marginally more friendly.

Liam cleared his throat. "I'm looking for a fellow named Duplin—" Liam began, but the bald man twitched, startled.

"Never heard of him," he said immediately. "Don't know him."

Mopsa nudged Liam, shook her head. "Are you sure?" Liam asked. "He comes here quite often, sometimes gets messages. He was telling me just a few days ago about your place, how much he likes it, and that I could leave word for him here."

The bald man pinched his nose between two fingers, and looked suspiciously at Liam. He began to say something, and then the dog behind him growled. He reached back and swatted at it.

"Shut your hole, mutt," he ordered, then turned to Liam. "Can't take a message for a man I don't know." He sounded sullen, like a child asked to wash behind his ears. "Couldn't even if I wanted to. Never heard of your friend. Got enough trouble here without taking messages for people I don't know."

Liam glanced around at the mess of the wineshop, the remains of bottles, the puddles of vomit and urine, and nodded. The place smelled like it had been festering for days. The bald man, however, was staring at the floor, chewing on his lower lip, considering. A troubled look passed over him as he absently reached one hand down to pat the dog.

"Friend," Liam said softly, unwilling to intrude upon the man's sudden reverie, "if you should see Duplin, could you—"

"I won't see him!" the bald man shouted, jumping up from his chair and setting the dog to barking. "I won't see him, I don't know him, now get out!"

The dog lunged between his legs at Liam and Mopsa, and they ran, not waiting to see him catch the beast by its spiked collar.

Halfway down Narrow Lane they stopped to catch their breath, the dog's deep-throated barking still barely audible.

"Duplin has nice friends," Liam commented. Mopsa frowned in the midst of her panting.

"He knows Duplin. He's lying."

"I gathered."

That much he had understood. But why? Nor did he understand the man's quick, irrational anger, or the vaguely sad mood that had preceded it. It was hardly to the point, however, and he put the question away at the back of his mind—adding to the pile already there—and focused on the important issue.

"All right, let's get on. There's only one more, eh? Then he's got to be there."

The last of Duplin's hideouts was as much of a disappointment as the others. In the neighborhood just next to the Point, it was a set of rooms on the fifth floor of a building with a large courtyard, and the owner told them that he had not seen Duplin in five days.

"Nor, his wife," the man added with an angry shake of his head, "but that in four days. And of course, that with her 'brother,' and the two of them cozier than a brother and sister should be, if you take my meaning."

"Cozy?"

The man laughed, a little bitterly. "I'll warrant Duplin's wife is now at sea with his brother-in-law." He laughed again, and Liam understood that he found Duplin's being cuckolded some consolation for the loss of a tenant.

"Ran out on him, did she?"

"My guess," the landlord said, shaking his head again and smiling ruefully. "And me not likely to see the rent for another month."

"What did you mean by 'at sea'?"

"Oh, that," the landlord said. "Her 'brother' was a sea captain, a passing tar, no land legs, even. Pray you," he said, changing the subject suddenly, "you wouldn't be looking for rooms, would you?"

"No," Liam said. "Sorry to bother you."

Mopsa held herself in until they were back in the street, the landlord safely out of earshot.

"She wasn't—" the girl began eagerly.

"Duplin's wife," Liam finished for her. "I know. Duplin isn't married."

Mopsa pouted a little, but Liam did not notice. He was thinking about Duplin's woman and his "brother-in-law," the sea captain, presumably the tar for whom Liam had been mistaken earlier. If she had run off with the man with whom Duplin was planning his job, what did that mean? No one had seen the thief since the time just before the night Liam was robbed, and now one of his women—his favorite, judging from the better neighborhood he kept her in—had disappeared with his accomplice.

He was making much of it up, piecing it together from inadequate clues, but if the story he was imagining held true, it was entirely possible that Duplin was dead, with Tarquin's enchanted things on their way to some distant port. He cursed.

"What?" Mopsa asked, driven out of her pout by curiosity. "What's that for?"

"That is for the fact that Duplin may well be dead, which means I'll never get my things back."

"Duplin dead? Nah, can't be. He's canny, I tell you. If you're thinking the sea captain and his punk . . . well, forget it. Not likely, not in the least. Duplin's too careful for that."

The way she said this, though, only planted the idea more firmly in Liam's head. She spoke as though Duplin were a hero, however, and the death Liam had suggested were unwelcome feet of clay on her idol. He did not press the idea.

"I think that's enough for now," he told her.

"No lunch?" she said, placing her fists on her boyish hips. "I got breakfast."

"Here," he produced a coin. "Buy yourself lunch."

"What about you?"

"I'm not hungry."

She rolled her eyes. "That's not what I mean, uncle. I mean, what are you going to do?"

"Not eat lunch," he said, puzzled.

"About Duplin," she prompted. "What are you going to do about Duplin?"

"Nothing," he said, though that was not true. He thought he might go down to the waterfront and look around there, but he did not need the girl for that. "I think I'm finished with Duplin."

"He's not dead," Mopsa insisted. "You should revisit his haunts tomorrow. I'll with you. What time will we meet?"

"We won't," he said, not wanting to tell her how sure he was that Duplin was dead. "I know where they are now. If I want to, I can find them myself."

"Ha! I doubt it! You couldn't find your way around the Warren, I warrant, let alone down on Narrow Lane. I'll with you."

Looking down at the girl, he was suddenly reminded of how young she was, and how hard it must be for her in the Guild. She probably wanted to continue helping him because it meant she would not be cuffed by the Werewolf or kicked around by Japer.

And because you buy her clothes and food, Liam told himself. He remembered a half-wild cat he had once given

food to, that had developed a persistent attachment to him.
He had eventually had to take it along with him on a sea
voyage—it refused to be left behind—and they had found
it in the hold halfway through the trip, dead in the midst
of a pack of giant rats.

He did not plan to take Mopsa to sea with him, though.

"All right," he said at last. "We'll meet at the same
time tomorrow, but down on the docks. Do you know
where Duke Street comes out on the waterfront?"

"I can find it," she said confidently. "No worry. I'll
meet you there."

"Don't be late," he called out, but she was already hurrying off down the street, his coin clutched tightly in her
fist.

Coeccias was seated by one of the hearths when Liam
came into the Guards' barracks, staring at the fire there,
and for a moment he wondered if the Aedile had moved
since he left him the night before. Seeing his friend's face,
he thought of the name Mopsa had given him and bit back
a guilty grin; Coeccias indeed looked addled, and his lips
moved soundlessly, as if he were working some complex
calculation in his head. Liam remembered then, with a pang
of regret, that he had forgotten to tell the girl to ask the
Werewolf if the Guild was involved in the business at Bellona's temple.

"Hello, Coeccias. Have you forgotten our lunch?"

The Aedile jumped up as if stung, flushing, and clutched
Liam's arm.

"Truth, Rhenford, you near frightened me to death. My
mind was wandering far and abroad—but I'd not forgotten.
I'm here, am I not?" He smiled, as if he had made a feeble
joke. "Then, where else would I be?"

"Trouble?"

"Say 'More trouble,' or the 'The same trouble twice

over with a new trouble added for spice,' and you come close.'' Liam's presence seemed to have invigorated him; he took a deep breath and snatched his jacket from a peg, bustled Liam to the door. ''But we'll have more on it over lunch. I'm passing sick of this room.''

He stamped across the square, Liam trailing in his wake, into a large tavern. The owner knew him, made a deferential bow; Coeccias hardly acknowledged it, leading the way up a narrow, twisting staircase to the second floor, where a number of tables stood by windows looking out over the square. They took a table by a window that looked out on the Duke's courts, the owner fussing over their chairs and gushing a list of specialties he was pleased to offer ''Your Eminence, Master Aedile.''

''Enough, Herlekin,'' Coeccias growled, ''two pies, two pints, and some privacy.''

Herlekin hurried away, not at all put off by the Aedile's gruff manner. When he was gone, Coeccias gave a long, exhausted sigh and rubbed briefly at his eyes.

''As bad as that?'' Liam had rarely seen his friend so harried, and felt bad for him.

''Worse.'' He launched into a description of Cloten's latest tantrums, the increased pressure the Hierarch was bringing to bear, the heightened tensions in Temple Street. Three more chandlers had come, demanding action on the *Heart of Oak*, the ship that weighed anchor without paying its bills—''As if I could whistle up a squadron and hunt them down!''—and someone had broken into a number of apothecaries' and herbalists' shops the night before.

''Not one, mind you, or two,'' he explained, ''but seven—all the ones in the city! No money taken, in course, that would make too much sense. Just a mess made, and some different herbs and things taken, some with value, some without. Most likely vandals, but passing thorough vandals, to hit seven different shops in seven different places, and take no coin and an odd assortment of plants.''

Liam thought of his own very particular thief, and began to wonder.

''Oh, but there's more . . .'' Coeccias paused as Herlekin returned with their meals and fulsome wishes for their enjoyment. When he had left, the Aedile pushed aside his plate and leaned close over the table. ''Remember the omens the priests wouldn't tell me about, and the lights all down Temples' Court being snuffed?''

''Yes?'' Liam felt himself falling prey to Coeccias's conspiratorial tone, leaning in himself, speaking in a hushed tone.

''No more on it, of course, no details, no telling points, but a deputation from Temples' Court to ask me to petition the Duke for the right to a cleansing.''

Liam gestured to indicate he did not know what a cleansing was. Coeccias had a definition ready; he knew that Liam was not familiar with Southwark's various rites and rituals.

''Do you remember Uris-tide Eve? The rite here and the procession and blessing around the city?'' Liam did remember it; he had sat at that very table to watch the ceremony in the square. ''It's much like that, only more so. The whole pantheon participates, priests and acolytes from all the gods in Temples' Court, and there's a great number of sacrifices—little boats burned in the harbor, calves and goats on all the altars, a general fast for a day. There's usually one before the trading season starts, to propitiate all and sundry above in hopes of a good return. But they want one now, and they have to get the Duke's permission, for it fair shuts the whole city down for a day and a night.''

''All the temples participate?''

''There y'have the thorny part. The Duke'd be glad to have a cleansing—he's strong for the old rites and ways— but will Bellona be included? Cloten has made himself so noxious to the others that none know if She'll be allowed in. Her worship is new, Her godhead unproven to many. While the cleansing might make things right with the gods, it might make things worse among Their priests."

"And Temple Street is not a very comfortable place as it is," Liam pointed out. "I passed near it this morning, and it felt like there was a pall over the whole neighborhood."

"Aye, I don't doubt you'd notice it, sharp as y'are. I swear it's colder there than anywhere else in the city. The air fair freezes in your lungs."

"So what did you do?"

"What could I? When the Hierarchs of twelve temples ask you to ask for a cleansing, you ask. What's more, I think it wise, if it can be worked. It'll take a day for my courier to reach the Duke, he'll make a quick answer, a day to return. The temples have promised to reach a decision on whether to include Bellona, and have agreed that I can cancel the cleansing, even if the Duke approves it."

Liam was impressed. "They said that?"

"I stand well with the priests," Coeccias said, without trace of pride; rather as if it were an unpleasant burden. "They trust me to do what's fit." What exactly was fit was left unexplored, and in a heavy, contemplative silence the two men picked at their meals.

It was a complicated set of affairs, and Liam could understand the distracted look he had seen on the other man's face in the barracks. He was sorry he had not sent a message to the Werewolf, and sorry he could not be of much help to the Aedile. On the other hand, his own business had grown far more complicated than he had envisioned four days earlier riding into Southwark and realizing he was bored. Something to do was one thing; a million things and a practically unsolvable crime were another. A small, cringing part of him was glad that Coeccias was so distracted with his own worries he did not think to ask Liam about his.

They sat that way, eating disinterestedly, for almost a quarter of an hour, and then Coeccias pushed away his plate and glanced out the window. Something caught his eye and he leaned closer, his breath fogging the glass. He wiped impatiently at the spot, craning his neck to look down into the square.

"What is that idiot doing?" he asked, more of himself than Liam.

"What's going on?"

"It's that Boult, waving his arms like a madman. I've never seen him like that." He stood, fumbled with the window latch, swung it open. "Boult!" Then louder, a roar that turned heads across the square: "*Boult!*"

Liam saw the man, a Guard who had helped him find Tarquin's murderer and was as completely unflappable as anyone he had ever met, jumping up and down on the stairs of the barracks, shouting at the Guard there.

"*Boult, you ass!*" Coeccias bellowed, and the Guard spun around so fast on the stairs that he almost fell off. Then he was sprinting across the square, skidding to a halt beneath the window and gasping up at the Aedile.

"Fighting—fighting in Temples' Court!"

With a curse, Coeccias dashed away from the table and down the stairs, his speed surprising in so heavy a man, leaving Liam alone at the table.

Liam himself, a little stunned, sat at the table for a few seconds after Coeccias's heavy footsteps had faded down the staircase. Then he shook his head and stood up quickly, dropping coins on the table and running after his friend.

Fanuilh? he projected from the stairs, remembering that the dragon had said it would follow him into the city. *Where are you?*

On top of the inn, master.

Go to Temple Street, Liam ordered. *Wait for me there.*

He came out of the inn just as Coeccias emerged from the barracks, a small buckler in one hand and two wooden truncheons in the other. Boult and the Guard from the door were right behind him, bucklers and truncheons ready.

The Aedile saw him, pointed toward the way to Temple Street. They met at the northeast corner of the square, and Coeccias tossed Liam his extra truncheon.

Master? Fanuilh asked.

Go, Liam projected, falling into step next to Coeccias. He mouthed the word to himself: "Go."

CHAPTER 9

WHAT AM I doing? Liam thought, loping alongside the grimly puffing Aedile, in front of the two Guards. He clarified his thought for himself: *What do you think you're going to do?*

Temple Street was like a drain, like a sinkhole that had opened up in Southwark and was drawing the city inexorably toward itself. As they ran, others joined them, little tributaries mixing into the main flood that coursed down the crooked street, past the staid fronts of the established temples toward the cul-de-sac where the fighting undoubtedly was.

Vendors, beggars, shopkeepers, even women and a crowd of children became part of the group led by Coeccias, and Liam was relieved to see at least ten more Guards, drawn by the shouting, fall in behind them. He clutched the heavy truncheon, had a moment to notice the button of metal at the base of the handle—*An iron core?* he wondered—and then the entire mass rumbled to a stop at the entrance to the cul-de-sac, halting raggedly behind the Aedile's outflung arms.

Almost thirty men struggled around the fountain, a tangled mess of writhing, flailing figures, pressed too close for real sword work and mostly striking with pommels or fists. Bellona's men wore chain shirts, Strife's only brown robes, but it was not clear if either had the advantage. Liam could see two men calmly surveying the scene from the steps of

Bellona's temple, presumably Cloten and Alastor; another man, presumably Guiderius, raged and shouted in the gateway to Strife's walled compound. The noise was what Liam remembered of battle—confusion made audible, a hundred wordless shouts, the clang and thump—and for the better part of a second, he wondered whether Strife and Bellona should meet in so common a manner, like feuding lords. There was no style to this fight, only a milling, mindless brawl.

Then Coeccias was calling out instructions: "Half the men with Boult, to the left, half the men with me to the right, and for truth's sake don't hit each other!"

A second of confusion among the Guards, and then they split smoothly, running into the square as Coeccias had ordered, only twelve to separate thirty. Liam ran after the Aedile, his knuckles white on the truncheon, sparing a second to glance at the steps of Laomedon's temple, where a woman in a close-fitting hood and black robes stood smiling, as black-robed acolytes clustered about her.

Master.

The thought was a distraction; he was running, he had no time to answer.

This is not safe, master, Fanuilh thought to him again, but by then he was following Coeccias into the whirl of fighting men, dodging a sword at its edge. He whirled, trying to catch the blade on his truncheon, missed, hit the owner in the side of the head, stumbled backward into another man, bore him to the ground.

He was disentangling himself from the man's legs when another sword flashed above him. He thrust the truncheon forward by both ends, praying, *An iron core, please*, and the sword hit his stick, jarred his arms practically out of their sockets and threw him back onto the man he had knocked down a second before. The sword came with him, lodged in the wood, and a Guard decked Liam's disarmed opponent with a shrewd blow to the head from the haft of a pike.

And it was over.

The Guards were pushing the men apart, kicking and shoving with pikes and truncheons, angry blows and loud curses. Wounded men—there was blood in the fountain, blood on the cobbles around it—staggered to their feet, some were helped up by their companions. Liam scrambled upright, stepped away from the man he had knocked down, and looked around, breathing a vast, happy sigh.

From the corner of his eye he saw Coeccias's truncheon flash out, and just after the Aedile's curse heard bones cracking; a follower of Bellona howled and dropped his sword.

"Back off, you bastard!" Liam had never seen his friend like this—so angry. If he could have, he would have warned Cloten not to shove his way forward, through his retreating men, to confront the Aedile.

"Well, Master Aedile," the Hierarch said, his thick, half-swallowed Caernarvon consonants making him almost unintelligible. "I hope you are happy!"

Coeccias twitched—visibly twitched, the truncheon jerking an inch like a reflex—and Liam turned away, wondering which of Cloten's bones would break first.

He found himself looking at the Death, the hooded woman on the steps of Laomedon's temple, and she was staring directly at him. He could tell she was staring at him, had singled him out from all the men around the fountain, all the men in the cul-de-sac, and when she was sure he knew, she smiled and bowed. It was a knowing smile, and a very slight bow, but it unnerved him more than the whole fight. He turned quickly back to Cloten and Coeccias.

"What . . . ," the Aedile was saying, struggling for control of himself, "what do you mean, Hierarch?"

"I mean," Cloten said, tilting his chin up, "that if you

had arrested only the men responsible for the attack on me, none of this would have happened." He was wearing a long purple robe under a steel breastplate, but his hands were empty. His hair was cropped in a bowl shape just above his ears; his lips were thin and bloodless; the chin he tilted at the Aedile was sharp. Liam disliked him instantly.

"I trust," said a new, cold voice, "that y'are not referring to my brothers." It was Guiderius, a tall man in a simple brown robe. He had a neatly trimmed, graying chin beard and a heavy mace in one hand. He bowed to Coeccias. "I must apologize for my brothers, Master Aedile; they were provoked."

Coeccias was grinding his teeth, glaring at Cloten, who spoke immediately: "I am referring precisely to your brothers, Guiderius, who first attacked me in my temple—"

Master. There was an emphasis to Fanuilh's thought, a hint of urgency, but Liam shrugged it off.

"—and have now called for open battle in the street!"

Master!

"Hush!" Liam said aloud, meaning Fanuilh but drawing the attention of the two Hierarchs and the Aedile.

Guiderius almost smiled, but Cloten goggled.

"Can you not restrain your . . . your constables, Aedile?" he demanded.

"He's not of the Guard," Coeccias grated, flashing Liam an irritated glance, "he's a Quaestor, the Duke's servant, and you, sir, will remember it. More," he went on, his voice gaining volume, "you will all go into your temple and not leave it without my permission. No man is to enter this street armed again, or I'll clap him in. And you"—he jabbed at Cloten with his truncheon, making the Hierarch jump back a step—"you'll await my pleasure. Is it clear? You'll wait on me, and not say a word, nor stir forth from the fane, until I've come to you. Is it clear?"

Cloten gasped like a fish out of water.

"Is it clear?" Coeccias asked again, a dangerous low rumble.

"It is clear," the Hierarch stammered, and stalked off to Bellona's temple.

Coeccias turned to the other priest, his anger hardly abated, but tempered a little by his apology. "It ranks me, Guiderius, but I must ask the same of you. No armed men in the street, and I'll have to come to you with questions. If you'd wait on me . . ."

"Certainly," the old priest said, not easily. "I understand, Coeccias. I'll wait on you." He bowed and turned away, calling for his men to follow him. The brown-robed acolytes moved as a unit, bearing their wounded with them, and disappeared into Strife's crenellated compound. Bellona's men, however, straggled back into her temple in some disarray, their Hierarch already gone. Liam caught a glimpse of Scaevola helping a man with a deep cut on his leg, practically carrying him up the steps.

I didn't see him in the fight, he thought. *Was he there?* He decided not: he did not think Guiderius's men would have stood long against the sick man. *Not with his speed*, Liam thought. *I'd pit him against a score any day.*

He had a vision, for a moment, of Scaevola dancing through the cul-de-sac, his sword flickering like lightning, men falling behind him like reeds. Then Coeccias barked a laugh at him, and Fanuilh thrust a dense block of thought into his head.

"Truth, Rhenford! 'Hush,' indeed!"

MASTER!

What is it? he projected, trying to shape the question to include his exasperation while forcing himself to smile sheepishly at the Aedile—no mean task, he discovered. It was not easy to divorce his outward expression from his inward thought, like holding two conversations at once, on wildly different subjects. Which was exactly what he was doing.

Coeccias shook his head, as if he were not sure whether he was amused by Liam's outburst, or annoyed by it. "Now what made you do that, I wonder?"

I have found the rug.

"What?" Liam could not help it; the word slipped out just as "Hush" had a moment before. Fortunately, Coeccias had already turned away, putting off his judgment and his question, barking orders to the Guards, who were the only people left in the cul-de-sac.

I have found the rug.

Liam took a deep breath, reminding himself to keep this conversation silent.

Where?

On the roof of Bellona's temple. Do you wish to see?

Yes.

The Guards had been dispatched on various errands— gathering the scattered weapons around the fountain, clearing away the crowd farther up Temple Street, taking position by the entrances of the two fighting temples—before Coeccias sought Liam out.

He was sitting on the edge of the fountain. By the time the Aedile came to stand before him, he had already seen the rug through Fanuilh's eyes. It lay flat on the roof of Bellona's temple, next to one of the windows in the dome, invisible from the street. Fanuilh had flown up and switched its own sight for Liam's, and he had experienced a dizzying moment, hanging above the street, peering down at the splash of purple on gray stone, the tiny figures—himself included—far below.

Are you sure it's Tarquin's rug? he projected, when his vision was restored. He could see his hands, clutching at the fabric of his pants.

There is the eagle, and the color is correct.

"Stupid question," he muttered to himself; it was obviously Tarquin's rug, and just as obviously stuck up on Cloten's roof.

Can you bring it down?

Then Coeccias was in front of him, concern on his face. "Rhenford? Is all well?"

He realized he must have looked strange, perched on the fountain, lost to the world. He jumped up quickly. "Yes, I'm fine, fine. Just tired. The fight—"

Coeccias's jaw dropped, making a round O of his mouth. "Gods, Rhenford, you should not have been in that! What were you thinking? Y'are no bruiser!"

Liam brushed the Aedile's hand from his shoulder. "Don't worry about it. I'm fine. But I have to talk to you, now."

"In course, in course. Y'are sure all is well?"

"No," he said deliberately. "All is not well. We need to talk, right now. It's about this whole business." He gestured all around, at the temples, the blood on the cobblestones.

Master, is this wise?

Never mind, Liam projected, faster and with more assurance than he had ever displayed before, *I should tell him, and I should tell him now, before he goes to meet the Hierarchs.*

Aloud, he said: "Is there someplace we can go that is private, and has access to a roof?"

Coeccias's look of concern grew careful and placating. "Certainly. Certainly."

"Don't look at me like that," Liam snapped, "I'm not mad, and I haven't gone battle crazy. The rug that was stolen from me is up on top of Bellona's temple, and I'm sure it was used in the robbery."

"Rhenford," the Aedile began, then stopped and shrugged. "I'll not argue. Y'are sure?"

"Yes."

"And you want a roof? Any roof, or Bellona's roof?"

"Any roof, but it can't be seen from the street."

"Right, then, the Duke's courts would be the place, Milord May-Do-Aught."

It was a name he had given Liam during the search for Tarquin's murderer, and by it he meant that he had decided never to be surprised by anything Liam did. So with no further argument, he started walking out of Temple Street.

Liam walked beside him, projecting to Fanuilh.

Can you bring the rug?

Yes, though people might see.

Let them see. They've seen enough strange things—a dragon with a carpet won't seem out of place.

As you wish, master.

Exactly, Liam finished, though he found he could not give the mental phrase the ironic twist he wished. *I'll work on that*, he added, more to himself than to Fanuilh.

Coeccias was mumbling to himself as well, and Liam caught only a few of his phrases, but the irony in them was clear. "Charges into a fray like he's berserk . . . finds his rug where my thief should be . . . can't be seen from the street . . . Milord May . . ."

Liam was only half listening; he was revising the list of things he had promised himself he would tell his friend that morning. There was little point explaining his experiences with war or corpses: they were not relevant to the fact of Tarquin's rug and Bellona's temple. His relationship with Fanuilh, on the other hand, was completely relevant. He could not explain how he knew where to find the rug without exposing the link between them, nor the fact that the little dragon was about to bring the rug to them.

There might have been an easier way to do it; he could

have had Fanuilh bring the rug back to the house on the beach after dark, and tell Coeccias the next day that he had found it on a tip from an anonymous thief. But that would take too long, and the Aedile was going to speak with the Hierarchs that afternoon. If he knew about the rug, it might change his approach.

Their approach, Liam realized, because it seemed plain to him now that their two thieves were connected, if not one and the same. Though why a thief who could break through Tarquin's wards would need the rug to break into Bellona's temple was beyond him.

Still muttering, Coeccias led the way through streets buzzing with the news of the fighting, shrugging off questions and shouts from the townsfolk with a gruff: "Naught to worry on, all over, out of the way."

They crossed the square and mounted the steps of the Duke's courts; Coeccias pounded a fist on the oak boards and, when the surly porter appeared, shouldered him aside.

"We're going upstairs and don't wish to be disturbed. Give me the key to the bell tower."

"The bell ringer has it," the porter shot back.

"He's up there?"

"It's almost the hour, isn't it?"

Coeccias growled and hefted his truncheon; the porter jumped back.

"Let's up, then," he said to Liam.

Fanuilh, Liam projected, *do you know where we're going?*

I am already there, master.

Liam glanced up at the ceiling of the hallway instinctively. *I did not see you.*

I saw you, Fanuilh returned. *You were looking at your feet.*

They were on the stairs, climbing up.

Did anyone see you?

I do not think so.

They passed three landings, the stairs changing at the second from stone to wood—dark, massive beams. Thin arrow-slits threw narrow beams of light into the stairwell.

And you have the rug?

It is here. But the bell ringer is here as well. He has not seen me, the dragon added, before Liam could ask.

They reached the top of the staircase, and Coeccias opened a door onto a small passageway. It broadened after a few yards into a long attic with steeply pitched sides, rough plank floors layered in dust. A set of footprints ran from the passageway straight to a rack of bells, which a man was polishing. His legs were crooked, so he appeared to stoop even when standing upright, but his arms and torso were thick with muscle, which made him look top-heavy. He did not respond to Coeccias's calls until the Aedile touched his back.

Then he turned slowly from his bells, a smile creeping across his face when he saw who it was.

"Master Aedile," he said, recognizing a friend.

"Yes, Tundal," Coeccias shouted. "I need you to leave the bells for a minute."

Tundal was only deaf, not slow, and he pointed to a sand clock attached to the rack. The mound in the lower half almost filled the glass.

"It's the hour soon, Master Coeccias. I have to ring them." He spoke in a barely audible whisper.

"I know, Tundal, but this will only take a moment. The bells can wait."

The bell ringer shrugged and walked off, nodding politely to Liam as he passed. His twisted legs gave him a peculiar up-and-down gait. When he had closed the door at the top of the stairwell, Coeccias turned to Liam.

"This won't take long, will it?"

"No," Liam said, looking quickly around the attic. *Come in, Fanuilh.*

The bell rack stood in the center of the attic, where a tower pierced the roof, rising an additional two stories. Open shutters allowed the sound to reach the city. The dragon flew in through one of these, the rug clutched in its claws, rolled up now. It turned smoothly and fluttered down to land in front of Liam and the astonished Aedile.

How did you roll it up? Liam projected.

With my claws, the dragon answered, and Liam was again sure that there should have been a qualifier to the statement, something along the lines of *How else?*

"Tarquin's familiar?" Coeccias said, pointing at Fanuilh and waiting for an explanation.

"My familiar," Liam corrected.

"Then y'are a wizard!" To Liam's surprise, his friend looked triumphant, as if a long-held suspicion had proved right.

"No," Liam hastened to say. "Not at all." He quickly outlined the beginning and extent of his link to Fanuilh—how he had found the dragon the night Tarquin was killed, how it had bonded to him against his will, taking part of his soul with a bite, how they communicated, could share sight—as much as was necessary to explain the finding of the rug.

"So he found it?" Coeccias asked at last, to clarify.

"Yes. And that's why I wanted to tell you right away, because—"

"Because then our thieves are one and the same," the Aedile finished, and a sly smile lit up his face. "Which means that I did no wrong to label you Quaestor in Temples' Court, for that you'll now help me to sort out Cloten!"

Liam was at a loss for words for a moment. He had expected to offer his help, not have it taken for granted.

That did not bother him, though; what puzzled him was
how quickly Coeccias had understood, how quickly he had
connected the crimes and known that Liam would be willing to help.

He knew the other man considered him a human bloodhound, a master thieftaker, but he thought he had made it
clear that he was not any of those things. Now he wondered
if he really had those skills, or if he just seemed that way
to others.

"Y'are sure y'are not a wizard?"

"Positive," Liam said at once. "I am definitely not a
wizard."

"And he," Coeccias asked, pointing at Fanuilh, "he is
not a wizard?"

"I . . . I don't know. I'm not sure. Are you a wizard?"

The dragon peered up at him for a moment, a quizzical
expression in its slit eyes. *You know I am not a wizard,
master*, it told him.

"No. Fanuilh is no wizard."

"More's the pity," Coeccias said. "A wizard could
solve this in a moment. For us to do it will require at least
another lunch. Come, I'm hungry."

With the rug tucked under his arm, Liam followed Coeccias down the narrow staircase. Above them, Tundal rang
the bells as quickly as he could, trying to make up for their
lateness with speed. Above Tundal, Liam assumed, Fanuilh
would be flying back to the house on the beach, there to
wait for him to return home.

They went back to Herlekin's restaurant, and their table
on the second floor. New pies were brought, and new mugs
of beer, and both men made significant inroads before they
began to speak.

"I won't ask," Coeccias started, "about your joining the
fray in Temples' Court. I won't ask about the way you

handled your truncheon, and I won't ask why you didn't tell me about Fanuilh when we were conning out that woman.''

"That woman" had killed Tarquin, and Liam was happy not to have to explain; he had kept the matter secret for fear that suspicion would fall on him. He said nothing, though, waiting for what Coeccias would ask.

"I needs must know, though," he continued, "what you've learned about your thief. You can see that, eh?"

"Yes," Liam said gravely. "It makes sense." He had realized that as soon as Fanuilh told him where the rug lay, and had hastily organized his thoughts, seeking a way to tell what was necessary without exposing the Guild.

"You've made contact with the thieves here, then?"

Liam admitted that he had, and started in on his round-about explanation. Coeccias stopped him.

"No. I'll ask, and you answer. If there're those you wish to protect, it'll be easier."

Liam nodded eagerly, surprised again at the Aedile's comprehension of his dilemma, and relieved by his delicacy.

"Do you know your thief?"

"I think so," Liam said, "but I can't find him."

"And it'd not do to have the Guard searching for him?"

"No, it wouldn't, but that's not the real problem. The real problem is that I think he's dead."

With as little detail as possible and no names, Liam told what he had learned with Mopsa: the outlines of Duplin's plan, the fact that no one had seen him since the night before the twin robberies, the disappearance of the woman he kept near the Point and her "brother," the sailor.

"So your thief takes a boat from the harbor with this sailor, steals your rug, and then returns to Southwark to use the rug to get to the roof of Bellona's fane. He drops onto the altar, tries to lift the treasury, and is surprised by Cloten.

He drops Cloten and flees, the rug left behind. And then you think the sailor killed him and fled with the girl?''

"That's my guess," Liam said, "but there are problems with it. First of all, why leave the rug?''

"Easy enough—they weren't with him, or couldn't get to it. He left it on the roof in his haste.''

"Possible, but why would he need the rug in the first place? From what I've heard, he was an excellent thief, so he should have been able to climb that wall easily.''

"He needed it to take that heavy chest from the altar,'' Coeccias suggested, but even he could see the problem with that. "How did he plan to get the chest off the altar?''

"Exactly. He might have used the wand—Fanuilh said it was for levitating objects—but then why have the rug at all? And what did he need the spellbook for? Only a wizard could use it. For that matter, I don't think anybody but a wizard could use the rug or the wand. I know I couldn't. But at the same time, everyone tells me there are no wizards in Southwark now.''

"I'd warrant it.''

"Then why didn't my thief take everything in the cases?''

"Or naught at all? Why visit your home if nothing there was of any use to him? No, we needs must assume that your thief could use what he stole.''

"Or that he was put up to it by someone who could. And that brings us back to how my thief got past Tarquin's wards. Fanuilh says they are still in force, and will only open for the owner of the house.''

It was a very strange conversation for Liam, and different parts of his mind stood at different distances from it. On one level, he was perplexed and frustrated by the intricacies of the puzzle at hand, the competing and often contradictory facts, the general lack of important information. On another, he was both concerned about what he said, avoiding any specific mention of the Guild, and a little skeptical as to the need for doing so. And on another, final level, he was amazed by the whole conversation, the things he was saying about Fanuilh, about whom he had never spoken to anyone, and the ease with which Coeccias accepted the situation.

Finally, after they had pursued the mystery for almost half an hour, they both agreed that further discussion was pointless.

"We need a solid path, Coeccias. We're going in circles."

"Aye, that's the truth. A solid path, and a direction to take on it. But what path? What direction? I've the Hierarchs waiting; perhaps we can start there."

"All right," Liam said, though inwardly he cringed at the idea. He did not want to have to face either priest, given the questions he thought he would have to ask. "And there's another thing: the sailor and the woman. I think we can safely assume that they've left Southwark."

"Can we?" Coeccias objected. "Is it so sure?"

"I think so. Or at least, I think we can safely assume it as a place to start. We have to start somewhere." With the Aedile's grudging acceptance, Liam went on: "From there, I think we can assume that they left by ship. The snows recently would make travel overland difficult, and since this other man was a sailor, it would make sense."

"Agreed, but what then?"

"We need to check the docks, to know what ships have left recently. There can't be many, in winter."

"No," Coeccias agreed, reminded of his other problems. "There's that damned *Heart of Oak*, though they could hardly have planned to passage on a ship that fled its creditors in the middle of the night. In any case, what will that tell us?"

"It might give us a name—something, anything. I don't

know. Perhaps a clue as to what happened to my thief. And I think I will go down to the docks and find out if anyone saw my thief. One of his women mentioned a 'little boat ride,' and people in Southwark know the difference between a boat and a ship. So perhaps he tried to hire one, before he met the sailor. Or perhaps the sailor is known down there.''

''You'll look for that? If you will, I'll have a man look into ships that have weighed anchor recently.''

''Good enough. Now, there's one other question we have to look into, but I have no idea who might help us. It has to do with magic.''

Coeccias grimaced. ''There's none in Southwark can help us.'' He brightened then: ''But there is one I know of, though he's not in the city now. Acrasius Saffian—he might be able to answer a question of magic. Though what question?''

''We need to know if theurgy can work with wizardry.'' Theurgy was religious magic, the power of the gods as channeled through their priests. Wizardry was an open book compared to theurgy; the secrets of the power were jealously guarded by the priests and never discussed outside temple walls.

''Y'are thinking that Guiderius worked a miracle to get the thief into your house?''

''Not necessarily Guiderius—perhaps some other priest—but yes. I don't know anything about theurgy, but I know it can be powerful. And if it's anything like wizardry, a priest against whom it was practiced would know it. So that if Guiderius used power from Strife to enter Bellona's temple, Cloten would know.''

''But if he used it to enter your house, then used some of Tarquin's enchantments to enter the fane, Cloten wouldn't.'' Coeccias nodded judiciously. ''It sings, Rhenford, it fair sings—though it would like me not if Guiderius were in it.''

Liam shrugged apologetically. He knew the old priest of Strife had an excellent reputation, but that did not mean he could not be a thief. ''Who is this Saffian? Can we get in touch with him?''

''Acrasius Saffian. He's a scholar, and the judge of the Areopagus, the Duke's circuit court for magic. The Duke's laws include a mass of statutes on offenses involving all types of magic, though mostly they touch on black magic, demonology, the like. Not many are ever invoked, so Saffian only rides the circuit once a year. For the rest he's a scholar, a delver into deep wells of all sorts. He summers in Southwark, but he winters with the Duke in Deepenmoor. If needs must, I can send a rider this day, to task him with your questions. We'd hear back in a day, more like two.''

''Too long,'' Liam said.

Coeccias agreed. ''I've a feeling things will turn even uglier in Temples' Court. And with the odd mood of the city these past two days, it might spread. Still, there's nothing for it. We'll send the word, hope for an answer, and in the meanwhile proceed as if the answer were yes.''

''You mean, 'Yes, a priest could overcome the wards on Tarquin's house'?''

''Aye.''

''All right. Then we have a plan.''

''No, Rhenford,'' the Aedile said, picking up his mug to drain the last of his beer, ''we have too many plans.''

They stopped at the barracks briefly, long enough for Coeccias to send a Guard down to the waterfront to ask after ships and for Liam to write out his question for Acrasius Saffian. Coeccias signed it, and told another Guard to see that it was sent by courier to the Duke's Seat at Deepenmoor. Then they set out for Temple Street.

CHAPTER 10

THERE WAS A disturbing lull in the streets, a quiet and tense aftermath to the fight between the temples. The news was disseminated in whispers, which grew excited as Coeccias and Liam passed.

"Word has spread," Liam commented.

"Aye," the Aedile said, worrying at his lower lip, "they'll note our passing into Temples' Court and make much of it." He cast a speculative eye at the sky. The earlier brightness was gone and the sun slowly began to sink behind gray clouds. "It'll be dark soon, and the story'll be over the whole city how I bearded Cloten in his own den—regardless of whether I do it or not.

"I tell you, Rhenford," he said after a pause, "these days like me not. There is too much to do, and too little to do it with." They had reached the cul-de-sac; an old man in the brown robe of Strife was using a bucket to splash water over the bloody cobbles, and six Guards stood in a tight knot near him, talking among themselves. One noticed the Aedile as he gestured at them, and alerted the others. "That's a half dozen men that'll not be of use elsewhere in the city this night. Which means the patrols in the Warren'll be smaller, and there'll be complaints from those wights that I'm ignoring their woes to the benefit of the rich in the Point."

"But this isn't the Point."

"I know that, as do you, but to those in the Warren, it's

always the Point. The Guard entire could die of the plague, and they'd say it was a trick of mine to pander to the rich.''

The Guards now stood roughly to attention, and the one who had noticed Coeccias's approach now came over to them. It was Boult.

"Not that I much blame them," the Aedile said ruefully. "I've never enough men for patrolling there at the best of times, and now they've a ghost—did I tell you?—a proper ghost, haunting the ways.''

Boult knuckled his forehead to Coeccias and nodded politely to Liam, but he managed to inject a sense of familiarity into both gestures. "Master Aedile, Quaestor Rhenford.''

"All quiet here, Boult?"

"Aye, sir. Just the elder with the bucket abroad, though we heard the Hierarch raising a fuss." There was no need to ask which Hierarch; Boult jerked a disdainful thumb over his shoulder at Bellona's temple. "He's quiet now.''

"Grand," Coeccias said sarcastically. "I'm sure he'll be the soul of reason now.''

"We could postpone this for a year or so," Liam suggested.

His friend smiled briefly. "Aye, or until the man died of old age—but I don't think he'll oblige. We'll be going in, Boult. Try and have the men look like soldiers, eh? Not a gaggle of gossiping fishwives.''

Boult saluted again with a lazy grin, and returned to the knot of Guards. Neither Coeccias nor Liam, however, made any move toward Bellona's temple.

Liam was thinking about the ghost in the Warren, and a word Mopsa had used. She had called Duplin's hideouts "haunts.''

"Coeccias," he asked diffidently, unsure if the idea was worth broaching, "where is the ghost seen in the Warren?"

"Eh? Where?" The other man had been glaring at the

tall doors to the temple at the end of the street.

"I mean, does it stay in one place, or does it wander around?"

"Truth, Rhenford, I've no clue. It's a ghost, it doesn't have a fixed address!"

"In all the ghost stories I've ever heard, the ghost haunts one or two special places—a favorite room, a particular castle, the place it died. . . ."

"Y'are thinking of Duplin," Coeccias guessed, and sighed. "I'll send a man to ask." He singled out a Guard, called him over, and explained the mission. The man looked uneasy, but on seeing his master's menacing frown, saluted quickly and dashed off toward the Warren. Coeccias shook his head in disbelief. "Do you know, half the men have asked to be switched to the day watch? But enough— we dawdle. We'll never beard the lion standing outside his den."

Liam could not imagine Cloten as a lion—a bleating sheep, perhaps, or a weasel—but his steps were no quicker than his friend's as they crossed the cobbles to Bellona's temple.

The differences from their first visit were legion. The gray gryphon still hung in its cage, far up in the dome, the supporting chain angling down the altar, behind which the temple treasury sat untouched. But on the altar itself, red-stained swords lay in a heap. The fire pit, cold the last time Liam had seen it, was now roaring, and water was being boiled by its heat. Bruised and bloody men were scattered around the temple floor, propped up against the walls, hobbling back and forth for hot water and bandages, cleaning armor.

It seemed to Liam like an armed camp, not a temple, and he was a little surprised to notice how familiar it all was. He had seen a hundred such camps, and this one differed only in being indoors—that, and the fact that he was not part of the camp. A dozen pairs of eyes jumped suspiciously to the doors as he and Coeccias entered, and two guards, untouched in the fight, sprang to bar their way with spears.

"Stand aside," the Aedile growled, "or fetch Hierarch Cloten here. I would speak with him."

The guards shared a look and one of them began to answer back, when Scaevola appeared behind them.

"It is all right," he said in his hoarse, wet whisper, and lightly touched one of the guards on the shoulder. "Ask Keeper of Arms Alastor to come here."

When the men had stepped away, Scaevola bowed. "I apologize, Master Aedile, Master Rhenford. They are no longer in Caernarvon, and have not realized it yet."

"No matter," Liam said, intrigued by the quickness with which the two men had obeyed the sick man.

Scaevola spread his hands and shrugged. His face was hidden within the depths of his hood, but the blasted skin of his hands showed in the light from the fire pit. "I have wanted to speak with you, Liam Rhenford. I did not think you would come here, but if I may?"

Liam heard a strange note in Scaevola's voice, an edge of weariness and, he guessed, desperation. "Of course," he said, then saw a man wearing a solid breastplate much like the one Cloten wore hurrying toward them. "As soon as we've spoken with the Keeper of Arms."

Bowing again, Scaevola stepped back to allow the priest to come forward.

"Aedile Coeccias," the Hierarch said with a slight bow. Alastor's face was flat and almost perfectly round, which made him seem fat, despite the leanness of his body. His head bristled with stubble; Liam guessed it was a soldier's haircut, not a priest's, shaved for comfort under a helmet and not a religious principle. The Keeper of Arms' gaze was direct, and frankly troubled.

"Hierarch." Coeccias offered a civil nod, but he was clearly displeased. "Is Hierarch Cloten not able to attend me? I specifically asked him to be available."

Alastor frowned. "Hierarch Cloten is closeted at prayer just now, Aedile Coeccias. He is trying to receive guidance from the Mistress of Battle."

Liam detected a hint of sarcasm in the way the priest said "trying."

Crossing his arms, Coeccias pointed at Liam with a finger. "Quaestor Rhenford has been seconded to me by the Duke to assist with the investigation into the attempted thievery. It was my wish that Hierarch Cloten meet with him, to go over the details of that evening. You can well see that his indisposition will make that difficult, and slow the investigation."

The casual lie—he had certainly not been seconded by the Duke—did not surprise Liam, but the formality of his friend's little speech took him aback, and he was not sure what direction Coeccias was going in.

"Yes," he stammered in the sudden pause, as the other two men looked to him. "It will make things difficult. Without Hierarch Cloten's comments, I do not know if I can form a clear understanding of the events."

"I believe I can help you there," Alastor said smoothly. "I have heard all Hierarch Cloten can remember, and can tell it to you somewhat less . . . heatedly than he could. And Scaevola here was the man on watch when it happened. He can add his part himself."

"I suppose that will have to do," Liam said, with a shrug to indicate that it might not be enough.

"For the moment," Coeccias added significantly. "I'll still have to speak with Hierarch Cloten later, at the very least about today's incident, if not about the other matter."

Alastor nodded acceptance of the condition. "Shall I begin?" At a gesture from Liam, he recounted Cloten's story of the night.

Unable to sleep, the Hierarch had been in his room, reading, when he heard the sound of footsteps and the clanking of metal from the main temple. His room was midway along a corridor that ran from the rear of the temple, where a door opened onto the alley behind, to the entrance to the hall they stood in. Cloten went down the hallway, drawn by the sound, and entered the temple proper through the door by the altar. Alastor indicated it, in a recessed alcove off to the left. By the dim light of the few candles, he saw a man by the temple treasury, gripping the chain that held up the gryphon's cage and tugging at the chest. He was about to call out when he was struck from behind and fell to the ground. When he regained consciousness a few moments later, he heard the sound of the front doors of the temple clanging shut.

"At first we assumed it was the thieves leaving," Alastor said, "but we later discovered it was only Scaevola, going out to look for them."

"I had come in only a moment before," the sick man volunteered, stepping forward to join the group and directing his comments at Liam with a new respect. "I was the guard on duty that night, and I had stepped outside for some air. I came back after almost fifteen minutes and found Hierarch Cloten lying by the altar. I ran out again, to look for his attackers, but they had already gone."

"They must have escaped out the back," Alastor said, "through the corridor Cloten had just come down. But then, Aedile Coeccias already knows that—and knows that that is strange, since we found the rear entrance locked."

Liam and Coeccias shared a brief, somewhat embarrassed glance. "Actually," Liam said, "we now know that they entered from the roof. We can assume they left the same way.''

''And how do you know that?''

''We found the, ah, instrument they used.'' He was being forced to revise his thoughts on the attempted robbery. If Cloten had been looking at the man by the treasury chest, and had been hit from behind, there must have been at least two of them. Duplin and his sailor brother-in-law, then, he decided. In the scramble to escape, they might have left the rug behind, though how they got down the outside of the building without being seen was beyond him. There was something else, though, that disturbed him.

''You said Hierarch Cloten was knocked down from behind?''

''Yes.''

''And that knocked him unconscious? Was he hit in the head, or did he hit his head when he fell down?''

Alastor looked briefly for support at Scaevola, who spread his hands to show he did not know. ''I'm not sure,'' the priest admitted.

''Well, did he have a bruise on the back of his head, or the front?''

''I am not sure,'' Alastor said after a moment, ''that he had a bruise at all.''

''Truth,'' Coeccias said, barely restraining his anger, ''you can see these are the kinds of things we needs must ask the Hierarch himself.''

''Yes,'' Alastor agreed thoughtfully. ''I can see that. But I am afraid he is praying at the moment, as I told you.''

''Very well,'' the Aedile said. ''Quaestor Rhenford, have you any more questions?'' Liam shook his head. ''In that case, we will leave you, but I must insist that as soon as Hierarch Cloten is available, word be sent to me. We will need to speak with him. You may tell one of my Guards outside, and they will inform me.''

Alastor bowed and turned away, moving among the wounded men; Liam and Coeccias had started to leave when Scaevola tugged lightly at Liam's sleeve.

"Quaestor Rhenford," he said, the title stressed. "May I have a word with you?"

"Oh, yes, Scaevola, I'm sorry. I forgot." He had been thinking of the dome and a quick experiment he wanted to make.

The hooded man indicated Coeccias. "Alone, if the Aedile does not mind."

Coeccias snorted with ill grace, but left; the doors of Bellona's temple were too heavy to slam, but he shoved them closed anyway.

"Actually, Scaevola," Liam said, "I wonder if you wouldn't mind stepping outside with me. There's something I want to see."

The other man agreed, and followed Liam out of the temple. They turned left, around the corner of the building to the alley on the south side. The walls of the temple were simple squared blocks of stone; the traces of an old facing of marble were still visible in places, and Liam lightly ran his hand over the pitted surface, calculating. The rug had been near the southeast corner of the roof, and there were enough irregularities in the wall there. It could be climbed, but that made little sense. Why climb down when the rug was there? And how could the thieves have escaped notice?

"Quaestor Rhenford?" Scaevola murmured politely.

Liam turned from his inspection of the wall, a little embarrassed. "Sorry. What did you want to talk about?"

"I wanted to ask you if you knew anything about visions."

"Visions?" Liam asked, confused. "You mean dreams, or hallucinations?"

"No," Scaevola said firmly, "visions. I . . . I have had

one, I think. I had hoped you might help me understand
it.''

There was a note of pleading in the sick man's voice, an
expectation of assistance. Liam frowned. He had been worried about Mopsa coming to expect things from him, and
now Scaevola was looking to him for help, no doubt because of his rash extension of sympathy. On one hand he
did not mind: he wanted to help the man, and he knew it
could not hurt to have the confidence of someone in the
temple, especially given the evident respect with which
Scaevola was treated. On the other hand, he was a little
annoyed with himself for getting involved. There was nothing he could really do for the other man, and he hated the
idea of people having unduly high expectations of him.

"Shouldn't you talk to the Keeper of Arms about it, or
even Hierarch Cloten? I think they might be more help than
I could be.''

"I cannot speak to them—or anyone else in the temple,''
Scaevola blurted, then whispered hurriedly, as if eager to
get it out: "Last night I saw Bellona, Quaestor, but I do
not know why.''

"You dreamed it.''

"I did not dream it. I do not sleep, Quaestor; people in
my position do not sleep.''

Liam considered the strange pride with which Scaevola
said this; he had not known that low-root fever stole sleep
from its victims.

"You never sleep?''

"Never.''

There was a long pause while Liam digested this. Then
he gave a low whistle and shook his head. "All right. Tell
me what you saw.''

In Tarquin's library there was a book on visions and
visitations; Liam had leafed through it once or twice, read-

ing passages at random. Scaevola's account matched many
of the ones he had read.

He had been in his cell (he had one to himself; though
they accepted him, none of the other acolytes would share
a room with him) lying on his pallet, when the walls suddenly shone with an unbearable light. He threw his arm
across his eyes, and when he removed it, the goddess was
standing before him.

Liam pressed for details on her appearance, but Scaevola
merely shook his head. "She was beautiful," was all he
could say, his hoarse voice trembling with awe. She carried
a breastplate and a sword, which she laid at the foot of the
pallet where he cowered. Then she put her hand to his
forehead and blessed him.

"She smiled at me, Quaestor, and then She disappeared."

"And the sword? The armor?"

"Gone as well—but they were a Hierarch's."

Then Liam understood why Scaevola could not mention
the vision to his superiors in the temple. If it was true,
Bellona had singled him out to be one of her high priests,
which he could hardly tell the present high priest and his
second in command without some sort of evidence.

"That could be difficult," he said. "Honestly, I can't
imagine Hierarch Cloten believing you."

"Nor I," Scaevola said as the euphoria with which he
had recounted the visit faded into misery. "But if She has
called me, how can I not answer?"

"You need proof, some open sign to convince them."

"But dare I . . . dare I ask Her? Should I pray for one?"

Liam sighed. "I don't know, Scaevola. I don't know
much about the gods in general, and still less about yours
in particular."

"I was afraid of that," the other answered, his disappointment well masked. "I had to ask, Quaestor, because

you are the only person I know here, besides my brothers in arms.''

''I'm sorry. I can't tell you whether prayer is proper or not. But I can tell you that you will need solid proof of Bellona's intentions, if you mean to act on them.''

It was difficult to read Scaevola's expression; his hood covered most of his face, and what little was visible was scarred and cracked. However, there was no mistaking the abrupt change in his tone, the false note of nonchalance with which he asked: ''Have you seen what you wanted to see, Quaestor?''

''What? Oh, yes, yes, I have, I think.'' He had not, but it could wait.

''Then I will leave you.'' With a quick bow he was gone, jogging back to the doors of the temple as if, in standing still for so long, he had accumulated energy that had to be expended.

Liam leaned back against the wall and ran a hand over his long face. *Visions*, he thought, *now there are visions. Robberies and fights between temples weren't enough, and ghosts and comets, too—now there's going to be a power struggle inside the temple.* For he was sure that Scaevola believed his vision, and would eventually be driven to act on it. The question was, would he get the proof he needed to make it easy? The vision seemed to indicate that Bellona had chosen Scaevola as her Hierarch as a way to settle the squabbles over doctrine, and Cloten did not strike him as the type to step aside with good grace.

Coeccias cleared his throat, bringing Liam out of his reverie. ''Something about the wall interests you?'' the Aedile asked, without a trace of sarcasm.

He expects me to do strange things, Liam thought, *so he can watch this.*

''Yes.'' He took off his cloak and handed it to the Aedile, and then pulled off his boots. "Hold these, will you? I want to climb up."

Cold from the cobblestones seeped immediately through his stockings, and he turned to the wall before Coeccias could argue.

In theory, climbing walls was simple; Stick had taught him, explaining the method in detail, and then made him practice until he was sick of it, and then a little more. The secret was in the fingers and toes, and not staying too long in one position. "Fast," the thief had told him, "go fast and don't think about it."

But with the iron cold of the stones alternately numbing and tearing at his fingers and toes, and the sharp wind that plucked at him once he was ten feet up, he cursed Stick and resorted to a trick he had devised himself. He pictured a lizard in his mind, a green, light lizard, swarming effortlessly up the wall, its digits splayed out. The image helped, took his mind off the pain in his hands, the small cuts from the sharp fragments left from the marble facade.

No lizard, he knew, would have panted quite as hoarsely on reaching the top of the wall, nor hauled itself up onto the roof there with quite as much relief. His hands were red and raw, prickles of blood on the fingertips, and he thrust them under his armpits to warm them up; his stockings were torn, and a dampness spread among his toes that he knew was not sweat.

So it can be done, he thought, and groaned a laugh. *Now all I have to do is get down.*

He crouched uncomfortably, resisting the urge to stand and stretch the cramped muscles in his calves and shoulders; the wind was stronger on the roof, and he did not want to be plucked off his narrow perch. He was on a triangular wedge at the southwest corner of the temple, where the rectangular body of the building met the base of the dome; three of the windows could be reached from the ledge, each a good six feet tall and frosted with ages of grime. He slid forward to examine the window directly in front of him.

Years of accumulated rust and dirt had been chipped away from the metal frame, and when he pushed at the glass, the window opened inward a few grudging inches.

Satisfied, he turned around and, with his hands braced against the frame, stood up, pressing his back flat to the dome. It was, he had to admit, a breathtaking view of Southwark: he could see the city square, the temple of the Storm King, all the way down to the harbor, to the jagged range of rocks called the Teeth, which formed the outer wall of the harbor, and beyond to the slate gray sea, choppy with whitecaps. He did not look long at the panorama, however; he was more interested in the neighboring buildings.

The roof of Laomedon's temple was a mere ten feet away, a relatively easy jump, but there was no room for a running start on his ledge. It would take a very brave—or a very desperate—man to make the leap, and though either description might have fit Duplin and his companion after Cloten discovered them, Liam did not think it likely. It had been snowing that night, and the ledge would have been slippery, even further reducing the chance of a good start. *And who would jump* there, *anyway?* Laomedon's home was just as eerie from the roof as from the street. The thieves would have to have been very desperate to brave the black temple.

They might have left by another window, and tried to cross the alley behind the temple, or the one to the north, but how would they have opened the window from the inside? If the windows there were as dirt-encrusted as the ones near his ledge, it would have been impossible.

Could they have used a spell? he wondered, and then nearly jumped from the ledge himself as a clanking noise and a muffled squawk from behind him set his heart thumping and dragged a shout from his throat.

Slowly, he twisted himself around, the blood roaring in his ears, and knelt before the window, looking into the temple. Through the grime, he could dimly see the gryphon's cage, swinging in wide arcs on its length of thick chain. It was oscillating toward him, the cage just on a level with the base of the dome, and the creature was staring at him, its giant black orbs above a sharp beak.

When it saw that he was looking at it, the gryphon simply stared back, occasionally bunching its hindquarters and thrusting against the cage when the arc of its swing shortened. It was gray all over, he saw, a dozen shades from tail to head, as if it had been cleverly carved out of stone from different quarries.

"Hello," Liam said, and tapped on the window. Then the creature squawked again, but it was not a challenge. To Liam, crouched shivering on the roof, it sounded like an appeal.

He shook his head slowly, finally breaking eye contact with the gryphon through force of will. *Get down*, he told himself, and quickly lowered himself over the edge without a backward glance.

The descent was, strangely, much easier. He was not thinking about the climb, and he had grown somewhat used to the cold. Nonetheless, when he reached the ground, having jumped the last ten feet, he fumbled hastily to put on his boots and his cloak. Coeccias crossed his arms and waited while Liam beat circulation back into his hands, and stomped his feet warm.

"Like a very spider," the Aedile commented approvingly. "Think you that was how our thieves got in?"

"Lizard," Liam corrected. "And yes, I do. At least, they got into the building by the window up there. I don't know if they climbed—it wouldn't make much sense, since they had the carpet. But I do know they didn't leave that way."

At the Aedile's questioning look, Liam explained about the distance between the buildings. "They could have reached only those windows so they couldn't try the other alleys around the temple. Since they didn't use the rug to escape, they would have had to climb down, or jump across—which I don't think they did. It's too far. And it also seems unlikely they climbed down—with all the noise and alarm in the temple, they couldn't have just come down off the wall and walked out through Temple Street."

"Aye, probably not," Coeccias agreed, "but then, how did they escape? They couldn't have just stayed up there till the search slackened . . . so how did they get away?"

Liam shook his head. He had no idea, but he was thinking more of the gryphon's black, depthless eyes and the squawk it had uttered, which had struck him as a cry for help.

It was getting late, the sun slipping away behind the clouds, an imperceptibly gradual darkening of the sky to herald the merging of afternoon into night. Liam's feet felt slippery in his boots, and he suggested to Coeccias as they left the cul-de-sac that he might buy some new socks and then go to the bathhouse. They were passing Laomedon's temple, and Liam paused to consider the empty portico, where the Death had stood only a few hours before and smiled at him. He could not see the doors through the shadows thrown by the pillars, and for a moment imagined that there were none: that there was nothing but darkness.

"Nonsense," Coeccias said, clapping him on the back and breaking the illusion. "No Quaestor seconded to me by the Duke'll go to a public bathhouse. You'll come home with me, and Burrus'll see to your feet."

Liam accepted the offer readily; Coeccias kept a small but comfortable home nearby, and his servant Burrus was a friendly man who played the flute well. In a companionable silence, Liam limping slightly, the two men made their way out of Temple Street. Night had taken hold by the time they reached the Aedile's home, and Coeccias threw open the door, calling loudly for candles and hot water.

"And stockings as well, Burrus, clean ones, if there are any!"

Burrus appeared from the kitchen, greeted Liam, and disappeared again, to follow Coeccias's instructions.

"I'll just wander around to the square," Coeccias said, as Liam slumped into a chair and started pulling off his boots. "Word should be back on what ships have parted Southwark, and on the haunts of your ghost."

Chuckling at his own wit, the Aedile left Liam to remove his tattered stockings, wincing at the crust of dried blood around his toes. Coeccias's joke brought to the fore his idea that the ghost in the Warren might be Duplin, and reinforced his conviction that the thief was dead. There were a number of ways to find out, but the surest did not appeal to him, and he put off considering it to deal with his battered feet.

"What have you been doing?" Burrus asked when he returned, a bowl of steaming water in his hands and towels thrown over his shoulder. "Fishing for sharks with your toes as bait?"

"Climbing temple walls," Liam replied, grinning. As he gingerly cleaned his feet, he was happy to see that there were only a few serious cuts; most of the blood had come from scrapes. Still, his own stockings were ruined, and he accepted a clean pair from the bald servant with a grateful smile.

"More trouble with that new goddess," Burrus guessed.

"Yes. There was a fight in Temple Street this afternoon."

"And you were climbing the walls to escape it?"

Liam laughed; he liked Coeccias's servant, his sense of humor and his familiarity. He was like Boult in his easy manners, and Liam was struck by the type of people the Aedile attracted. There were few fawners and scrapers in the Guard, and Burrus never failed to speak his mind, though he was by turns tactful or funny about it. He had been apprenticed to Coeccias's father when the latter was court bard at Deepenmoor, and had known the Aedile since he was a boy. For reasons Liam could not fathom, he had given up on his life as a bard to serve Coeccias when he was created Aedile of Southwark.

"Exactly. I stayed up there until Coeccias had it all sorted out."

"Which he did by boxing a few ears."

"More or less."

"But now you are helping him, I imagine." It was a shrewd guess, and Liam wondered how he had made it.

"Yes, I am, as a matter of fact. In what little ways I can."

Burrus offered a mysterious smile. "Coeccias lays great store in what little you can, Master Rhenford. I wonder if you know how much. Just the other evening, he explained to me at great length how sure he was that, if you would only help him, the problems in Temples' Court would be solved like that." He snapped his fingers, and Liam snorted. It was exactly what he did not want to hear.

"Hmm. Do me a favor, Burrus. When you hear him talking like that, try to talk him out of it."

The older man only laughed and went off to the kitchen, returning a moment later with a cup of wine.

"You are a young man, Master Rhenford, and for all that you have seen, you have not seen enough of yourself. You do not know your value."

The conversation was uncomfortable. Liam did not know his own value, but it did not interest him very much, and the wise smile on Burrus's lips made him fidget.

"Nicely put," he said, by way of shifting the discussion away from the personal, "but what man knows his own value? What man would want to know it, for that matter? Nine out of ten ignore all evidence of their real nature, or confuse it with what others perceive it to be."

"But not you," Burrus countered, refusing to be drawn into generalities. "Coeccias told me how distressed you were to hear that many in the city think you are a wizard. Nine out of ten would encourage that, not protest."

"Nine out of ten are fools," Liam muttered. Tarquin had been a wizard, and what did it get him, other than a knife in the chest?

"Yes, they are, but again: not you. You should have more faith in yourself, and drink your wine."

It was impossible to think of Burrus, with his rich, bard-trained voice and knowing smile, as a nag, but Liam came close. "I'll drink it, if we can talk of something else besides me and my value."

"As you please," the servant said, but he still smiled confidently, as if he had scored an important point.

CHAPTER 11

COECCIAS RETURNED BEFORE long, going straight to the kitchen to get a glass of wine. When he had settled himself in a chair opposite Liam, he told him what his men had found out during the afternoon:

"Only one ship's parted Southwark in the past se'ennight: the *Heart of Oak*, the one that cheated the chandlers—and that on the first tide five days ago."

Liam nodded; the morning after he had been robbed, and Cloten attacked.

"Now, for your ghost," Coeccias went on, swirling his wine thoughtfully, "he's been seen in four places."

There was a map of Southwark hung on the wall, which Liam approached as the Aedile listed the spots. Two of the four he mentioned were in the Warren. The map showed the twisting sprawl of tiny alleys and courtyards, but it did not give all their names; nonetheless, they were able to determine that the ghost had been seen outside the wineshop where Duplin often received messages, and at a corner only a block away from one of his hideouts. The other two sightings had taken place in Harbor Street and Coopers' Row, both roads that led up from the Warren toward the Point.

"What does the ghost do?"

"Do? What ghosts are wont to do, Rhenford—scare those that see them witless."

"But nothing specific? I mean, did anyone say what the ghost looked like, or wore, or said?"

"Not that I know," Coeccias replied. "Have you seen your thief?"

"No."

"Then what does it matter? You couldn't recognize it from a description, could you?"

He could not, but Mopsa could. If someone had said what the ghost looked like, he could have checked it with her or, better, with the Werewolf or one of the older members of the Guild. He did not want the girl involved, but that was beside the point in any case, because he did not have a description. Which meant he would have to get one.

"How often does the ghost appear?"

"Every night in the Warren, a few hours before midnight. It's been seen outside the Warren only twice, in Harbor Street and Coopers' Row."

A question occurred to him that he should have asked before: "When was it first seen?"

"It was reported two days ago," Coeccias said, "so it could be your thief, if he was taken off after the botch-up at the temple."

"Yes," Liam said thoughtfully. "And it appears every night?"

"For the past two."

"Can you lend me a man tonight?"

Coeccias shook his head and chuckled. "Milord May-Do-Aught wishes to go ghost-hunting, is that it?"

"Not willingly, but I have a feeling it would be worth our while to know. The sightings are all near my thief's hideouts, and it seems very strange that he should have disappeared."

"Perhaps he fled with his punk and his sailor friend on the *Heart of Oak*."

"I don't think so. I told you I spoke to some of his

friends, and they all seemed to expect him back.''

"Well, then, I can lend you Boult. He's the man to have if you needs must hunt ghosts.''

The suggestion pleased Liam. He had encountered a few ghosts in his travels, and had little physical fear of them. Most were tied impotently to a specific spot, and could do nothing to harm the living. Still, they were frightening, and the Guard's unflappable calm would be nice to have at his back.

The two men sipped at their wine for a while, quiet, content not to talk. The low crackling of the fire barely intruded on Liam's thoughts, as they jumped from one idea to another, back and forth fruitlessly. There were too many unresolved questions. How had Duplin gotten past the wards? How had the thieves gotten away from temple? Why had they taken only the book, the rug and the wand? Why did Cloten not have a bruise?

There were other thoughts, unwelcome things that cropped up in the the path of clear thinking, Scaevola's vision and the Death's smile chief among them. He did not want to mention the first to Coeccias, because he considered it the sick man's secret, but the other was his own, and he could share it.

"This afternoon,'' he began hesitantly, "during the fight, something . . . strange . . . happened.''

"Some *things* strange happened,'' the Aedile corrected. "Did you have a special one in mind?''

"Yes, I did. Something apart from the other strange things, an extra one. I'm not sure what it means, or if I'm just imagining it.''

"Well?'' Coeccias prompted after a moment. Liam had fallen silent, considering.

"I'm probably imagining it.''

"Rhenford!''

"All right. Just as we were going in, as we were running,

I saw the Death on the steps of Laomedon's temple. Now I know this will sound strange—"

"You've said that already; go to, go to!"

"... but afterward, I'd swear she smiled at me. At me in particular. She caught my eye, and she nodded and smiled at me."

He had hoped Coeccias would laugh at the idea, or at least put it down to the heat of the fight. The other man, however, tugged at his beard, twisting his mouth as if he had tasted something sour.

"Truth, did she?"

"I think so, though I might have been mistaken. There were other things happening at the moment."

Coeccias disagreed. "I doubt it. Y'are sharp, and the Death is not given to throwing smiles and nods to the wind. If you saw it, you saw it, and that worries me. We've enough to trouble us without another temple thrown into the mix. And certainly not Laomedon." His fingers crossed on the outside of his cup, then uncrossed as he remembered something. "Though now I think of it, the Death was not among the Hierarchs who requested the blessing."

"Great." Another riddle. "Should I do anything about it?"

"Aye, I think you should. I think you should attend the Death tomorrow, at her temple."

"Call on her? 'Excuse me, Death, but why did you smile at me yesterday?' "

"Something like," Coeccias said, ignoring Liam's sarcasm. "Y'are a Quaestor now, and can do it. Present yourself in that office, and pose a few questions about the robbery. If she meant anything by her smile, she'll tell."

"Or not."

"Or not, perhaps. But what else can you do?"

Liam frowned; he did not want to visit the black temple. Of all the gods in the pantheon, Laomedon was the one

with which he was least familiar—and he would have preferred to keep it that way. He had met the Storm King face-
to-face once, and lived not to tell of it, but he balked at the
idea of approaching a place whose priests were called
Deaths.

Nonetheless, he would go. There were simply too many
unresolved questions to ignore it, and a feeling was growing
on him that the thing they faced went beyond the robberies.
Finding Duplin might not put an end to it.

Burrus tentatively suggested a little music, but neither
Liam nor Coeccias was much in the mood, and they sat in
silence for over an hour, locked in their own thoughts. The
Aedile grunted from time to time, twisting in his chair as
if there were nettles in the seat.

The bells in the Duke's courts struck nine, jerking both
men to their feet.

"I should go," Liam said.

"Aye. Boult'll be at the barracks. Tell him I said to
attend you. And take care, Rhenford—if not of the ghosts,
then at least of the Warren."

Since both worried him, Liam promised to do so before
leaving.

The streets were empty, and a sharp wind blew off the
land, pushing him seaward. It whistled and keened over the
rooftops, hooting on the myriad chimneys.

A perfect night for chasing ghosts, Liam thought, and
until he reached the city square, he seriously considered
calling his familiar. When he saw the torches by the barracks and the reassuring presence of the Guards there, he
gave up the idea. *Boult will be as good as Fanuilh—I hope.*
He realized, then, how much he had come to accept the
little dragon's presence in his life. Since the day his father's
keep was burned, Liam had never been in one place long
enough to develop permanent relationships—moving from

camp to ship, from port to mountain fortress, from Taralon to the Freeports and beyond—and he was surprised at how often he thought of the dragon.

Boult was inside the barracks, a pile of battered truncheons at his feet and a sanding stone in his hand. He accepted Coeccias's orders without question, but without enthusiasm, dropping the stone next to the truncheons and grabbing a coat from a peg. When he reached for a halberd, Liam stopped him.

"You won't need that."

"We're going to the Warren?"

"Yes."

"Then I'll take it. Things are not so easy there as the last time we ventured in, Quaestor Rhenford."

The last time they had been looking for—and inadvertently found—Tarquin's killer, and Liam did not like to think about it. The object of their search this time, however, was scarcely better, and when Boult asked after their quarry, he was slow to divulge it.

"We're looking for a man," he said, taking an unlit torch from a barrel by the door. He occupied himself with catching a light for the torch from one of those burning outside the door, and waited until they were walking past the Duke's courts before expanding his statement. "A dead man."

To Liam's relief, Boult lived up to his expectations.

"The ghost, eh? I suppose I really don't need the pike, then." He did not pause, though, or try to turn back. "Can you tell me why, Quaestor, or is it secret?"

"No, no secret," Liam answered. "I think one of the men who tried to rob Bellona's temple has been killed, and I think the ghost in the Warren may be his."

They turned down Butchers' Road, now deserted. The shops were closed and barred, awnings rolled up, stands taken down. Offal lay frozen in gutters, flickering grotesquely in the erratic torchlight.

"And if you see the ghost?"

"I'll know if the thief is dead."

The answer satisfied Boult, and he lapsed into silence, but it did not satisfy Liam. What good would it do him to know if Duplin was dead? It would only put an end to his investigation. He did not think they could catch the ghost and put it in jail for Cloten's benefit, and even if they could, what sort of information could a ghost provide?

Enough of that, he told himself. *Stop trying to talk yourself out of this. It's just a ghost—what harm can it do you?*

That unfortunate question plagued him as they passed through Tripe Court and followed Butchers' Road to where a bend in the street marked the beginning of Coopers' Row. He hated his imagination then, as a picture of himself and Boult floated through his head, both of them addled with fear, their hair gone white.

Stop that, he ordered, and picked up his pace, marching down Coopers' Row so quickly that Boult had to jog to keep up with him. The buildings on either side of the street quickly grew seedier as they approached the edges of the Warren, but there was still no sign of life. Windows everywhere were shuttered tight, or empty, like eyeless sockets, opening on pitch black, abandoned rooms. These bothered Liam the most, and he carefully avoided looking too deeply into them.

He remembered his trip with Mopsa, and guided them to the wineshop where Duplin used to receive messages. A feeble glow slipped underneath its tightly shut door. Liam stopped in the street and heard a faint murmur of voices from inside.

"Do we go in?" Boult asked.

"I don't think so," Liam said. "We had better wait in the street. There wouldn't be people inside if the ghost came there, and Coeccias said the ghost appears here every night at ten."

Boult shrugged indifferently and positioned himself against the wall of the house opposite, only a few feet away. Liam leaned back beside the door of the wineshop, the torch held out in front of him, and they began to wait.

It seemed like an eternity, and Liam spent it questioning the wisdom of what he was doing. The torch hissed occasionally, the murmur of voices inside the wineshop died away, the wind rose up, whistling, then faded. Boult shifted position once or twice, coughed.

This is stupid, Liam thought again, and then they heard the distant tolling of the bells in the Duke's courts. Liam counted each chime, absurdly hoping that they would total nine, or eleven, that somehow they might have missed ten, missed the ghost.

It was ten, and there were no more. Liam caught Boult's eye, and knew that the Guard was holding his breath, just as Liam was holding his. The sound of the bell lingered in the clear winter air, trailing on unbearably, then died. A full second later, both men exhaled, and Liam gave an embarrassed grin.

Then they heard the weeping.

It was a low sound at first, barely distinguishable from the wind, from their own breathing. It rose, though, catching their attention, freezing them where they stood, erasing Liam's grin. It rose, a child's sobbing, then a man's, deep and broken, a rasping cry that raised the hackles on Liam's neck.

It went on, loud now, easily heard over the wind, and when Boult spread his hands, Liam put a finger to his lips, urging him to silence, to immobility.

The glow rose out of the street, seeping through the gaps between the cobbles, rising up as if it were following some invisible pattern, spreading upward to delineate legs. It moved smoothly, like paint trickling down only up, past the legs, to the waist, to the torso, a white glow haloing a man,

his back to Liam, his head down, clutching himself with
luminescent arms and sobbing.

Liam could see Boult past the ghost's shoulder; the
Guard was wide eyed, but he did not look afraid, only
amazed, stunned by the glowing, crying ghost.

"Boult," Liam whispered, and then the ghost looked up,
saw the Guard, whose head jerked back as if he had been
struck. Then the ghost was moving, spinning around and
running down the street. It wailed a long, desperate moan
and Liam, stung into action, ran after it, thinking only that
he had not seen its face.

He heard Boult's pounding footsteps behind him, heard
his own, but he could hear nothing of the ghost's, and was
not sure it even touched ground. The eerie glow that en-
cased it made such things difficult to tell, but it was moving
quickly, far faster than he was, dodging down the streets
of the Warren, trailing its wail like a banner.

The torch flared wildly, fanned by the wind as he picked
up speed, and Liam dropped it so that he could run even
faster. The ghost was a block away, but he could see it
clearly by its own glow, turning onto Harbor Street.

He burst onto Harbor Street seconds later, saw it receding
up toward the Point, and ran as fast as he could after it.
His throat burned with each gasp, the cold air searing deep
into his chest, and he was running in blackness, unable to
see his feet or the road before him. All he could see was
the glow of the ghost, loping up Harbor Street past the
closed shops, howling as though it were in pain, like an
animal unable to understand its hurt.

It disappeared.

He had lost it, and as he stumbled to a stop, he cursed
himself hoarsely for dropping the torch. The moon was
hidden behind clouds, and he was blind, doubled over and
gasping for breath, a stitch in his side. He forced himself
to straighten up, stepped uncertainly to the side of the road,

stretching out his hands in front of him, finally touching stone. With his hand lightly brushing the wall, he started jogging, following the dim wail of the ghost as it faded in the distance, determined, though it was pointless.

Once he stumbled, barking his shin on some unseen obstacle, but he regained his footing and inched forward, creeping now, both hands on the wall like a blind man. He was amazed at how dark it was.

If only that damn ghost would come back, I could see. He could hear it, still wailing, and then, after an eternity of groping, there was no more wall, and he was standing at the corner of an intersection. But what intersection?

"Quaestor!"

He jumped, frightened, and below him, an immeasurable distance down Harbor Street, he saw a torch bobbing along, a pinprick in the blackness.

"Boult!" he shouted, and blessed the man for picking up the torch. "Up here!"

The torch began bobbing violently, and a minute later the Guard ran up, awkwardly holding both his pike and the fitfully burning brand.

"Gods, Quaestor, I thought I'd lost you." He sounded nervous, but Liam paid no attention.

"Where are we?"

The flame, no longer moving, grew, the circle of orange light expanding to reveal the corner at which they stood. Boult held it high, then pointed to the left.

"Spice Court, and up there, Coopers' Row again."

Liam took the torch. He could barely hear the ghost's cry, somewhere to the east, up the hill. If it was Duplin, it might be going to his apartment in the Middle Quarter, but suddenly he did not think so; he was thinking of the barkeep in Narrow Lane, who had lied about not knowing the thief—and the corpse in Mother Japh's morgue, which he had thought that of a clerk.

"Come on," he said, and started jogging up Spice Court, tired from his sprint but with refreshed determination. Boult sighed behind him and then followed, not wanting to be left in darkness again.

Through Spice Court, onto Coopers' Row, going uphill this time, turning right at the bath house, past the three blind alleys. Neither man spoke, saving their smoking breath, and they were at the beginning of Narrow Lane. The wailing had stopped but Liam pressed on anyway, hoping now to meet the ghost, to get a look at its face. The street was even more like a tunnel at night, with the torchlight catching on the overhanging stories, throwing weird, elongated shadows all around them.

Liam slowed down as they approached the bend, moving close to the wall, the foundations of the Duke's courts just ahead. Motioning Boult to stop, he handed over the torch and edged around the corner, feeling his way again.

The ghost was standing outside the door of the bar Liam had visited with Mopsa, its white radiance playing around it, a fuzzy nimbus of light that pooled on the cobbles around it and sparkled on the dirty snow heaped in the bend of the road. It stretched out a hand and pawed at the door.

"Please, Faius, let me in," it begged. "It's bitter cold out here, Faius, and they're after me."

Liam paused, struck by the misery in the ghost's voice, and its thin frame. A thief could have calluses on the pads of his fingers, just like a clerk.

"Go away!" shouted a voice from behind the door, the voice of the lying barkeep. "Leave me alone!"

Why didn't I think of that before? Liam berated himself. *I wouldn't have to be here now.*

"Gods, Faius, you can't do this to me," the ghost moaned. "There's animals after me, and the Guard, and it's so cold, cold, and y'are my friend, Faius. Just look what they've done to me, Faius, they cut out my goddamned

heart.'' It started weeping, hitching sobs that made the
white glow jump and dance.

''*Go away!*'' Faius bellowed hysterically.

''My heart . . .''

''Duplin,'' Liam whispered softly. ''Duplin!''

The ghost turned its head slowly and saw him, poised a
few yards away.

''Look what they've done to me,'' it said, facing him
now and gesturing to its chest, where a dull purple stain
lay beneath the radiance, a knife wound and a face like the
corpse in Mother Japh's morgue, whose body had been
found in Narrow Lane the morning after Liam was robbed.

''Who did it to you, Duplin?''

''It's so cold,'' the ghost said, looking down at its
wound, ''and the birds won't leave me alone, but I can't
help them, and someone's cut out my heart.''

He's gone mad, Liam thought, with some pity. *And so
would you.* ''Who cut out your heart, Duplin?''

Duplin's ghost, though was not listening; it was staring
at the broad purple stain and starting to wail again, the
forlorn cry growing louder and louder even as the ghost
started to sink, dropping into the cobbles. Faius was shouting wordlessly behind the closed door, trying to drown out
the sound, and Liam jumped forward.

''Duplin!'' he shouted, even as the ghost disappeared.
He cursed and stomped his foot, then turned sharply.
''Boult!''

The Guard ran around the corner with the torch, shaking
his head. Faius was still shouting, and Liam kicked viciously at the door, gratified at the splintering of the lock
and the thud as it hit the barkeep, silencing him.

He pushed inside, Boult coming after with the torch held
high, and found the bald man huddled behind the door,
holding his forehead with one hand, the other stretched out.
He was weeping and pleading, but it did not deter Liam.

"Oh, gods, Duplin, I'm sorry, don't hurt me."

Liam reached down, grasped the man by the front of his shirt and hauled him roughly to his feet.

"How did he die?" Liam demanded, shoving the barkeep against the wall. "Who cut out his heart?"

"The sailor," Faius spluttered, "the sailor did it."

"When?" It was strange; from what he knew of him, Liam did not think he would have liked the living Duplin, but the sight of his ghost, pleading futilely at his friend's door, had roused in him an angry sense of injustice.

"Four, five nights ago, the night after the messenger." The bald man looked as if he were regaining his composure, so Liam pushed him hard against the wall again, making sure to bang his head in the process.

"Here?"

"No, in the street," the barkeep said, wiping at his teary face. "I swear I didn't see it, didn't know it, 'til the Guard found the body in the morning. I swear."

"Shut up," Liam told him.

"I swear it, master—"

"Shut up!" Liam growled, shoving the barkeep again. "Did they say anything? Do anything? What did they act like?"

"I don't know," the barkeep said, beginning to cry again. It seemed faintly ridiculous—he was big and mean looking, and the crying only made Liam angrier.

"Think, you idiot!"

"I don't know, master, I swear I don't. They might have been arguing, but the place was crowded—don't bang me again, please, master—I swear, I don't know anything, and he's been haunting me every night since!"

For a long moment Liam glared at the cowering man, his fists twisted in the cloth of his shirt, and then he relaxed his grip, as if he had just discovered that the shirt was dirty.

"Come on," he said to Boult, suddenly disgusted with Narrow Lane and eager to be gone.

The Guard once again had to jog to keep up with him, awkwardly managing the torch and his halberd. "We could clap him in," he suggested as they passed out of Narrow Lane. "For not telling what he knew."

"Better yet," Liam said viciously, "we could just leave him be, and let Duplin haunt him for the rest of his days."

"There is that," Boult agreed. "Seems fitting."

"No," Liam said after a long pause, his anger receding as quickly as it had sprung up. "There's no point. He's not responsible, and I think he's had enough of a scare. I certainly wouldn't want Duplin haunting me."

"Nor I," Boult said fervently. "So it was your man?"

"Yes," Liam said. They had reached the city square, and he looked thoughtfully at the Duke's courts. It had been stupid not to connect Duplin with the corpse in Mother Japh's morgue, but even belatedly it settled some questions. "Do me a favor, will you? Leave a message at the courts for Mother Japh, saying that I would like to speak with her tomorrow, and hope to find her in sometime during the morning. And also leave word for Aedile Coeccias about what we saw tonight, and that the ghost was Duplin."

"Y'are going home?"

"Yes. No, no, wait. Don't say the ghost was Duplin. Just say it was my thief. And forget the name yourself, will you?"

"No fears there," Boult assured him. "Once I leave your messages, it's me for the barrel in the barracks 'til I forget the whole damn evening."

Liam smiled grimly. "Don't get too drunk, Boult. There'll be work for you tomorrow night as well."

Taking the torch, and leaving the Guard to puzzle out what he meant, Liam set off for the stables.

• • •

By the time he reached home, his body felt drained, worn out by the long day, but his mind was curiously alert. He ran over his growing list of answers, and found that his list of questions had grown faster.

On the surface, he had found his thief, and presumably Coeccias's as well. With Duplin dead and his accomplice and murderer off at sea, the investigation should be at a close. He had his rug back, and would simply have to give up the wand and the spellbook. Coeccias could try to mollify Cloten with the information, and though Liam did not think it would work, what else was there?

The problem, he knew as he kicked the wet sand from his boots and entered the house, was that he felt there was something else, and it irritated him.

"Fanuilh," he called. "Where are you?"

In the workroom.

"Come into the kitchen. I want to talk to you."

He went there himself, tossing his cloak on the back of a chair and conjuring up a meal in the magical oven.

The dragon padded in, blinking its eyes sleepily, and flapped its wings once to rise onto the table.

Good evening, master, it thought.

"Good morning to you, familiar mine. Were you sleeping?"

Yes. There was no hint of reproach in the thought, but Liam apologized anyway, pulling a bowl of coffee from the oven with his meal.

"Sorry. Smell that. I want to tell you a story, and I want you to help me figure it out."

Very well, the dragon thought, arcing out its long neck to sniff daintily at the coffee.

"All right," Liam began, around a mouthful of food, "you know this story, I assume, but I want to tell it to you whole. We start with Duplin and his sailor friend. They have been planning this job for at least a week—we know from Mopsa that Duplin is a great one for planning—and then they do it, correct?''

Apparently.

Liam held up his spoon to show that he agreed. "Exactly. Apparently. They sail out here, and Duplin comes in and steals three of Tarquin's enchanted things.''

Your *enchanted things*, the dragon corrected.

"Whatever. We know only one person came in, because there was only one set of footprints.'' He paused to take another mouthful, and the dragon sent in a thought.

How did he get past Tarquin's wards?

"Leave that. Just the story as well as we can figure it— the problems will come later, and believe me, there are more than enough problems. Now, only one set of footprints.''

He went on, describing the night in as much detail as he could. Duplin, with Liam's things, returned to the boat, and the two men sailed back to the harbor. From there, they went to Bellona's temple, presumably using the rug to get to the roof. They opened the window and somehow got down to the floor, where one of them tried to get at the temple treasury, stuffed with unsigned notes of hand on the Caernarvon mines. Cloten interrupted them, and the other thief knocked him out. They then escaped by the roof—the back door was locked, and Scaevola was out front—leaving the rug behind.

"Sometime later," Liam concluded, "they went to Faius's place in Narrow Lane, where the sailor stabbed Duplin, and then fled with his supposed sister-in-law on the *Heart of Oak* the next morning. We have one thief's body in the morgue, and the other thief is at large, at sea, and out of reach. Story told.''

The problems . . .

"Yes. Can you name them?''

Liam counted them off on his long fingers as the dragon listed them.

1. How did Duplin get past Master Tarquin's wards? 2. How did the thieves get to the floor of the temple? 3. How did they escape? 4. Why did they leave the rug behind?

It looked like a list in Liam's head, complete with the numbers. He smiled. "Excellent! But you missed some—the most important ones."

Fanuilh cocked its head. *Which?*

Liam did not bother to count off his own points. "Why did they sail back to the harbor? It's easier to get from here to Bellona's temple by land than by sea, and even easier by air. Why didn't they use the rug? We have to assume they knew it was here—they chose what they took very carefully. So why come by sea at all? It's not a long walk, and they would know they could take the rug back. They must have known how to use it, because it was up on the roof. How they got to the floor of the temple doesn't interest me so much—they might have used a rope, and a sailor could climb a rope as well as a thief, probably better.

"The question is, why didn't the gryphon make any noise? I was only standing outside, and it nearly shouted me off the roof. How they got off the roof after Cloten found them is an excellent question, but so is the fact that he didn't have a bruise, or at least not one anyone can remember. And the last specific question, of course, is what did they want the spellbook and the wand for?"

There was a long silence; Liam toyed with his food and Fanuilh sat back on its haunches, the coffee grown cold and the odor stale. At last, it suggested, *A wizard hired them?*

"But who? Tarquin was the only wizard in Southwark that we know of, but he's dead. And you yourself said that you would know if a new one arrived."

He might have given Duplin an enchantment to break the ward's magic elsewhere.

"Yes, so that you wouldn't have noticed. But why bother? Why conceal wizardry, when there are no wizards in Southwark?"

You thought it might be one of the priests.

"Yes," Liam conceded, "I did. And it's still a possibility, but we won't know that until Coeccias gets a reply from this Acrasius Saffian."

Then we must wait until then.

"But I don't want to wait," Liam said irritably. "I want to know now."

Because there are other questions you have, the dragon observed. *Not "specific" questions.*

"Lots of them," Liam admitted. "For instance, what did the Death's smile mean? And I want to know if Scaevola really had a vision, and if he did, what it means—and whether it has anything to do with what's going on. And then there's the comet, and the candles in the temples blowing out a few days ago. And while we're discussing the bizarre and unnatural, what did Duplin mean about there being animals and birds after him? The gods only know the tortures of being a ghost, but that seems beyond even them."

Suddenly he was sick of talking, and of thinking. He was tired, and his feet hurt in his boots. "Are you finished with your coffee?"

Yes, master.

"I'm going to bed. Will you wake me early?"

Yes, master.

"No more pages from the bestiary, all right? And no ancient temples, either. Something simple—a pretty girl, with long brown hair." He closed his eyes and thought hard, imagining a dark-eyed beauty from a distant land. "Can you see her?"

I can, the dragon answered, and when Liam opened his eyes, he laughed. Its tail was curled around its legs, and its eyes were directed at the ceiling; it somehow looked the picture of prim disdain.

"Wake me with her," he ordered lightly, and went to the library to sleep.

CHAPTER 12

NIGHTMARES TROUBLED LIAM'S sleep, and when Fanuilh dutifully sent the exotic beauty into them to wake him, she was quickly incorporated. She cried "Wake!" from the cage of the gryphon in Bellona's temple, while Scaevola sat astride the creature as it flew around the dome. She called "Wake!" from the roof of the temple, holding the rope, slick with blood, that Duplin was using to climb down the outside of the building, beneath a sky swarming with thousands of brilliant comets. She called "Wake!" from the portico of Laomedon's temple, wearing the skullcap of the Death and the sheer robes of a dancer, while Cloten's men marched in a precise circle around Guiderius's men, who did the same, the two lines weaving in and out but maintaining an impossible integrity.

Finally the dream righted itself, and she was kneeling by the divan in the library, cooing "Wake!" at him, and he did.

"Gods," he grumbled, hauling himself out of bed and scrubbing at his face. Cold sweat clung to him, and he shivered. "Let's not try that again, shall we? At least not until you're better at it."

They are your *dreams.*

He could not think of a response, and slouched out of the library, rubbing his eyes. It was just past dawn, and the sun shone weakly out of a mackerel sky. He shaved and

197

washed perfunctorily, dressed and got breakfast before he was truly awake.

Will there be coffee, master? Fanuilh asked, padding curiously into the kitchen.

"Yes, there will be coffee, master," Liam muttered. "You know, you call me that, but I seem to do all the serving around here. Why can't you conjure up breakfast once in a while?"

The magic works only for the owner.

"But you have part of my soul. That makes you a part owner—or do you just want the part where the food is eaten, and not where it's made?"

Even if I could conjure the oven, the dragon objected, ignoring Liam's comment, *I could not get the food out. I have no hands.*

"Quite right," Liam conceded, retrieving their breakfast from the oven and setting it on the table. "We can't have you dropping the plates and making a general mess. I wonder if I could train you to balance them on your nose."

I do not think I would be good at it.

"Naturally. The question is, what would you be good at? The house cleans itself, I take care of Diamond, and there's nothing else to be done around here. Perhaps I should sell you to Madame Rhunrath's menagerie."

You would miss me.

"Not likely," Liam said, but he said it lightly, because he knew it was true. He would miss teasing the dragon, using it as a sounding board for his ideas, and as a comforting presence in the house. It filled a gap for him, somewhere between a pet and a friend, and he seemed to be aware of the fact.

"Would you miss me?" The dragon cocked its head and peered at him, as if the idea were alien to it. "All right, never mind that. Do you miss Tarquin?"

Master Tanaquil was a good master.

Liam puzzled over this equivocal answer for a moment, then gave it up. He was never sure if he should give up hope of understanding the little dragon.

You will meet the pickit today.

"Yes, and the Death, too, and Duplin's ghost again."

Why the ghost?

Liam searched for an answer. "I'm not sure. I have to talk with Mother Japh about that. Since she has the body in her morgue, there might be a way to lay him to rest. That at least would be something done, and it would get the 'wights' in the Warren to leave Coeccias alone."

You feel sorry for him—Duplin.

"Don't you?" He studied the dragon's reaction, the way it paused in the middle of a bite to consider.

I do not think so. He is dead, but does not know it. It is foolish.

"Foolish," Liam echoed. "You are very strange, Fanuilh." He said it fondly, though, and scratched the dragon's head as he left the kitchen.

I am single-handedly making that hostler the richest man in Southwark, he thought, frowning at the diminished pile of coins in his palm. Then he tossed them in his pocket and walked away from the stables, heading for the waterfront. He had more money at the house, enough for a long while, considering that he paid for food only when he was in the city. He had more money, in fact, than he had had for years, but the times he had been without had not taught him to be careful with it. As long as it was there, he would spend it as he saw fit, and when there was none left, he would see fit not to spend any more.

Harbor Street was crowded as he strolled down it, people taking advantage of even the weak, watery sunlight to open stands and hawk their various wares. It was heartening to see the mounds of fish and barrels of oysters, the crates of lobsters, the fishermen hauling their catches up from the docks and the shoppers bustling down from all over the city to buy. There was a cold, salt smell to the air, and he marveled at how much different the street was during the day.

How many of them know, he wondered, *that just a few hours ago there was a ghost running here? And a fool running after it?*

He came onto the docks and turned to the east, to the far end, where Duke Street trickled out, winding down a steep incline from the temple of the Storm King, and was content to wait there for Mopsa.

The docks were busy as well. Almost fifty ships sat at anchor in the harbor, or tied up alongside the wharves, but they were mostly quiet, settled in for the winter, decks stripped and masts denuded. It was the fishermen who filled the waterfront, maneuvering their small boats in and among the larger trading vessels, manhandling their catches up slimy water stairs and onto waiting wagons, which boomed on the foot-thick planks of the piers and jetties and rattled on the cobbles. It was a happy scene, for all the cursing and shouting, and it pleased Liam immensely, a pretense of normality in a city where ghosts ran the streets and temples clashed.

He knew Mopsa was behind him even before she slipped her hand into his pocket, and he let her grab his purse before touching her wrist. Then he frowned and shook his head at her.

"Is that the best you can do? No wonder you're still a pickit."

She handed back the purse with a sheepish smile. "I wasn't really trying, you know, just testing you."

"Of course not. And they wouldn't really cut your hand off for stealing, either."

She gave a superior smile. "Not in Southwark, Uncle.

I'm too young. A few days with the Addle, then I'd be out." At least she knew the law; still, she was too complacent. When Stick had taught him thieving, he had made the dangers clear.

"And have the Guard spreading your description, and every stall-keeper and merchant and hawker looking at you. Every time you get caught, it makes it twice as easy to get caught again."

She digested this soberly, and apparently did not like the taste. With a grimace, she changed the topic.

"Have you thought about where y'are going to start?"

He had not, he realized. Southwark's waterfront was not terribly big, but there were an awful lot of people about that morning, and he could not just work his way through all of them. He had been thinking more about the fact that he knew Duplin was dead, and the girl did not. Should he tell her?

"Well I have," Mopsa said impatiently, after about a second's delay. "I think you should go ask Valdas what he knows."

"Who's Valdas?"

"Just an old man who spends his time on the docks, but he knows more of what goes on than anyone else."

That made sense to Liam. Every port, no matter what its size, had a man like that, usually a retired sailor, who could recount the history of every ship, every sailor and every coil of rope. Bigger harbors usually had more than one; Harcourt had at least a dozen, and the giant roadstead at Dordrecht probably supported twice that.

"Do you know him?"

"Know him?" the girl said, as if he had insulted her. "Didn't he used to give me bread every Godsday?"

"Then lead me to him," Liam suggested, throwing out his arm and bowing over it.

She did, marching confidently through the crowds of

fishermen and fishmongers, checking over her shoulder every now and then to make sure he was following.

They found Valdas in the middle of the docks, unofficially supervising the unloading of a boat filled with eel pots. He was ancient but cheerful, long years at sea etched in his round white face, with a sunken mouth from which jutted three proud yellow teeth. He was practically swaddled in clothes, four layers visible at his neck, where a bright red scarf easily three yards long had gotten loose. One of his sleeves was empty, and Mopsa tugged at it.

"Valdas," she said, tugging again. "Can I talk to you?"

He turned, and delight crinkled his doughy face. "By the gods, if it isn't . . . no, it isn't either, not Tarpeia, nor Dorcas neither—but it is! It's little Mopsa, though grown now, and dressed like a boy!"

"I'm not dressed like a boy!"

His delight undimmed, the old man beamed on. "Your hair's cut short, like a boy's."

"But I'm not dressed like a boy!"

"Aye, but your hair is. Now come, little Mopsa, and talk with old Valdas. Y'are not as much about the docks as was your wont, nor with a clean jacket and shift, neither."

The girl stifled a sigh, and indicated Liam. "My uncle would like to talk to you."

"Ah! And you've an uncle now—how fine!—and a gentlemen, too! Good day to you, master, and good days. And a fine wind, too, for you, sir. Buying Mopsa a clean coat— that's good on you, sir, for that she's usually a dirty little whelp, though I haven't seen her in over a year, and get to wondering where's she's gone."

He continued to smile, bobbing and bowing at Liam with befuddled amiability.

"Good day to you, Valdas," Liam said. "Mopsa was telling me that you know a great deal about what goes on down here."

"Oh, aye, one way or another, I throw my net wide, and pretty near everything comes into it," the old man said happily, "though not as wide a net as yours, sir, I'm sure, you a gentleman and all, with such fine clothes. I mostly sit in my old shack there"—he pointed vaguely down the waterfront—"and I hear what there is to be heard. Not that such would be of interest to you, a gentleman and all. And sure, isn't it a cold day?"

"It's not that cold," Mopsa protested, but Liam quickly agreed. He had seen the open, almost innocent, appraisal in the old sailor's eyes.

"It is very cold," he said. "Perhaps, if you have the time, we could go somewhere and have something warm to drink, and you could see if you can answer my questions."

"Well!" said Valdas, apparently greatly surprised. "Well! That would be a rare honor, and a passing pleasure, and would do a man's heart good! Why we could go to the Green Eel—no, we couldn't, either, it's closed at this hour—and the other, the Freeporter's Wife, why that's not been open in years—no, not the Pot and Mess, either, he never sells a drink before noon—why, sir, I don't think there's a decent place for something hot that'll be open for hours!" He scratched his head, indignant at this state of affairs, and then winced. "And come to think of it, sir, I'm busy at the moment, with the unloading, you see"—he jerked a thumb over his shoulder, where most of the eelpots had been removed without his indispensable aid—"for all that I've only one arm, I've two eyes and twice as many brains, and the morning's not for wasting in taverns."

"I see what you mean," Liam said, smiling politely. "Perhaps we could forgo the drink and speak here. I'd be immensely grateful if you could spare just a minute—and perhaps you would be good enough to accept a token of my gratitude, and have a drink on me later, at your convenience." He put a hand meaningfully into his pocket, and jingled the purse there.

"Oh, sir, I don't know how I could," Valdas protested, lying with a sincerity that Liam found strangely refreshing. "A token, at most, sir, a mere token—for your sake and the girl's, not my own. To drink your health with, only, sir, and only if you were to insist."

Liam produced a silver coin and pressed it into the old man's hand. "I do insist, Valdas."

"Sir, you are too kind, a gentleman, sir. Mopsa, your uncle is a gentleman, as any can see by his bearing and his fine clothes—and the fine clothes he's bought for you. Sir! Your health! Now, your questions?"

It took some time, because of Valdas's roundabout manner of speaking and his digressive habits, but they managed to discover that he had indeed seen a man and a woman go aboard the *Heart of Oak* the night of the two robberies, and had seen the ship put to sea the next morning with all haste. But when Liam suggested that the man and the woman had bought passage, the old sailor cackled long and hard.

"Ha! Bought passage! Oh, sir, y'are a passing jester, fair—no offense meant, sir, but what I mean—bought passage!—why, do you see? Why buy passage?"

"Why not?" Liam said, unable to see the humor but smiling anyway. "How else would they get on board?"

Valdas's cackles faded away, stopping with a brief coughing spell. "How else, sir? Why, by walking up the gangplank of his own ship, is how! For the man was the captain, and the captain the man, do you see?"

"Are you sure?"

"Sure as the sea is wet, sir. I don't sleep as much now as I used to, and I saw them board her myself—Captain Perelhos, and his woman. I remember it well, sir, very well, for that he was storming and swearing, and ordering all things well, and kept me up half the night, though that was no great loss, do you see, for that I don't sleep neither sound nor deep, being old.''

"And they were the only people to go aboard, this Captain Perelhos and the woman? There were no other passengers?'' He waited tensely for the reply; this was not news he wanted to hear, though he had half expected something like it.

"None, not a one, sir," Valdas beamed, "and how could there be, on the *Heart of Oak*? She's but a poor schooner, sir, only the one mast and no great weight of sail, though sturdy, and one for a storm. She carries no great cargo, either—a regular packet ship, letters and small parcels and, of course, the pay.''

Things were changing rapidly in Liam's mind, lists rearranging themselves, chronologies shifting, and then the word *pay* hit the whole structure like a hammer, shattering it.

"Pay?"

"Aye, sir, coin, two or three heavy chests of it. For that any number of merchants use the *Heart of Oak* to pay their factors—the little merchants up and down the coast who vend their wares. She carries an extra complement of soldiers, and is reliable—not likely to founder in the heavy seas—so every month or so Perelhos takes aboard the money from different merchants and guarantees to distribute it to their outposts or their creditors or what have you, and returns with accounts and reports and sometimes revenues, though it's mostly going out that he has any money.''

"Two or three chests of it," Liam murmured absently. "Close to a fortune."

"Aye," Valdas said, chuckling, and held up a finger. "Which, mark you, is what makes it passing strange that he should fleece his chandlers, do you see? Chests of money on the *Heart of Oak*, and he leaves the port with a host of unpaid debts! And him no doubt needing to come back in a month for supplies!"

"I doubt he'll be coming back," Liam said slowly, sifting through the wreckage of his ideas. Perelhos had not fled his creditors, but the Guard, afraid because he had stabbed Duplin in Narrow Lane. The reason for the murder could be almost anything; they might have argued over the woman, for instance, or the plan or the division of the loot—but he was sure it had not involved the rug, the spellbook or the wand, or Bellona's temple. With a sinking feeling, Liam concluded that the robbery Duplin planned had nothing to do with the crimes he was investigating.

Going out of the harbor in winter was no "simple boat ride," and he berated himself for not thinking of it earlier; the currents outside the Teeth could be vicious, and the winds were unpredictable. Inside the harbor was a different thing altogether, and any man born in a seaport could row a dinghy out to an anchored ship, particularly if the captain of that ship was willing to help. And with two or three chests of money there, it would be well worth the trip.

Instead of two connected crimes, Liam suddenly found himself facing three, and the one he knew the most about was the one he was least interested in. Duplin had not planned to rob him, or Bellona's temple; he and Perelhos had concocted a scheme to steal the captain's own cargo. Perelhos would express his sincere regrets to the merchants whose money had been stolen, and then split it with the thief.

"Sir?" Valdas asked. "Are you sick?"

"No, not at all," Liam said quickly, the concerned expression on the old sailor's face and the disapproving pout Mopsa wore telling him how stunned he must look. *I am stunned*, he thought, *and very, very confused.* "I'm fine, thank you. And thank you for taking time to speak with me, Valdas. You have been a great help."

He found another silver coin for the old man, and turned away in the midst of his thanks.

No, he corrected himself, *I'm not confused at all. I'm just at a dead end*. He could not prove that Perelhos and Duplin had planned the crime he imagined, but he did not want to. He wanted to know who had stolen Tarquin's things and then tried to steal the temple treasury, and now he had no one to suspect, no clues, and nowhere to begin.

"Hey! Uncle!" Mopsa appeared at his side, running next to him as he paced along the waterfront. "Hey, where are you going?"

Liam stopped, and the girl went on a few steps before stopping herself.

"Where are you going? What's wrong with you? You look ill."

He wondered that his disappointment should show so much on his face. And yet he was not as disappointed as he might have been. Valdas's words had made sense only of the questions he had raised with Fanuilh the night before. There had been too many holes in the supposition that Duplin was his thief; the old sailor had helped him discard an unsuitable hypothesis.

"Where am I going?" He did not know; he had not gotten as far as thinking out his next step. To Coeccias, he imagined, but he could not tell the girl that. And what would he do about her? He ought to let the Werewolf know that Duplin was dead, but he did not want Mopsa to hear it from him. He could write a note—she could not read—but then she had said she was not sure if the princeps could, either. "I have to meet someone," he said, "and I want you to send word to the Werewolf. Duplin is not the man I was looking for, but I need to see him tonight." A vague idea struck him, the merest outlines, but it seemed fitting. "Ask him to meet me in Narrow Lane at ten. Tell him I'll have his gift then."

Mopsa looked suspiciously at his small smile. "Why?"

"To give him my gift. The one I promised."

"Yes, but why Narrow Lane, and why tonight? And what if he won't come?"

"Don't ask, pickit, just do as you're told. Ten in Narrow Lane, where it bends. All right?"

"All right," she said sullenly.

"And buy yourself a lunch," he said, but though she took the offered coin, she did not seem pleased.

"Can't I come with you now?"

"As told, pickit," he repeated, and made a shooing gesture.

She walked off, pouting over her shoulder every few steps.

When he could no longer see her, Liam started up Chandlers' Street for the Guard barracks.

Coeccias was not there when he arrived. "More trouble in Temples' Court," the Guard told him at the door, and Liam groaned. As he walked over to the Duke's courts, though, he had a consoling thought: the trouble the day before had led Fanuilh to discover the rug. If the newest trouble yielded a clue even half as significant, he would welcome it with open arms.

He knocked at the tall doors of the courts for five minutes before trying the handle, and found them open. The porter was nowhere in sight, so he slipped quickly down the hallway to the staircase. The darkness after the first twist of the spiral was complete, as it had been on his last visit, but he cursed the creeping fears stirring in his imagination and groped his way down to the cellar.

Just like last night, he thought, and squeezed his eyes shut, shuffling hastily down the corridor to Mother Japh's door. The old woman opened it almost immediately, and he stepped in.

"Rhenford! What would you? I had your message from the Guard," she said irritably, "and have been attending you all the morning."

The morning was not old, but Liam ignored her frustration. "I've found your ghost."

Her expression changed; he had caught her interest. "The one in the morgue? The clerk?"

"Not a clerk—a thief, and he wanders past here every night just after ten."

"Does he?" Mother Japh asked, excited. "To where he was taken off?" Liam nodded. "There's fortune for you— the time and the place. If I can get his body there, he'll find it himself! That'll like Coeccias no end!"

He had expected just such a reaction, and stopped her. "Before we do that, I want to ask you something. Is it possible to trap him?"

"Trap him?" The old woman's eyes narrowed suspiciously. "For what?"

"Not really trap him," Liam said hastily, "but just hold him for a minute. I want to ask him some questions."

Her expression softened, and she nodded sagely. "Ah, I see now. You said he was a thief in life. Is this your thief?"

"No, not exactly. Actually, not at all. But when I saw him last night, he said some things that I did not understand. I was hoping we might, well, lure him somewhere with his body, ask him a few questions, and then let him go."

Tapping at her chin, she spoke thoughtfully: "Aye, it's possible . . . a bit of lead over the mouth and nose, someone outside . . . aye, it could be done. Though not for long, see you. Most ghosts are stupid, do you see? Addled a little. They can pass through walls like nothing, but they often forget. With lead over the face, we could hold him, at least until he thought to go through the wall."

"Would you help?"

"Help? With a will, Rhenford, with a will! It'd like me to see him properly buried."

"And you can arrange it? I mean, put lead on his mouth and nose? And why lead?"

"In course I can. Spirits cannot pass through lead, for that it's a gross metal, a base element, and withstands their airy nature. Though it would be best if we had someone he knew in life on hand."

"A friend?"

"Aye, a friend would do us nicely."

"I can arrange that." He could probably arrange two friends, he realized, and decided he would with a mean little smile. It was petty, but he thought Faius deserved it, and the Werewolf, too.

"Rhenford," Mother Japh said suddenly, "are you being careful?"

"What?"

"Mind you, I told you to be careful. Just then, you did not look like you were being careful."

He remembered her warning, and protested feebly: "Of course. What do you mean?"

She leveled a short finger at him. "There's more here than this ghost, Rhenford. I said it before, and'll say it again. This morning's news only proves it."

He was confused. "What news?"

"Have not heard?" She waited, and when he shrugged, spoke soberly. "A host passed through the city this morning, at dawn. Thundered out of the north, clattered like Hell through the streets, and drew rein in Temples' Court."

A host? "An army? In Southwark?" Was that the trouble the Guard had referred to? "That's impossible! How could there be an army in Southwark? I didn't see any soldiers!"

"That," she said pointedly, "is exactly it. No one *saw* soldiers—they only *heard* them, a noise like legions in the streets, and shouted orders and horses and all the trappings, but nothing to be seen at all. And all camped in Temples' Court.''

Liam whistled. "In front of the temple of Bellona?"

"Where else? I told you there was more here, and that new goddess is at the very heart of it.''

"No doubt," Liam said, wondering how hard Scaevola had prayed, and if this was his sign. "Did they do anything else?"

"No, they didn't. My house is down the hill aways. I didn't hear that they did anything other than wake all of Temples' Court, but isn't that enough?''

"No," he said, "it's not enough. Thank you, Mother Japh. If you would arrange those things for me, I would be grateful. I'll come back around nine.''

She raised her eyes to the ceiling. "Y'are not going to be careful, Rhenford, I can tell.''

"I don't need to be careful," he told her, "I'm very lucky."

Liam did not feel lucky five minutes later. His head full of the phantom host that had paraded down Temple Street, he walked out of the Duke's court and called out to the Guard.

"Is the Aedile back?"

"No, Quaestor Rhenford," the Guard replied.

Liam turned, meaning to head for Temple Street, and saw Japer across the square, lounging against the wall of Her-lekin's restaurant. For a moment their eyes locked, and the thief touched his forehead, smirked, and disappeared into the crowd.

"Damn!" Liam exploded, and when people stared at him, he clenched his fists and headed off in his original direction. There was no chance of catching Japer.

It had been bound to happen: his precaution of waiting until Mopsa was out of sight before going to see the Aedile had been silly, if not completely careless. It had never occurred to him to be more circumspect, but his few experiences as a spy had been brief, forthright things: sneaking into an enemy camp, scouting out unknown territory. He wondered that he had not been spotted before, and then realized that he probably had.

Then why didn't they do anything about it?

There was no satisfactory answer, but he knew that he had underestimated the Southwark Guild. What the price might be, he had no idea, so he ignored it. After scolding himself thoroughly for his stupidity, he put thoughts of the Guild aside, and concentrated on Temple Street.

CHAPTER 13

IF WORD OF the nighttime host had not spread as far as Harbor Street and the waterfront, it had at least completely infected the neighborhood around Temple Street, exaggerating and, perhaps, justifying its already fearful mood. Many of the shops in the nearby streets were closed, and a group of old women stood by the entrance to the row of temples, some still in their nightclothes. They had been awakened by the passing of the invisible army and now they hung by the corner, glancing down the row of columned facades, as if desperate to enter and pray but afraid of what they might find there.

Liam passed them without a second glance, his boots echoing in the empty road. The temples loomed on either hand, their doors shut. It was early yet; the sun had not penetrated into Temple Street, and in the shadows the houses of the Taralonian gods were mute and unhelpful. Greasy smoke oozed from the dome of Pity, burnt offerings creeping humbly to the heavens. He noted it, strode on.

The six Guards in the cul-de-sac looked pathetic, too tiny a force in the empty space, huddled in a circle and warily eyeing the walls around them. Liam did not know them, but one recognized him.

"The Aedile," he said, as if he did not expect to see his commander again, "is in there." He pointed at Bellona's temple.

No one answered Liam's impatient knock, so he pushed open the door himself, and stepped inside.

Now it looks like a temple, he thought, and it did. All resemblance to a military camp was gone; acolytes littered the floor in uneven ranks as though stricken, some kneeling, a few lying prone, with their arms flung out and their faces pressed to the cold stone. A fierce whispering reached him from the altar, Coeccias and Cloten facing each other, Alastor off to one side, and then the Aedile's voice boomed through the temple: "And I tell you you will not!"

Cloten hissed a reply, and Liam hurriedly picked his way among the praying acolytes. There were tears on many of the men's faces.

"No! I'll not have it!" Coeccias insisted. His face was red.

"It is not your will," Cloten said icily, stepping behind the altar; it did not seem that he was retreating, but more as if he were taking up his official position. "It is Her will." He jabbed a finger toward the ceiling.

"The Duke's will rules this city," Coeccias said.

"Then send word to your Duke," Cloten replied disdainfully, "and while we wait his answer, I will have satisfaction!"

Alastor saw Liam approaching, and stepped away from the altar to meet him.

"It would not be well to interrupt them, Quaestor," he whispered.

"What are they arguing about?"

Looking quickly over his shoulder, the Keeper of Arms explained: "Hierarch Cloten has challenged Strife to a duel."

"He challenged Strife?"

"His temple," Alastor clarified. "A champion from each, to do battle tomorrow. Hierarch Guiderius has accepted the challenge. It is Bellona's will," he finished, but it was clear from his tone that he had his doubts about that.

"Did something happen here this morning?" Alastor was a man he could speak to, Liam had decided, more reasonable than Cloten and more disposed to cooperate.

The Keeper of Arms glanced at him, startled. "What do you mean?"

"When the host arrived, what happened here?"

Alastor was quiet for a moment, considering, then shook his head with regret. "I cannot say, Quaestor. It is a matter for the temple to deal with, not the Duke."

"Does it involve Scaevola?" Liam pressed.

Again the priest was surprised, his hasty denial serving only to confirm Liam's suspicions. "Not at all, Quaestor. As I said, it is a matter for the temple, not the Duke."

"Then you would not mind if I spoke with him?"

"With Scaevola?" the priest asked uneasily. "I am afraid that is not possible. He is . . . in retreat. He will be Bellona's champion in the duel tomorrow." Alastor's tone was ambiguous, and Liam guessed that Scaevola's retreat involved guards at the door of his cell.

"Alastor!" Cloten snapped from the altar. "Who is that?"

"Quaestor Liam Rhenford," the priest answered quickly.

"Seconded to the Aedile by the Duke," Liam added politely, with a deep bow in Cloten's direction. "I am here to help find the men who assaulted you, Hierarch."

Cloten sniffed, taken aback by Liam's good manners. "There is no need. They will be discovered tomorrow, on the field of honor."

"Of course," he said smoothly, walking over to the altar. "But perhaps in the meantime you could spare me a moment, Hierarch. There are just a few things I hoped you could clear up for me."

Unsure of himself in the face of Liam's apparent deference, Cloten stammered.

"It will take only a moment," Liam assured him, "and I would greatly appreciate it. For instance, perhaps you could describe the man you saw standing here." He put his hand on the shelf where the temple treasury sat, and smiled expectantly at the high priest.

"I have already gone over this with the Aedile—" Cloten began, and Coeccias started to speak, until Liam overrode him gently.

"I know, Hierarch, and I regret the inconvenience, but it is different to hear it from the person directly involved. Could you just describe the man?"

"Very well," he said with an exasperated sigh, "he was of average height, with a beard."

"Could you say what color beard, or what he was wearing?"

"No. It was dark."

"Of course—forgive me. But could you guess the shape of the beard, for instance? Was it like the Aedile's, or Hierarch Guiderius's?"

"Neither," Cloten said, his face flushing at the mention of the high priest of Strife. "It was full and long—it reached to his chest."

Liam nodded approvingly, trying to keep the man talking and cooperative. "Now, could you tell me what he was doing?"

"I have already been through all this!"

"I know," Liam said sympathetically, "but please, exactly what was he doing?"

"Oh, very well. He was tugging at the chest, trying to move it."

There were leather straps on either side of the chest, Liam took hold of one and pulled experimentally. "Like this?"

Wood grated on stone as the chest slid an inch on the shelf. Behind the chest, he could see the bolt stapled into the wall, the chain running straight up the wall to another bolt, where it angled across the dome. He ran a finger around the edges of the staple; the mortar there was old and thick, sunk deeply in the stone of the walls. There was no way he could see to lower it.

"How do you feed the gryphon?"

"We do not," Cloten said, irritated by the question, as if there were no reason to feed it. "We are going to sacrifice it to the goddess." He looked at Alastor meaningfully, and repeated himself: "We are going to sacrifice it."

"But how will you get it down?"

"With ropes," the priest said shortly, rapidly growing impatient. "Now, if that is all—"

"Just one more question," Liam interrupted. "Did you see the man who knocked you down?"

"I did not. The coward struck me from behind."

"And where did he hit you? He hit you in the head, didn't he?"

"No," Cloten said, suddenly stiff. "He shoved me in the back."

"But you lost consciousness?"

"I must have hit my head when I fell."

"Ah, you had a bruise, then?"

"I do not recall," Cloten said, and Liam knew he had pushed the priest to his limit. "Perhaps I was only stunned. I fail to see the importance of these questions, sir, as the cowards will be exposed tomorrow. Good day."

His purple robe swirled dramatically as he spun on his heel and stalked off to the door in the alcove.

"It will not!" Coeccias shouted. He had kept silent until then, for which Liam was grateful, but the high priest ignored his comment, slamming the door behind him. The Aedile ground his teeth with rage, and turned on Liam. "Did see? Did see that? The man is a fool!"

Alastor, who had watched his superior's departure with

a worried frown, cleared his throat, and Liam hurried to quiet Coeccias.

"We should discuss this elsewhere," he said. "I have to tell you some things."

Coeccias lowered his voice. "Truth, Rhenford, I've heard too much—but I'll attend you." He forced himself to nod politely at Alastor. "I apologize for shouting. Yet you must make him understand that there can be no duel."

Alastor shook his head. "It is Her will," he said, this time with a hint of resignation. Then he too retreated to the door in the alcove.

Liam and Coeccias made their way out of the temple, moving quietly through the rows of praying men. Only a few raised their eyes to note their passing, and Liam noticed that none seemed resentful: only curious, or confused. If that indicated an ambivalence toward Cloten, Liam would not be surprised. On the other hand, between the theological and hierarchical disputes, the visions and visitations that plagued her temple, Bellona's worshipers had more than enough reasons for confusion.

Something had clearly happened when the invisible army arrived in the cul-de-sac, something that almost certainly involved Scaevola, and it had set almost the entire community of Bellona's worshipers to serious praying.

Once outside, Coeccias vented his rage by shaking his fist at the closed door and cursing Cloten vigorously. He finished his opinion with: "The arrogant, blind, pox-ridden bastard!" and then stopped, out of breath, huffing his anger when new curses failed him.

"You can't stop the fight?"

"No," the Aedile said. "It would take the Duke's written hand, and that cannot be had for at least two days. There's no ban on dueling in Southwark, though there should be. The Duke has a faith in the field of honor, and's not above applying it himself. Mind you, it would be no large affair, were it not that the champions will each have one or two score of seconds, all armed to the teeth. And I can't tell them to go unarmed, and Cloten knows it, for that their very weapons are holy to them, and I can't interfere with their 'worship.' Now just think you, what will Cloten do if his man loses? Will he take it like a man? It doubts me—he'll order a general massacre!''

"I don't think Cloten's man will lose. Alastor said it would be Scaevola, and he's one of the best swordsmen I've ever seen."

"Truth, these are good news. I think I can trust Guiderius not to rage if he loses. I'll just have to hope that Cloten'll take his satisfaction from winning, and demand no more." He rolled his eyes to show how much faith he placed in the likelihood of Cloten demanding no more, and blew out a heavy sigh. "But come, Rhenford, do you have more news?"

"I do," Liam said, "but it's not good." He briefly explained what he had learned the night before in Narrow Lane, and on the docks that morning: the identity of the ghost, and the fact that he had almost certainly been chasing the wrong thief. "So now, at the very least, you know why the *Heart of Oak* slipped anchor so quickly, and we can get rid of the ghost in the Warren."

Coeccias smiled grimly. "Aye, that's something. Though now I have to tell all the merchants who had money with Perelhos that they're like never to see it more, and you have to trap a ghost. And we've no direction to take here at all."

"There is still the possibility of one of the other temples being involved. We have not heard from your judge, Saffian."

"That we'll hear tomorrow, I think, though I would not put much faith in it. It makes little sense for another temple to have done it. They're all old, well rooted. Even Strife has little to fear in the poaching of worshipers—not with

Cloten presiding for Bellona. None'll approach. And even if he weren't a complete ass, there're enough mysteries and split hairs at work in her rites to keep all but the most learned away. And what do the learned need with a warrior goddess?''

"Still, you have to admit that it's all we have. Who else would have done it? The only thief who might have been involved is dead, and the only wizard who has been near Southwark in years is dead, and buried right by my house."

Coeccias turned a pensive look at the fortress walls of Strife's temple compound, and Liam wondered how much of his reluctance to suspect the other priests in Temple Street sprang from his own personal bias. These were the gods the Aedile had grown up with, and from what Liam could see, he was friends with many of their priests. It must be difficult for him to imagine them as sneak-thieves.

Nonetheless, the possibility remained, and really was their only avenue. Who else could it be? With the best thief and the only wizard in the city both safely out of the question, who else would have the power to break the wards on Tarquin's house and want to steal Bellona's treasury?

Even as he thought that, something in the formula nagged at him; some awkward phrase, something out of place. He wondered if he was framing the question correctly, but could not conceive of another way to put it.

"I wonder," he said at last, "if we should go speak to Guiderius."

"I already have. He's accepted the damn challenge—had to, he said, for the honor of Strife, and I must say I see where he stands—regrets it, but has accepted. There's no moving him." He looked at Liam, who was chewing lightly at his lower lip, and rolled his eyes again. "Truth, what am I thinking? You don't want to talk him from the duel; you want to put him to the question, and sound him as to whether he could play the thief."

Liam blushed. "You have to admit—"

"Aye, aye," Coeccias said, waving aside his protests. "You've the right of it. We needs must be thorough. And I suppose it's only fair to try Guiderius, after the way you prized the facts from Cloten. I haven't seen the man so open since he came to Southwark."

"Can we go now?"

With a shrug, Coeccias led the way across the cul-de-sac and knocked at the gate of Strife's temple. A brown-robed acolyte with a naked sword in his hand let them in, and asked them politely to wait while he informed Guiderius of their presence.

There was a courtyard inside the gate, and the temple proper stood at the far end of it, a square structure with four towers rising from the corners. Sheds and wooden buildings lined the inside of the courtyard, plain, sturdy barracks, a small smithy, a number of pens and stalls for different animals. There was even a mews for hawks. It seemed more like the manor of a rural nobleman than a temple, except for the blood red marble of the temple itself, and the richly detailed carvings that covered its walls.

Guiderius came out of one of the small buildings, dusting his hands on a brown robe like the gatekeeper's. There was a fletching feather stuck in his goatee; he bowed with a patient air.

"Again, Coeccias?"

"No," the Aedile said, managing a rueful smile. "If you must, you must, Guiderius, and I cannot change that. But it would like me if you could spare a moment for my friend, Quaestor Rhenford. He is helping me to try and sort out this mess."

"I believe I saw him doing just that yesterday afternoon. Good day, Quaestor Rhenford. You wield a cudgel well."

Liam blushed again. "Thank you, Hierarch. I am more lucky than skilled, but the two are often mistaken."

The priest smiled his appreciation of the joke. "Very true, especially in battle. Y'are much a soldier?" He sounded like Coeccias, the same southern dialect, the slurring together of words.

"No, more a scholar than anything else. There are a few questions—"

"Rhenford," the priest said suddenly. "Liam Rhenford? The wizard? Old Tarquin Tanaquil's apprentice?"

Liam goggled at the older man for a moment. "No," he stammered, then got control of himself when he saw Coeccias trying to hide a smirk. "No, Hierarch, I am not a wizard. My name is Rhenford, and I do live in Tarquin Tanaquil's house, but he left it to me because we were friends. I was never his apprentice, and know nothing of magic."

"Ah, I see," Guiderius said. "I apologize. One hears these things bruited about, and they take on the color of truth."

"Not at all," Liam said. "It seems everyone thinks I am a wizard. But there were some questions. . . ."

"By all means, Quaestor. What would you know?"

The priest folded his hands and smiled expectantly.

Liam realized he did not know where to begin.

"First," he began, and then a question occurred to him. "First, can you tell me, are there any in your temple who resent the appearance of Bellona?"

To his surprise, Guiderius chuckled. "I can assure you," he said with perfect confidence, "that Strife has no grudge against Bellona. While it is surely false that She is His daughter, our temple accepts Her happily. Coeccias knows this—we were among the first to welcome Cloten to Southwark."

"A great mistake," the Aedile muttered, drawing a rueful nod from the Hierarch.

"It would seem so," Guiderius concurred.

"I understand that," Liam said, "officially, of course, and personally for you. But perhaps not everyone feels the same way. There might be one or more of your community who do not feel the same. Is that possible?"

Guiderius shook his head, and said flatly: "No. Not in the least. We are a warrior cult—we all take a vow of discipline. The man who violated a stated principle of the temple would be liable to expulsion. It is inconceivable."

"And yet some of your men participated in the fight yesterday. Surely brawling in public is not a mark of discipline."

"They were attacked," the priest pointed out reasonably. "Of course they may defend themselves. But as for the possibility of some of mine breaking into Bellona's temple, it is not even remotely possible."

In the face of the man's iron bound certainty, Liam could not think of any more questions. He did not believe that Strife's discipline could extend so far, but he could not contradict the Hierarch, for Coeccias's sake.

"Well, that is good to hear. But perhaps another temple? Laomedon, for instance, or the Peacekeeper?"

The idea amused Guiderius. "I hardly think the Peacekeeper would be happy to have His priests breaking into other temples, let alone assaulting other priests. And Laomedon is little concerned with the doings of the other gods."

Liam frowned. "Then perhaps some of your lay worshipers?"

"I can't imagine that, either. The people of Southwark are passing tolerant, Quaestor; short of human sacrifice and worshiping the Dark Gods, we'll allow almost aught."

"What about the money lending?" Liam asked, switching to his last suspicion.

"You mean those notes-of-hand on the Caernarvon mines? I would not bother with that, Quaestor. Trade is high in Southwark, and next season promises to be rich, no temple that I know of is unduly worried about Bellona's wealth.''

All his questions neatly deflected, Liam spread his hands and smiled. ''Well, Hierarch, I think that is all I wanted to ask. It seems as though no one in Southwark could possibly be involved.''

''No one of Southwark,'' the priest said. ''Have thought that it might be someone from Caernarvon?''

''Yes,'' Liam said, thinking of Scaevola and the doctrinal disputes he had heard of within Bellona's temple. ''We have thought of that, but unfortunately it seems as unlikely as anything else.''

''It truly is a mystery.''

''Aye,'' Coeccias said sourly. ''Sorry to pester you, Guiderius. We'll part now. You'll keep your men on a tight rein tomorrow?''

''In course. Though there'll be no need: on the field of honor, the righteous will always triumph.''

He smiled and bowed, then returned to the outbuilding from which he had come.

''The righteous almost never win on the field of honor,'' Liam commented. He had seen a few duels, and they always went to the better fighter. ''Guiderius's man will lose.''

''Truth, y'are a doomsayer, Rhenford. Have you no faith?''

''Not in this,'' he answered. ''You wait.''

Coeccias yawned suddenly, stretching tiredly. ''I am hungry. Come, let's get something.''

It was early, an hour or more to noon, but Liam did not object. He was at a loss, and a feeling of futility swept over him. Thieves, wizards and now priests seemed beyond the reach of suspicion; there was no one left. He began to wonder if there was any point to continuing, but still the few

facts he had fluttered through his mind maddeningly, like
flies on a hot summer day.

They left Temple Street, passing a new group of people
waiting there, who stared at Coeccias as the two men went
by, but did not approach. The Aedile led the way to a small
tavern nearby, and called for food. When the meal arrived,
he attacked it with more fierceness than hunger. Liam
sipped at a mug of cider and drummed his fingers on the
tabletop, running over and over his basic assumption.

Someone had bypassed Tarquin's wards, stolen his book,
wand and carpet, and then broken into Bellona's temple to
steal her treasury.

He played with the phrases, rearranging them, deleting
some, keeping only those he knew were absolutely true.

Someone had definitely bypassed Tarquin's wards. Fanuilh insisted they were still intact, and that it had not been
done by another wizard, which meant either theurgy or a
thief with the proper enchantment.

They had stolen the three items. That was undeniable, as
was the fact that at least one of them, the rug, had later
ended up on the roof of the temple, which meant that his
house had been robbed first. He toyed briefly with the idea
that the two were unconnected, but decided that would get
him nowhere.

Then they had broken into the temple. That, too, was
undeniable, because Cloten had discovered them in the act
of stealing the treasury.

"Hold on," he muttered to himself.

What if they were not trying to steal the treasury?

Coeccias heard him, and looked up instantly from his
meal. "Hold what?"

It was the only one of his assumptions that he could
safely discard, the only event in the whole night that had
not actually happened. Cloten had seen a man tugging at

the treasury—not a man taking the chest out of the temple, or opening it to take out the notes-of-hand.

"I had a thought," Liam said, not sure if he should share it.

"Out with it," the Aedile demanded, and the hopeful look in his eyes made Liam wish he had kept silent.

"What if—and this is just a guess—what if our thieves weren't thieves at all? What if they weren't trying to take the treasury?"

Coeccias snorted, the hope going out of his eyes. "What if they were just there to pray? What if they were just taking a stroll in the middle of the night? What if I suddenly grew wings and flew to the moon?"

Perversely, his friend's ridicule increased Liam's interest in the idea. "No, wait, just listen. All Cloten saw them doing was tugging at the chest—and only one man at that. I tried to pull that thing, and believe me, it would take at least two strong men to carry it."

"So? There was another there."

"I know," Liam said patiently. "Indulge me for a minute. Have you got any better ideas?"

"We could book passage on the next ship out of Southwark," Coeccias replied, but he pushed aside his plate and prepared to listen. "Go to, Rhenford. Spit it out. What do the men want, if they don't want the treasury?"

"What's on that shelf?"

"Nothing."

"Vandalism, then. Like those people who broke into all the apothecaries' shops in Northfield. Maybe they wanted to smash up the place, to discredit Bellona, because they don't want her worshiped here."

"Laypeople, you mean—not priests."

"Probably, yes. I'm willing to take Guiderius at his word when he says no one on Temple Street disapproves of Bellona."

"It seems a great deal of trouble just for a mess—stealing your things, going up to the roof. A pot of paint, good red paint, splashed on the door, a dead cat on the steps, both'd be easier, and more visible to the world at large."

Liam admitted this, and then thought of something else. "You know, there is something else on the shelf." It was, perhaps, even more improbable than vandalism.

"And that's?"

"The chain that holds up the gryphon's cage."

"There is that," Coeccias said slowly, considering the idea, and then rejecting it. "But who in Southwark would care about the gryphon?"

Liam thought of Madame Rhunrath, who would have been delighted to have the creature, but she did not have a beard, and what would she have done with it anyway? She could hardly exhibit it.

Still, when he said, "No one," he qualified the statement: "But then, no one could get past Tarquin's wards, either."

The Aedile studied him intently for a moment. "Y'are thinking of something, Rhenford. Is it of value, or just a fancy?"

"A fancy, I think. But worth looking into, if only I knew how." Who would be interested in the gryphon? What if it was a stone gryphon, the rarer type mentioned in one of Tarquin's bestiaries? He tried to call to mind the brief passage: they were rumored to eat the souls of the dead, and they could walk in the Gray Lands, the places where dead souls went. That seemed a contradiction, because the Gray Lands were supposed to be a place of peace, except for those small sections reserved for the punishment of the evil.

No one would be interested in an ordinary gryphon, but Laomedon might be interested in a stone gryphon. The Gray Lands, after all, were his domain.

"I think I will go visit the Death now," he said.

"Then it's not a fancy," Coeccias accused. "Y'are thinking of something, and it involves the Death. And do you know, Rhenford? I've no interest. It'd like me not to know. If your visit is fruitful, I'll be happy, but otherwise, I'd rather let you be wrong alone."

Liam was not surprised at his friend; his attitude only mirrored Liam's own. He had no desire to speak to the Death, but his aversion to entering the shrouded temple of Laomedon was weaker than his frustration at their dead end. Where else could he go?

And besides, he reasoned, *you met a ghost just the other day. How much worse can the temple be?*

CHAPTER 14

LIAM REPEATED THE phrase to himself in the cul-de-sac while he stared up at the grim portals of the temple of Laomedon, and summoned his nerve. For no reason, he was afraid, more afraid than he had been outside the Guild's abandoned house in the Point, more afraid than in the Warren, waiting for Duplin's ghost.

There had been no temple to Laomedon in the Midlands. The dead there were simply burned or buried, with a few observances and sometimes a funeral feast that was more melancholy than frightening. In the city of Torquay, where he had been a student, however, there had been a temple, and it was the focus of any number of ghost stories and dark rumors. He did not try to remember them, but they came to mind unbidden as he hesitated in the cul-de-sac, and he had to force them down.

The Southwark temple was smaller than the one in Torquay, but it maintained the same sinister appearance, like an outsize mausoleum. The walls were of a black, dull stone that drank in light; the columns of its small portico were smooth cylinders of the same stone, without fluting or capitals, and they cast thick shadows on the single door.

This is silly.

He took the steps two at a time, with a jauntiness he did not feel, and knocked three times quickly, before he could stop himself. The door looked like that of a tomb, but it did not creak when the black-robed man opened it.

"My name is Liam Rhenford," Liam said in rush, "and I would like to see the Death."

The man nodded, as if this were the most normal thing in the world, and ushered Liam in.

"If you'll wait here, I'll bring her word of you."

Without waiting for a reply, the acolyte slipped away, leaving Liam alone in the long hall. It was dark at his end, near the door, and at the far end, but in the middle of the hall the walls were pierced by wide arches open to the sky, letting light in. A row of columns of the same unreflective stone ran down either wall, and between them were statues, dimly seen in the shadows by the door, crouching like dogs or lions. He fidgeted for a moment, then stepped to one side and peered closely at a statue, put out his hand and touched the head of a carved gryphon.

"Ha," he breathed, most of his apprehension draining away, and then the acolyte was behind him, his approach unheard.

"If you will come with me, sir?"

Liam stood quickly, and for a moment considered making his excuses and leaving. But he was there, and there were questions he could ask.

"Yes, thank you."

He walked next to the acolyte down the hall, the gryphon statues between the columns revealed as they neared the light from the arches.

"Those statues," he asked, "what are they?"

"Gryphons," the acolyte answered easily. "The servants of Laomedon, Whom all serve."

Was it that easy? Liam could not believe it. *It looks like Cloten and I were barking up the wrong side of the street*, he thought.

The arches opened on identical cloistered gardens; the acolyte turned into the one on the left. The bushes were withered with winter, the beds were covered with straw, but Liam was sure that in the spring and summer the gardens would be beautiful, which surprised him. He had not expected gardens in the temple whose Hierarch was called the Death.

She was waiting for him just off the arcade that ran on three sides of the garden, in a low-ceilinged room with a large fireplace. It was a cheerful place, with vivid tapestries on the walls and comfortable chairs.

"Please sit, Sir Liam," she said, rising as he entered and dismissing the acolyte. "I have been expecting you for some time."

The greeting was odd, but she did not seem threatening. She wore a long black dress, buttoned from her neck to her feet, and a snug skullcap covered the nape of her neck and ended in a point like a widow's peak on her forehead. Her features were too finely cut for prettiness, with wide and childlike eyes, and her voice was high and girlish. She was not at all what he had expected, and it put him on his guard.

"I have been meaning to come since yesterday, Death," he said, standing behind the chair she had indicated. "You smiled at me during the fight."

"I did," she affirmed, smiling again. "I thought you would come much sooner."

"I was not sure it was meant for me." This was not at all what he had anticipated, and he was impatient to ask her about the gryphons in her hall, but he was unsure of himself, put off by her easy, open manner. Her next statement threw him even more.

"It was, Sir Liam. The gods are much interested in you these days. Please sit."

He choked briefly. "Me?"

"Yes, you. Do sit, please."

He sat gingerly, as if the chair might be a trap. "Why are they interested in me?"

"Things are happening in Southwark, Sir Liam, important things, and you have a part in them."

This was so far from the interview he had imagined that he abandoned his planned questions entirely. "I'm sorry. I don't understand."

She steepled her fingers and looked to the fire, as if searching for inspiration. "There are four ways the gods reveal themselves in this world," she said, carefully picking her words. "Really, there are more than four, but for the moment we can say that there are only four. Do you know them?"

"I can guess," he said, but he did not want to; he did not, in fact, want to hear any more. He had been in the presence of a god once, and thought it once too often.

"Do not trouble yourself; I will tell you. First, there are signs—messengers, the flight of certain birds, omens, and the like. Second, there are those to whom the gods speak directly—prophets, some madmen and, occasionally, priests—who do the bidding of Heaven by express command. And then there are those who, without knowing it, follow that bidding—by accident, as it were. Do you understand?"

"By accident," Liam repeated. He had a strange feeling, like the world was telescoping in on the room where he sat, telescoping inward, so that there was nothing beyond the room and the girlish priest who smiled and nodded at him. Nothing but words and mysterious smiles, no arcade, no gardens, no temple, no city.

"You do understand, Sir Liam. You have done the bidding of Heaven before, by accident. Have you not?"

He shook himself, the feeling gone but the glimmer of comprehension remaining. "The Storm King thought so," he said, and remembered that it had not seemed that way when he cowered before the cloud-wrapped god, begging pardon for the crime he thought he had committed.

"So He did. Have you been to His temple here in Southwark?"

"No." He had been in the city for over six months, but had chosen to avoid the edifice that brooded over the harbor, separate from the other temples. "It did not seem proper."

She waved the question of propriety aside. "It is not to the point. That is the past, and we are discussing the present. There is something I am permitted to tell you, and you may make of it what you will. It is this: no one will die tomorrow in Southwark."

The change was too abrupt; he was still absorbed in his memory. "No one will die?"

"No one."

"How do you know?"

She giggled, and he was struck again by how young she seemed. "How do you think, Sir Liam?"

He raised his eyebrows, then lowered them. "Ah. Of course."

"That is all I am permitted to tell you. As I said, you may make of it what you will, but I should think it will effect how you will proceed from here."

How he would proceed? How *would* he proceed? He had no idea, and her vagueness stirred a spark of rebellion in him. "I was hoping you could tell me something else."

"There is nothing else," she said, with a hint of sadness.

"Yes, there is," he persisted. "You can tell me what service stone gryphons perform for Laomedon."

For a long moment she stared wide-eyed at him, and then burst out laughing. "Oh, Sir Liam, I can assure you, no one in this temple had anything to do with that."

"With what?" he asked, as innocently as he could.

"You know very well what," she chided him lightly. "With the attempted theft at Bellona's temple, if you insist that I say it out. For one thing, there are no bearded men in this temple.''

How did she know the man had a beard? And why had she so quickly made the connection between his question and the incident in the other temple?

''In that case, you should have no objection to telling me what service they perform.'' He was excited now, suddenly more interested in the investigation than he had been in days; even though it might be tied to broader events in which he did not particularly want to be involved, he was at least beginning to see their outlines.

The Death wagged a finger at him, but conceded the point. ''Y'are right, Sir Liam. I should have no objection. The question is, would anyone else?''

''You would know better than I.''

Her eyes turned to the fire then, and he was suddenly aware of a maturity in her that had not been apparent before. His sense that she was inappropriate for her position faded; Laomedon might weigh a question as soberly as she did at that moment, he imagined, and with just such a pensive look.

She roused herself eventually, after nearly a minute. ''What do you know of stone gryphons, Sir Liam?''

''Only that there is one in the temple of Bellona, and two dozen statues of them here.''

The Death did not smile. ''No more?''

He hesitated. ''I read that they haunt graveyards and battlefields, and eat the souls of the dead.''

''A misconception. Battlefields sometimes, but never graveyards. And they do not eat the souls of the dead. They are the most special servants of Laomedon, more so than I or any acolyte in this temple. They carry the souls of the elect to the Gray Lands, those marked out by Fortune or greatness to dwell in the most beautiful quarters of those lands. Auric the Great went to the Gray Lands on the back of a stone gryphon, and Ascelin Edara, and the poet Rhaeadr, and many you would not know, nameless in this world but blessed beyond. Does that answer your question?''

Scaevola had said they caught the gryphon after a battle with bandits, and that none of the worshipers of Bellona had been hurt; he wondered which bandit had been among the elect.

''If they are the most special servants of Laomedon, surely he would not like to see one sacrificed?''

''No,'' she agreed, ''He would not.'' She left implicit the contradiction that no one from her temple had done anything about it. There was a long pause, in which he gathered together and reordered his thoughts.

''I suppose I will go,'' he said finally.

''There is nothing more for you here,'' the Death said, spreading her empty arms. ''I will see you out.''

She led him through the wintering garden and down the hall of columns and gryphons to the street door. He stopped there, and gestured at the statues.

''Does no one ever see them?''

''The statues, or the real ones?''

He had meant the statues. ''Both.''

''There is a real one on view in Bellona's temple,'' she said, with no trace of emotion. ''But the statues? No. The dead are brought in by a separate door, purified, and sent back out for burial. No one but His servants have been in Laomedon's home—and now you.''

Liam was not sure how much of an honor it was. ''I see.'' He reached for the door, then stopped. ''The fourth way—the fourth way the gods reveal themselves. You didn't say.''

She might have smiled, but it was dark, and by the time he opened the door and let the light in, her face was serious.

"They reveal themselves," she said. "Good day, Sir Liam."

At least she *didn't think I was a wizard*, he thought as the door closed behind him, and he looked out at the cul-de-sac. He realized then that, though it had been a busy place in the last few weeks, before the arrival of Bellona it would have been secluded, the neglected end of Temple Street—an appropriate place for a temple that admitted none but the dead.

There were more important things, however, than how the cul-de-sac might have been before Bellona came from Caernarvon. What he had learned—he corrected himself: what he had been told—put a completely new spin on all of his and Coeccias's investigations and, while he was not sure what they could do with the information, he knew he should tell the Aedile at once.

Temple Street was still quiet as he went out of it, and the unnatural hush seemed to have infected more than just the immediate neighborhood. The city square was almost deserted, a few men huddled near the entrance to a wine-shop, a lone woman hurrying across, her skirts billowed out in front of her by the wind, like a ship carried uncontrollably across the surface of the sea. He wondered how far beyond the square the mood of uneasiness had spread. *Soon enough*, he thought, *the whole damn city will be hiding under their beds.*

Coeccias was in the barracks, crouched over a table and rapidly filling a sheet of pure white, expensive paper with his unruly handwriting. He looked up when Liam came in, laid aside his quill, and held up another, cheaper sheet of paper, folded in quarters.

"One of Cloten's boys gave this to the Guards by the temple—fair demanded they deliver it that very moment."

Liam took the note, turned it over; apart from his name,

misspelled, there was nothing on the outside.

"Go to," Coeccias urged, "read it. You can tell me of the Death when I've finished my missive to the Duke."

Liam stopped in the middle of unfolding his letter. "You are writing to the Duke? What about?"

"To tell him I've taken it upon myself to stop this damned duel. I've thought it through, and there's no chance of it turning out well. If I halt it, Guiderius and Cloten can both maintain their honor, and I can avoid a passing mess." His tone was defiant, as if he were daring Liam to disagree.

"I don't think you should do that."

"And why?"

Liam held up the letter. "Let me read this, and then I'll tell you."

Coeccias gave an exaggerated shrug, picked up his quill and threw it in the inkwell.

The letter had been written in block capitals, with the elaborate care of the near illiterate, and contained many misspellings and crossed-out words.

Master Liam Rhenford, it began, *I am writing this to you for Hierarch Scaevola, who begs you to come see him next morning before the duel. Hierarch Cloten has said he will allow it. The time will be just at dawn. Again, he urgently begs you to come.*

There was no name signed to it, but Liam imagined one of the praying acolytes laboriously printing out the message. If he needed any proof that something had happened in the temple after the arrival of the phantom host, Scaevola's new title was more than enough. The question was whether Cloten had authorized it, and he doubted the obnoxious priest had. More likely the temple was split, with some accepting whatever sign had come that morning, and others, certainly Cloten, denying it.

Liam handed the note to Coeccias, and when he had read it, explained what he thought. "And what's more, I would guess that that's why Cloten pushed ahead with the challenge. Scaevola would be the obvious choice, but he may be hoping he'll lose, and get rid of him. That would put an end to any discord in the temple."

"And leave that knave safe as its head," Coeccias agreed. "All the more reason to cancel the duel."

"It would be, but there is something else."

"The Death."

"Yes." He recounted his conversation with Laomedon's priestess, omitting nothing, not even the mention of his own past. He had considered skipping over it, but decided not to; he did not want to have any more secrets from his friend.

Naturally, it was that part that intrigued Coeccias the most.

"And what was it, then, this task of the gods you performed by accident?"

"It's not important now," he said, and then, at a twinge from his conscience: "I'll tell you later. What should concern us more is what she said about no one dying tomorrow, and all those gryphons in Laomedon's temple. I'm not sure I believe her when she says no one there was involved."

Coeccias was staring intently at him. "But you do believe her about tomorrow, eh?"

Liam started to answer, then paused, frowning. "I am not sure. I think I do—but you are right, it does not make any sense. Why would she tell the truth about one thing, and not the other?"

"Truth," the Aedile said, shrugging, "I know not. Perhaps she's telling the truth about both. In either case, let me ask you: should I send this letter?"

The burden was unfair; if Coeccias did not stop the duel, and there was trouble, Liam would feel responsible. On the other hand, he knew his friend would not blame him; in fact, he would take the responsibility himself—but that would not lessen Liam's guilt.

Cross your fingers, he told himself, *and hope your Luck is with you.*

"Let the challenge stand."

Crumpling the letter he had begun, Coeccias let loose a heavy sigh. "Aye, I thought you'd say that." He threw the wad of paper into the fire. "So now, how do we proceed? Will you follow this with the gryphons? I suppose I should apologize for being so short with the idea earlier."

"Who would have guessed? I certainly did not think I would find Laomedon's temple decorated with them. The problem is, how do we follow it? We can't very well march back there and ask to see if any of the acolytes have beards."

"They don't," Coeccias said. "Like Uris's, Laomedon's are completely shaven—head as well. Even the Death herself."

Liam did not question the statement; Coeccias had forgotten more about Taralon's gods and the ways of their priests than he had ever known. "And we can't arrest every man with a beard and have Cloten look at them."

"No, we can't," the Aedile said, stroking his own beard. "Some of us would take it ill."

They both sank into their own thoughts; Coeccias doodling absently on another sheet of paper, Liam pacing back and forth in front of the fire. He noticed his friend's sketchings, and wondered at the waste. Truly, white paper was expensive. He thought the Aedile had realized this when, with a puzzled expression, he pushed the paper aside and looked up.

"Think you they would try again?"

"Try what?" Liam asked.

"Whatever it is they were trying in the first place—lib-

erating that gryphon, plundering the treasury—whatever.
Might they try again?''

"They might," Liam said, but he did not see that it mat-
tered. "Why?"

"When would they try? Cloten's had a heavy guard
mounted since that night, eh? No chance for a repeat." An
expectant smile spread across his face; he was waiting for
Liam to catch on. "When would they try again? When
would the guard be smallest?"

Liam caught on. "During the duel!"

"Truth, it sings, Rhenford. During the duel is right—and
so you'll go? You'll answer the new Hierarch's sum-
mons?"

It does *sing*, Liam thought, and nodded. It was a slim
chance, but it made sense at least for him to be there. He
could visit Scaevola, and stay behind after the acolytes left.
If necessary, he could even say he was there to protect the
treasury, in case the thieves returned.

"It is not foreordained," Coeccias warned. "They may
not return, you know. The guilty returning to the scene of
their crime is more myth than truth."

"No," Liam agreed, "but it's something to try."

"That it is. But in the meantime? Will you still do this
with the ghost?"

He said he would, and mostly because he pitied the lost,
mad soul. However, there was something else he was interested in, and he was glad he had told Mother Japh he
wanted to corner the ghost for a while.

"I need to go home for a while," he told the Aedile.
"I'll be back in a few hours."

"Will you need men tonight?"

He thought about Japer spotting him in the square; a few
Guards at his back might be a good thing. At the same
time, he did not want to betray the Werewolf, should he
come. It did not seem likely, given that they now knew he

was in touch with the Aedile, but he did not want to risk it.

"No, only Boult."

"And that, I'll warrant, for that Boult knows to hold of his tongue."

Liam smiled, refusing to be surprised anymore by his friend's quick grasp.

"Exactly. Do you want to eat dinner?"

They agreed to meet at Herlekin's, and then Liam left for the stables.

The traps, if they could be called that, pleased Liam as he rode back to the house on the beach. Holding Duplin's ghost for a few minutes might give him some information, tell him whether a suspicion he was holding was true—and it was an active thing, more than just wandering around asking questions. Waiting in the temple during the duel and hoping the thieves returned was not very active, but at least it would feel like action, and a quiet voice at the back of his head told him it would be worth his while.

The same voice prompted him to go to the library, leaving Diamond tethered by the door, loosening the girth but leaving the horse saddled.

It is strange, Fanuilh thought at him while he scanned the shelves, *that the Death knew those things about you.*

"You think so?" he said absently, his mind and his eyes on the spines of Tarquin's books. He was familiar with most of them, having gone through the library thoroughly over the past two months, but he was not sure which might provide him with the information for which he was searching.

Yes. Could she be right?

Liam pulled his eyes from the books and looked to the doorway, where Fanuilh now sat. "About my accidentally helping the gods? Why not? It's happened before. The question is, which gods? Whose plans am I supposed to further? And, for the philosophers among us, I might ask whether I have any choice.''

You do not believe in predestination.

''No, but it doesn't matter what I believe—it's what the gods believe. And if they believe in predestination, then the rest of us just have to go along, don't we?''

I do not know.

''It was a rhetorical question.''

The dragon's snout wrinkled, an expression that Liam knew meant it was thinking hard.

Your thoughts are scattered, it told him after a pause.

Liam agreed; he had allowed himself to get caught up in the unresolvable problems of predestination. With a shrug, he returned to the shelves, tapping each spine as he read the title.

The books of fables and travelers' tales would not have what he was interested in, nor would the many history texts. He ignored the thick tomes on magic and wizardry, though they might have something: he knew from paging through them that they were mostly impenetrable, and he did not have the time to check hundreds of pages in hopes of spotting a morsel of intelligible information. That left the philosophies, of which there were over a hundred. Liam frowned, then sighed and started checking their spines.

What are you looking for?

The dragon knew, of course, or could know, if it chose, but Liam was glad to see his familiar upholding the polite fiction.

''I want to know more about the differences between the planes—the ethereal and astral planes, is that what you call them? And the Gray Lands and the real world. You said Tarquin could see into them easily, and I was hoping he might have a book on it.''

He does. The bottom shelf, on the right. It is called On the Planes.

"Naturally." The book was where Fanuilh had said it would be, and it stuck to the covers of the volumes beside it, coming free with a leathery rustle. Dust lay thick on its top, a dirty puff when Liam blew on it. "Consulted it often, did he?"

I do not think so, the dragon thought; Liam abandoned the joke and opened the book. The writing inside was tiny, and packed together so tightly that the descenders of one line often overlapped the line below. Cradling the heavy book in the crook of his arm, he flipped randomly through the pages, hoping at the very least for a diagram or illustration, but the book was solid with text from cover to cover.

"I'm not reading this," he said at last, closing the book with a thump and wedging it back onto the shelf. "I don't have a year and a day, and I'd be blind in six months anyway."

I have read it.

Liam looked up, surprised. "You have? How did you read it?" He imagined his familiar, crouched over the open book with its snout close to the words. "How did you turn the pages, with your tail?"

Fanuilh sniffed. *When Master Tanaquil read it, I followed along in his head. He always let me read with him, because I remember everything.*

"Everything?"

Everything.

"So I've been wasting my time here. You could have told me all this."

I did not think—

Liam held up a hand for the dragon to stop. "Never mind. It doesn't matter. Just tell me what I want to know."

You wish to know about the planes.

"Fanuilh!" he shouted, in exasperation. "I know what I want to know, because I don't know it! I want you to help me stop not knowing it."

I was going to, master.

Liam slowly unclenched his fists. "Right. About the planes."

The dragon narrowed its eyes and looked up at him, then shook itself, like a dog shedding water, and started telling him about the planes.

There were four: terrestrial, heavenly, ethereal and astral. The book suggested there might be more, but there was no proof. The terrestrial plane was what Liam had called the real world, and the heavenly was where the gods lived and where the Gray Lands were.

The ethereal and astral planes are not so much places, Fanuilh recalled, *but borders, where the other two planes intersect. The silver cord that binds us can be seen in the ethereal plane, because that plane is attuned to things spiritual.*

"Spiritual, as in spirits? Souls, that sort of thing?"

Yes.

"So that is why the stone gryphons need to walk in the ethereal plane, to guide the souls of dead people to the Gray Lands."

It would seem so. The witchcraft Mother Japh used to show you that Duplin's soul was lost touched the ethereal plane.

"And Tarquin could see this plane at will?"

Yes.

Liam crossed his arms and leaned back against the bookcase, mulling this over. Duplin's ghost should have crossed the ethereal plane to get to the Gray Lands, but it had not. Presumably it was either barred from it, or lost in it. Outside Faius's wineshop, it had said something about being chased by birds and animals, and that it could not help them. Had the stone gryphons come for Duplin when he died? That did not make much sense—the Death had said they only fetched great men, and Duplin was hardly even a good man.

Do you wish to hear about the astral plane?

"Is it relevant?"

Not particularly. It is even less understood than the ethereal plane. It is where magic seems to come from.

"I thought magic came from the gods," Liam said.

Apparently not. According to the book, and Master Tanaquil's own beliefs, it has a source apart from the gods. When I notice magic being performed, it is in the astral plane.

"You can see it?"

It is more like sensing—like heat, a burst of warmth. The dragon paused, and it struck Liam that it was struggling for words. *I cannot explain,* it thought finally, *but it is not seeing.*

"That's all right," Liam said. "As long as you don't think it is relevant. I'm more interested in the fact that Tarquin could see into the ethereal plane. Could he go into it?"

It is not so much a place. He could travel it a little, but it is not like traveling. Again, the dragon paused, but Liam did not leave it hanging.

"Never mind," he said. "He was familiar with it, though?"

Yes, very familiar.

Leaning against the bookcase, Liam was suddenly aware of being tired. He breathed out heavily, letting his shoulders slump.

"Questions, questions, questions. Gods, I hate asking questions."

You should take a nap. If you plan to find the ghost, it will be a late night for you.

The divan he slept on was right in front of him, and he considered it, the soft, cool brocaded fabric, the thick pad-

ding. A nap would be a good thing, and with the sunlight
from the window in the ceiling, he would be sure not to
sleep too long.

"I believe I will do just that, familiar mine."

He slouched over to the divan, noticing how comfortable
it was to have his shoulders loose, the tension dissipating
even as he let himself down onto the cushions.

I will leave you then. May I fly?

"Yes," Liam murmured, stretched out at full length, one
arm over his face. "Just make sure I get up in a couple of
hours."

The dragon left, and Liam took a couple of deep breaths
to prepare himself for sleep.

It did not come.

His muscles relaxed, knots and cramps he had not recognized fading away, his whole body adjusting itself for
sleep. His thoughts started jumping, however, as soon as
Fanuilh's padding steps faded away.

"Damn," he murmured.

Fanuilh had once described his thoughts as a flock of
startled birds, rising in panicked confusion. They were like
birds now, he knew, except that they circled different ideas,
randomly lighting on one after another, touching any of a
thousand subjects except sleep.

If the dragon could remember everything, why did it
have such a hard time explaining certain concepts about the
planes? He wondered how its memory worked. It might be
eidetic, so that it could quote whole sections of a book, but
be unable to explain them to the uninitiated. Then again, it
might be entirely different—the mind of a creature as ut-
terly humorless as Fanuilh must be.

Liam let his arm drop away from his face but kept his
eyes closed.

Had Duplin been referring to stone gryphons? The Death

had suggested that they sometimes came for people who were unknown, but she had also said they were great people. He doubted that Duplin had been secretly a great person. Of course, it had been fairly obvious that the ghost was unhinged, and its ramblings about birds and animals might have been just that, ramblings.

Liam opened his eyes and stared at the ceiling.

What was he supposed to do for Laomedon? When she said he would unwittingly serve the gods, the Death had not specified her own deity, but if it was not him, then why would she have been the one to relay the message? He was wary of the gods, and the fact that they expected his help without telling him directly what they wanted made him uneasy. If he acted wrongly, would they be displeased? *Could* he act wrongly?

He rolled over and pressed his face into the cushions, trying to force sleep.

What had happened in the temple of Bellona? Scaevola called himself a Hierarch, but was apparently Cloten's prisoner—and he would fight at Cloten's command.

"Damn," he said, and sat up. There was no chance he was going to sleep, and as comfortable as the divan was, he could not stand lying there and wallowing in his own questions. Closing his eyes, he sent a thought to Fanuilh.

I am going riding. I will not be back until after tonight.

Should I come to the city tonight? the dragon asked immediately.

Yes, Liam projected, after a moment's thought. *Come to Narrow Lane at nine.*

He imagined a roll in the kitchen, and was munching it as he went outside to get Diamond. From the doorway he could see Fanuilh far out over the slate gray winter ocean, skimming along the whitecaps. He watched it fly, driven by occasional thrusts of its tiny wings, and then went back inside.

When he came back out he had another roll, and his sword at his belt.

CHAPTER 15

IT WAS LATE in the afternoon before Liam reentered Southwark by the city gate. He did not take his usual route along the muddy road, but guided Diamond to the north, over the winter-bare fields. There was a thin belt of farmland, which gave way shortly to rolling moors interrupted by rare drainage ditches and the occasional swale.

Houses sometimes huddled in the swales, often sheltered from the sea wind by a screen of hardy trees, and Liam rode along the rough arc they described around the city. Some were the homes of merchants from Southwark, those rich enough to keep a country establishment, but most belonged to the nobility of the Southern Tier. They tended to keep to themselves, apart from the society of the Point, but Liam could tell by the design of their homes that they relied on the city for other things. There were no outbuildings, none of the messy appendages that marked the hold of a Midlands lord and made it self-sufficient; the buildings themselves were defenseless, many windowed and erected in hollows beneath hills.

He counted seventeen structures as he rode in a wide semicircle around the city, crossing their lands with impunity. At one, a man grooming a horse even waved to him. In the Midlands, the man would have mounted and given chase the moment he saw Liam, demanding toll or at least an explanation for his trespass.

To keep his mind from his present business, Liam pretended his ride was a reconnaissance, and planned a siege of Southwark as he went. It could not be in the winter of course, with the ground covered in snow as it was now, and the weather uncertain. Nor in the early spring, when the rains would turn the moors muddy. In the summer, though, the city would be an easy prize, a simple matter of marching straight south. The lords' manors would offer little resistance, and once past them, the artisans' quarters were wide open.

He could see them, the inviting sprawl of Northfield and Auric's Park, the cobbled roads petering out into dirt tracks, completely indefensible. An army could invest Southwark in a single day.

Even if it wasn't invisible, he thought, and started looking for a road into the city. He had tried to avoid the thorny questions awaiting him, but they had followed him into the countryside, and as Diamond trotted southward, he puzzled over his many riddles.

If the situation at Bellona's temple were any indication, the invisible host had done more than just make noise in Temple Street, and the most likely thing was that it had been the sign for which Scaevola had prayed. That fit with his use of the new title, but it did not fit with the fact that he seemed to be Cloten's prisoner.

And it was strange that he was going along with the duel. The Death had insisted that no one was going to die, but what did that mean? She had also said that no one from her temple was involved in the attempted robbery, but he was firmly convinced that whoever the bearded man and his companion were, they were after the stone gryphon, not the treasury. An odd and disturbing thought occurred to him: what did Laomedon look like? There had been no depictions of him in his temple, and Liam did not remember ever hearing any stories that described him.

"He probably has a beard," he said to himself. "And when he comes tomorrow to free his servant, you will have to tell Coeccias that he has to arrest a god for knocking Cloten on the head." It was ridiculous, he knew; if Laomedon himself had been the bearded man, he would not have been deterred by Cloten's doubling the guard on the temple. Who would have been, though?

Diamond found his own way into the city, slowing to a walk as he entered the outskirts of Northfield, and Liam scarcely held the reins as the road became cobbled, the buildings rising higher on either side. Many of the stores were closed, and there were few people in the streets. Word of the strange things in Temple Street must have spread.

If the thieves did return during the duel, who would he find? As sick as he was of looking, he wanted to know the answers. It was like riddles from his childhood: he heard them eagerly, and pondered them avidly for a while, but there was always a gap between giving up and learning the answers, in which his interest in knowing was high but his interest in figuring them out ebbed. He had always spent the interim dutifully mulling over the riddles, knowing that in the end he would have to be given the answers.

Only those were riddles, he thought, *not gods and duels and priests, and I never had to guess how to act before I knew the answer. How am I supposed to know what to do? If they want something from me, I just wish they would ask.*

That was not the gods' way, though, which was one of the reasons he had as little to do with them as possible.

Diamond found the stables on his own as well, and Liam was drawn out of his musings when the horse stopped and looked over his shoulder.

"Are we here, then?"

The horse blew and stamped a hoof.

"It's hardly five yet," he scolded. "You go too fast."

Diamond whickered an apology but refused to move, so Liam dismounted and called for the hostler's boy.

He was half an hour early for his dinner appointment with Coeccias, but he settled himself into a quiet table on the second floor of Herlekin's restaurant, and nursed a mug of beer until the Aedile arrived.

The dinner was slow. Liam did not particularly want to talk, knowing that almost any conversation would turn treacherous, doubling back to pointless speculation on the next day's events. Coeccias seemed to sense his mood, and devoted himself silently to his meal.

They lingered over cups of mulled wine after the serving girl had cleared the table. Liam studied his fingers, drumming them slowly on the tabletop, and Coeccias's eyes roved aimlessly around the near-empty restaurant. Finally, he cleared his throat.

"Truth, we're a gloomy pair." He chuckled, but with little humor.

Liam nodded. "It's been a long week."

"And'll get longer—at least 'til the morrow." The Aedile coughed behind his fist, hesitated, then struck out: "I wonder, Rhenford, the time y'unwittingly aided the gods. Would you . . . ?"

"Tell you about it?" Liam frowned. He had promised, not thinking to do it so soon. It had happened when he was much younger, and he had tried not to think about it for years. Still, he could understand his friend's curiosity. Coeccias was much more interested in the gods than he was, and Liam's earlier hint must have caught his imagination.

"Aye, if you've no objection. That is, it can wait, if you'd rather."

Liam spread his hands out on the table. "No, no reason for that. But you must remember, this happened almost twelve years ago. I may not remember it all.''

Coeccias pulled his chair closer to the table, and the look on his face and the way he said, ''In course, in course,'' showed that he did not believe that Liam might have forgotten.

If he met a god, Liam thought, *he wouldn't forget a thing*.

''Right. As I said, it was twelve years ago. I was living in Carad Llan—the border city built on the ruins of Auric the Great's fortress—working as a clerk. There were always caravans going north of the King's Range, or coming back south, and plenty of people who could not read or write, so business was good. And one day this mad old noble, Baron Keillie, came into the city with a troop of mercenaries and an ancient map he needed translated.''

Liam told the story in broad outlines, leaving out many of the details. Baron Keillie's map had shown the way to a building hidden in a valley deep in the King's Range; the old script indicated that it had belonged to someone named Duke Thunder. Keillie had organized an expedition to find the place, expecting to find either a tomb or an abandoned keep, and hoping, because of certain clues on the map, to find treasure there as well. He brought Liam along because he could read the near-forgotten language with which the map had been inscribed.

It had seemed like a grand adventure at the time, with the promise of riches at the end, but when they reached the valley they found that Duke Thunder still lived there—and that he was no musty Taralonian nobleman, but a god gone mad and made prisoner there by his father, the Storm King.

There were complications Liam chose not explain, but in the end Thunder had trapped the expedition in the valley, and they had to kill him to get away. Liam's part had been small—he found the weapon, a spike of stone created by the wind spirits Thunder had enslaved—but apart from the captain of Keillie's mercenaries, he was the only survivor.

"I don't see it," Coeccias said, when the story was done. "How did that serve the gods?"

"The Storm King wanted his son killed. Thunder was mad, absolutely mad, like a rabid dog. He was a danger to everyone, gods and men alike, but the King could not kill his own son."

Coeccias shook his head. "But if the Storm King could not kill him, how could you?"

They were questions Liam himself had asked at the time, fleeing the valley with the mercenary captain. "It was not a question of the power to kill him," he explained, "but of the will, and the right. I don't understand it fully myself," he went on, "though the Storm King had tried to make it clear; for some reason Thunder's father could not kill him himself. It had to be someone else, and that was where Keillie and his expedition and I came in."

With a grunt, Coeccias dropped his eyes to his wine, pondering. "I did not know gods could go mad."

"Neither did I," Liam said simply. He could tell his friend was dissatisfied with the story, but then so was he. There were details of the expedition that still puzzled him, and memories that were still troubling. At the time he had shrugged them off, joining up with the mercenary captain to form a troop and later traveling south, where he met Stick; now the questions came back, like dimly remembered wounds aching with the arrival of cold weather.

The bells over the Duke's courts started ringing, and Liam counted along with them up to eight; it had taken longer than he thought to tell the story.

"What time are you to meet Mother Japh?"

"Nine, but I think I will go over there now, and make sure everything is ready."

"Do you really think this necessary? All this with the spirit, that is. Could not Mother Japh see it through? You do not look well, Rhenford."

He was tired, and knew that it showed in his face and the way he kept rubbing his eyes, but the Aedile's voice registered more than just nominal concern.

"I'm fine," he assured him, "and yes, I do think it's necessary. I want to ask Duplin a few questions before Mother Japh does whatever she must for his soul."

"Very well, if y'insist. Only remember you've to meet that Scaevola on the morrow, early."

"I'll be there, don't worry." He wanted to avoid talking about it, so he stood up. "I'm going to see Mother Japh now. Could you send Boult over to the morgue?"

"I can," Coeccias said. "Will he need aught?"

"Aught?"

The Aedile pointed at the sword leaning against Liam's chair. "Aught like that, Rhenford. Arms."

Liam picked up the sword and guiltily buckled it on. "I doubt it—maybe one of those cudgels, just in case. But I doubt it."

"He'll bring one."

"All right. I'll see you tomorrow sometime."

Coeccias nodded and touched his forehead. " 'Til the morrow."

With a wave, Liam strode out of the restaurant.

Mother Japh was waiting in her room in the basement of the Duke's courts. She opened the door within a second of Liam's knock, pulling him inside and shutting the door in the sullen porter's face.

"Faith, Liam Rhenford, I thought you'd never come!"

"I am early," he pointed out, but not as sarcastically as he might have. The old witch's nerves showed plainly on her face, and he was surprised at how apprehensive she seemed. "Is everything ready?"

"Ready? Oh, aye, all is ready, but I have come to doubt the wisdom of this."

He did not want to hear it, and laughed to hide his own nervousness. "What wisdom? We're trying to catch a ghost, Mother Japh. There's no wisdom involved to doubt."

"It's not catching the ghost that I doubt." She cast a glance toward the morgue. "It's this with holding him. Showing him his body is right and good, helping him find peace is all right. But this with holding him . . . it likes me not the more I think on it. Ghosts are tricksy things, Liam Rhenford, and of unknown parts. Who knows what he might do if we present him his body, and then keep him from it? There are strange things in Southwark these days, and a ghost may not be just a ghost."

She gave the last sentence a strange emphasis, and he frowned.

"What do you mean by that?"

He had never seen her like this: dithering, unsure of herself. She looked from the door of the morgue to him, then back, then spoke in a whisper: "I mean, what if this ghost is somehow a part of the troubles in Temples' Court? What if it's a part with the messengers, and the invisible host of this morning? What if it's the work of the gods?"

Liam almost laughed, switched to a gentle smile. *You don't understand*, he wanted to say, *I'm doing the work of the gods these days. The Death told me so.* Instead, he reached out and gently touched her arm. "Mother Japh, I cannot think of a single reason the gods would want Duplin's soul to wander the streets without peace. It is only right that he should be put at rest. And if it makes you feel any better, I promise that if there is even the slightest indication that we cannot hold him, we won't try. We will just let him go. All right?"

She pushed lightly at his hand, looked away. "Very well, very well. I don't know why I should be so skittish. The mood of the city is terrible just now. It must be wearing on my nerves.''

"It wears on everyone's nerves. Now, is there anything we need to do?''

Sniffling, she drew herself upright and shuffled toward the morgue. "Just move the body. I've made the mask ready, and put a shroud on him. Did you think how you would move him?''

Standing at the door, she looked expectantly over her shoulder at him.

"I . . . ,'' he began, and was saved from admitting that he had not when a knock sounded at the outer door. Boult entered without waiting for an answer, trying to escape the complaints of the porter.

"The courts aren't open,'' the man was saying, and raised his voice when he saw Mother Japh. "And you know it, woman! There's no call for all this tramping in and out!''

"Go to!'' she shouted back, "go to, you rogue! Back to your pot and your couch, for that's all y'are good for! Go to!''

Boult shut the door on the porter's protests, forestalling a shouting match, and grinned doubtfully at Liam.

"Good evening, Quaestor.''

"Evening, Boult.''

"Good evening, Mother Japh.''

"Who's this, Rhenford?'' she demanded, looking with disapproval at the crossbow resting on the Guard's shoulder. "Is this the thief's friend?''

"No,'' Liam said, quickly covering his lapse in planning, "he's going to help me move the body. Aren't you, Boult?''

Grin fading, Boult sketched a mockery of a bow. "In course, Quaestor. I'm at your service. What body did you have in mind?''

Mother Japh harrumphed at his tone, and pushed open

the door to the morgue. "This one, Guard."

Liam went into the morgue, Boult at his shoulder, and walked over to the slab where Duplin's corpse lay. The body was bound in strips of white cloth up to the neck, and a curved piece of lead lay on the chest, beneath the crossed arms. The two men stood to one side of the slab; Mother Japh went to the other.

"We can bury him as soon as the spirit's recovered," she said, indicating the wrappings, "and the lead should keep the ghost out."

"This is your ghost," Boult said. "Are we moving it to Faius's?"

"Yes," Liam said, prepared to explain, but the Guard merely nodded.

"Very well. Am I to forget this part?"

"This part, no. What comes later, perhaps."

"What is he talking about?" Mother Japh asked.

"I have been in Quaestor Rhenford's service several times," Boult said with a wink, "but I cannot remember any of them. I am in danger of forgetting him entirely." The wink irritated the old woman, but Liam laughed.

"You may wish it all you want, Boult. In the meantime, however, we have to move this"—he pointed at Duplin's body—"down to Narrow Lane."

Boult shrugged. "Very well. Will the porter forget, do you think?"

"Damn that porter," Mother Japh said. "He's a sozzled knave."

Liam had not considered the porter; he did not need a reputation for body snatching added to his one for wizardry. Nor did he want to have to maneuver Duplin's body through the maze of streets leading to Narrow Lane. "Is there any other way than out the front door?"

Mother Japh shook her head, but Boult pointed to the window. "We could lower him out."

To Liam's surprise, the ghost witch did not object. "There's sure to be some rope down the hall, if y'insist on this foolishness." She went off without waiting for his reply, leaving him to exchange amused looks with Boult, and then the two men took hold of Duplin's body.

It was far easier than Liam had expected; the body had none of the stiffness and weight he associated with old corpses, nor any of the smell. Duplin might have been asleep, despite the pinkish stain revealed when they took away the lead plate. They hoisted the limp figure over to a slab near the shuttered window. Boult undid the clasp, shoved the shutter aside, and looked down into the inky blackness of Narrow Lane.

"We could drop him down," he suggested with a straight face. "It's not so far, and he wouldn't feel it in any case."

"You will not drop him down," Mother Japh said angrily, struggling in the doorway with a heavy coil of rope. "How would you feel if it was your corse, Guardsman?"

"It was only a jest," Boult said, so meekly that Liam almost laughed again. He relieved the ghost witch of her burden, and measured out lengths while she berated the sheepish Guard.

" 'It was only a jest,' " she mimicked, waggling a finger at him. "Only a jest, ha! Y'are a rude rascal, Boult of Crosston, and should be ashamed of yourself."

"How did you know where I'm from?"

"Never mind that," Liam said, wondering himself. She had said it as if just remembering it. "Help me get this rope around him."

Wrapped in the shroud and tied with the rope, Duplin's body looked like a bundle of sailcloth, which made it easier for Liam to stomach the idea of lowering it into the black well of Narrow Lane.

"They'd never do this in Crosston, I'd warrant," Mother Japh muttered.

"They've done stranger," Boult countered. "Anyway, we burn our dead there."

"Where is Crosston?" Liam asked. They were all talking just to hear themselves, he could tell, to take the edge off the thing they were doing, like soldiers before a battle.

"Nowhere," Mother Japh offered, helping to guide the bundled body through the window, while Liam and Boult took the strain on the ropes.

"A day's ride north," Boult grunted, easing his rope down so that Duplin's feet dropped below his head.

"At a crossroads," Mother Japh said, with a little sneer. "Can imagine? The town is at a crossroads, so they call it Crosston!"

Duplin's shrouded feet scraped the stones of Narrow Lane; the pressure eased on Boult's rope. Liam paid his out slowly, the muscles of his arms bunching, letting the corpse sink to the ground.

"And Southwark?" Boult asked. "Is that so very clever, Mother?"

"Cleverer than Crosston," she answered, with a toss of her head.

"But not half as clever as the Midlands," Liam said. He could not see the body, sunk in the darkness below. "We can't just leave him there. I'll jump down and wait while you two go around by the street."

Neither Boult nor Mother Japh objected, so he climbed onto the wide windowsill and swung his legs out. Twisting around, he lowered himself down by his arms, legs hanging, and only at the last minute thought of the body below, kicking frantically against the wall to arc out into the street.

It was an ungraceful landing. Liam's heels hit the cobbles—not the body, he realized gratefully—at an awkward angle, and he sprawled backward, arms flailing. He scrambled quickly to his feet, but not before the chill dampness of the street penetrated his cloak.

Boult tied a lantern to a rope and lowered it down to him, and whispered that they would come around to meet him. Liam urged them to hurry, also whispering, though ten o'clock was still far away and there was no one to hear. There was something about standing there, in the meager light of the lantern, looking up at the window in the Duke's courts that made whispering appropriate.

When the Guard had shut the window, Liam tucked his hands into his armpits, prepared to wait, then looked at the bundled corpse and remembered the wetness of his cloak.

Muttering an apology, he stooped and lifted the body, cradling it in his arms and leaning back against the wall for support. The cloth of the shroud was damp and cold. He apologized again to the night air, unwilling to look at where Duplin's head would be. There was an eery stillness all around; he could hear the wind above him, but it was baffled by the height of the surrounding buildings, leaving Narrow Lane a cold, quiet backwater. As at Laomedon's temple, the world seemed to contract, so that there was nothing but the bend in the road, the light of his lantern, the corpse in his arms. He imagined the scene as if from a distance, the strangeness of it.

Like a grave robber, or a ghoul. The shadows beyond the lantern light seemed to shift. *Distractions. Think of something else.* They did not appear to have met before, but Mother Japh knew Boult's name, and where he was from. She knew he was a Guard, just as he knew what her position was—just as they both knew his. The difference was that in his case they were most likely wrong. Boult, thanks undoubtedly to Coeccias, thought he was a human bloodhound, fully deserving his borrowed title of Quaestor. The gods alone knew what Mother Japh thought he was now, but until a few days earlier she had believed him a wizard.

*A poor one, but a wizard nonetheless. And Mopsa thinks
I am a thief, unless Japer has spread the word, in which
case the whole Guild thinks I am an informer.* The old man
on the docks—Valdas, he recalled—had thought him a rich
lord, which was probably the closest guess of them all.
*Though my riches are fairly limited, and my estate long
burned to the ground,* he qualified. *Still, what can you expect? You're not much of anything, really, are you? Not
much of a scholar, not much a lord, certainly not a wizard
or a thief. An apprentice of all trades, and master of none.*

Before he could go further along this maudlin line of
thought, Boult and Mother Japh came around the corner,
the old woman ordering the Guard to slow down.

"*Shh!*" Liam said automatically, though there was no
real reason to be quiet. Both obliged. He pushed away from
the wall and carried the body across the alley to stand in
front of Faius's. "Boult, open the door." His arms were
beginning to ache, and it was cold. He wanted to be finished.

Faius's door was locked, and no one answered when
Boult knocked.

Have I ever been this stupid before? Liam wondered.
What else have I not thought of?

There was no sound from within, and no light under the
door.

"It seems the barkeep has decamped," Boult said.

"Yes." Liam forced the frustration from his voice, trying
to sound calm and authoritative. "Break it down."

Boult shrugged, then kicked at the door. There was a
small crash and it banged open, rebounding from the inside
wall. The interior of the wineshop was dark and empty.
The Guard took the lantern and advanced cautiously, his
crossbow held in front of him.

"No one here."

"Just as well," Liam said, carrying Duplin's corpse in-

side and to the back of the shop. There was less litter on
the floor there, and he cleared a space before setting his
burden down. Then he dusted his hands, and turned to face
his two companions. Boult was standing by the door, pointing his crossbow into the street, and Mother Japh was looking around the wineshop and wrinkling her nose.

"Is this where he died?"

"Yes," Liam answered.

"Well then," the old woman said, gathering her skirts
around her and squatting against one wall, "there's nothing
for it but to wait. At the stroke of ten we'll unveil the
corse."

"We should have brought dice," Boult said from the
door, "to pass the time."

Liam shrugged. He did not think he would want to game
in an abandoned wineshop with a corpse for company. Broken pottery crunching under his boots, he followed Mother
Japh's example, squatting against the wall and resigning
himself to the wait.

In a dozen wars and hundreds of night watches at sea,
Liam had never been able to condition himself to waiting.
He hated it, all the more intensely for the vain efforts he
made to be patient. Shifting on his haunches, he frowned
at the grating noise the movement made, and settled himself
once again. The same noise came from the door, where
Boult was standing, and it annoyed him. Waiting did that,
made him prickly and irritable.

The bells rang nine eventually, and he got up and began
pacing. The tolling sounded distant, even though the tower
was close by, and somehow mournful. In the wan light of
the single lantern, his monstrous shadow paced behind him.
The old woman against the wall, the armed Guard at the
door, the corpse at the back of the room: the scene was
disconcerting, and he had the strange impression that it was

not just the wineshop that was abandoned, but all of Southwark, and that they were camping in a dead city.

As he paced he tried to think, running over everything
he knew and all the things he did not. The bearded man in
Bellona's temple and his impossible escape, Cloten overcome without a scratch, Scaevola and his visions and his
new title, the Death and her warnings and assurances. The
gods and their plans, into which he was supposed to fit.

He was not sure whether he wanted to know their plans,
the better to fit in with them or the better to avoid them. In
the back of his mind he held an image, planted by an old
teacher, of the gods in the heavens holding strings on which
men jumped. He did not like the image.

Master?

The thought in his head brought him up short, and then
he projected. *Where are you?*

On top of the Duke's courts.

Come down here.

There was a pause, and Liam looked to the door, expecting the dragon to appear.

You are expecting the princeps.

Yes, he projected, trying to inject some urgency into the
thought.

You think he knows you work with the Aedile.

YES. He actually formed the words in capital letters, and
instead of projecting them, he shoved them at the dragon.
COME DOWN HERE.

*He may wish to harm you. Perhaps I should wait outside
and watch, where I cannot be seen.*

Liam blew out a heavy breath and nodded. *That makes
sense. I did not think of it.* More, he realized he did not
want Boult or Mother Japh to see his familiar. It was difficult enough to convince them he was not a wizard without
Fanuilh adding weight to their belief.

"Eh?" Mother Japh looked up at him. "Thinking again?"

"No," he said, smiling wryly. "I just hate waiting."

"Hmph."

I will watch the street then.

That would be good. You can also watch for the ghost.

Mother Japh looked up at him skeptically. "Is this friend of the ghost going to arrive early?"

Liam cleared his throat. "I had arranged two, actually, but one of them seems to have gone. He owned the wineshop. Is a friend absolutely necessary?"

She frowned, waiting a moment before responding: "No, it's not absolutely necessary, but it's best. Y'are not sure of the other, then?"

"No," he admitted, "I am not." Would the Werewolf come? He must know by now about Liam's connection with Coeccias, but if he knew that, he would know that Liam could have turned him in to the Aedile at any time. And Liam guessed—hoped—that the Werewolf would be curious. The more he thought about it, the more the hope faded. Curiosity was a weak thing to put against a spell in the Duke's jails or the loss of a hand, the common punishment for stealing.

He eventually gave up on trying to figure out whether the Werewolf would come or not. If it came to that, there would be time enough later on to deal with the Southwark Guild. He had done such a thing once before, when a powerful merchant had tried to force him to leave Southwark. With Fanuilh's help, he had convinced the merchant he was a wizard, and thus not to be fooled with. . . .

And if Ancus Marcius did not spread the word that you were a wizard, then those bodyguards of his probably did, you idiot. He shook his head, recalling how Fanuilh had put them to sleep, so that he could confront the merchant. The irony did not escape him, and he appreciated it fully.

So now you are angry that people think you are a wizard, eh?

Mother Japh had her head down and Boult was watching the street through the half-opened door, so they did not see the smile of self-derision that crossed Liam's face.

There is a man on the roof above you, and three approaching the bend in the road, one from one direction and two from the other.

Liam's head jerked up. *Are they armed?*

Not with swords. Only knives.

No bows?

No.

"Damn," he muttered aloud. So the Werewolf had come after all. He went to the door, gesturing for Boult to stand aside. There was nothing he could see in the street, and nothing to hear, but he knew it nonetheless. The Werewolf had come, and brought friends.

There was no back way out of the wineshop, and they could hold the front door if necessary. But first he wanted to see if the princeps would talk.

"Stand here," Liam whispered, placing Boult to his right and behind him. "If I hold up my hand, step forward and show your crossbow. Aim it at whoever I am talking to. Do you understand?"

The Guard nodded. Mother Japh stood up stiffly and took a hesitant step toward the door.

"Is this our corse's friend?"

"I think so. You should step back, and shutter the lantern."

He did not wait to see if she would comply. Opening the door completely, he leaned forward and peered into the street.

How close are they?

You will see the two in a moment. The other is waiting

at the corner, hiding, and the man on the roof has not moved. If you wish I can put them to sleep.

Only if I say so. How close are the two?

They have rounded the corner, but they are hiding in the shadows. The light from the lantern does not reach them.

Liam looked at the ground; a weak tongue of light spread from the door a few yards into the street. Taking a moment to gather his wits, he stepped just outside the doorway.

"Avé, princeps."

There was a sharp intake of breath to his left, and he turned that way.

He did not bother any more with chant. "I am glad you could come. I need your help."

The Werewolf's wary voice came from the shadows, and he could sense the man looking around the dark street. "I should think so, Liam Rhenford—or should I say, Quaestor Rhenford?"

Liam appreciated the princeps's flare for the dramatic: he stepped forward as he mentioned the title, placed his fists on his hips and smiled, showing his overlong eyeteeth.

The best defense. "Come now, princeps, you knew I worked with the Aedile when we first met. And you also knew that if I wanted you arrested, I would have managed it that night, instead of coming in and chatting. Have you moved your carad yet?"

It was a bluff, a wild shot in the dark, but it made the Werewolf's smile deepen. "As it happens, we have. And we did. Think you I set Mopsa on you for the promise of a gift? We were passing curious about this attendant of the Addle who could chant, this wizard who sought us out. And it seems we were right to be, eh?"

For just a moment, Liam faltered. It made perfect sense of Mopsa's determination to stay with him. He had thought it was because he was kind to her, when she had been spying on him all along.

Then he rallied: "And yet you did nothing."

"You could have had us that first night, Quaestor, but you didn't. And once we'd moved our carad and were safe, we wanted to know more about you. Y'are a man of parts, Rhenford—chanter, wizard, aide to the Addle. What else can you do?"

He decided not to contradict the part about his being a wizard. "I can tell you that your man on the roof should have a bow, if he is to be of any use."

The Werewolf laughed, but his eyes narrowed, and his mock bow was stiff. "A bow's unhandy on the rooftops, Quaestor. But he can throw a dagger as well as the next, if not better. So you know it would be bloody to try to clap me in here. Now come, what do you want of me?"

"Have you heard of the ghost in the Warren?"

"Aye."

"It's Duplin. He was murdered here a few nights ago. I have his body here. I think he will come back to it and I want to ask him a few questions, but I need someone to be there who knew him. Someone he will listen to."

Suddenly another figure appeared out of the darkness behind the Werewolf.

"I say we kill the bastard," Japer hissed, stopping just behind his chief.

"How many Guards have you got in there, Rhenford?" the Werewolf asked, as if he had not heard Japer's suggestion.

"Just one," Liam said, "and he will forget everything, won't you?" He raised one hand.

"I will," Boult said, "unless I quarrel with it." He stepped forward to show his crossbow, giving the pun meaning, and they were mirrored: Liam and Boult, the princeps and the angry thief.

Japer started to say something, but the Werewolf raised

his hand and silenced him. His lips lifted at the corner, turning his smile feral.

"I will come in, then, Quaestor, on your word there'll be no trouble, and that I'll leave unmolested."

"You have it."

The bells started tolling ten as the Werewolf entered the wineshop.

CHAPTER 16

BOULT AND JAPER eyed each other like dogs who had not met, distrust plain on their faces and in every line of their bodies. Liam, however, was watching the Werewolf as he walked to Duplin's body. Mother Japh had pulled away the shroud, revealing the dead man's face.

"Aye, that's Duplin," the thief said, crouching down. He took hold of the corpse's chin, moved the face from one side to the other, examining it. Then he pushed the shroud down, looked for a moment at the knife wound, and pulled the cloth back up. "Who took him off?"

"A ship's captain, someone he was working a job with."

"His name?" The Werewolf stood up, and his voice was tight.

"Perelhos, but he has left Southwark."

"He may return."

"He may," Liam conceded. He knew what the other man was thinking. "And if he does, you can have him. In the meantime, Duplin's ghost is wandering the city. We can put him to rest, but I need to ask him some questions first. Will you help?"

"What sort of questions?"

"It has to do with what's going on in Temple Street."

The princeps crossed his fingers. "Well enough. What do I do?"

Liam looked at Mother Japh for help.

"Look, you," the woman said, "when the ghost arrives,

speak to it. Reassure it. Show it the corse, and explain, as gentle as you can, that it's dead, and that it must leave this world. Can you do that?''

"Here now," Japer said, "how do we know that the Quaestor didn't take him? This could be a trap! Wolf—"

"Shut it," Boult ordered.

"Yes," the Werewolf said. "Shut it, Japer."

Fuming, Japer shut it.

"I can do that," the Werewolf went on. "Is that all?"

"No. Once you've calmed it, Rhenford'll have his questions. Present him as a friend, point him out. All as gentle as you can, for that ghosts are skittish, confused. And the same for you, Rhenford, go lightly."

The ghost is here.

"It's come," Liam told them. Then Japer cursed and he and Boult both stepped away from the door. The ghost was there, white radiant in the doorway, peering fearfully around the room.

"Faius?" it said.

Mother Japh nudged the Werewolf, whose jaw dropped at the sight of his friend.

"Faius?" the ghost repeated.

At another nudge, the Werewolf spoke, trying to sound soothing. "Faius is not here, Duplin. But it's me, do you see? The Wolf. And Japer's here, too. Remember Japer?"

The other thieves have run away, Fanuilh told Liam.

"Oh, Wolf, look at what they've done to me, the bastards." Duplin gestured at his chest, where the purple stain stood out like a blossom. "They've cut out my heart, Wolf."

"They've killed you, Duplin, I know. But all will be well. We'll take the one who did it. We'll kill him, Duplin, I swear."

"The body," Mother Japh whispered urgently. "Show

him the body." She had placed the piece of lead over the corpse's mouth.

"It's bitter cold, Wolf, and I've no heart to keep me warm."

"Don't you worry," the thief said, and Liam was impressed by his composure. "You need to get back into your body, Duplin, and we've brought it for you. It's got a heart, and you'll be warm there."

The ghost stood hesitantly in the doorway, looking unhappily at the Werewolf. Then it began to sob.

"I'm so cold, Wolf, and it's dangerous out here. Can I come in? There's people after me, and animals. Everybody's out for me."

"Come in, Duplin. Look, you, y'are dead, do you see? That Perelhos has killed you, but you've got to see your body. It's warm there. Will you come in?"

"There's people here," the ghost said, sniffling a little and looking around the wineshop.

"All friends," the Werewolf told him. "They all want to help you . . . but you've got to go into your body." He gestured to the back of the room. "Can you see it? It's warm there."

Duplin's ghost walked forward a few feet, then stopped. Liam repressed an urge to shout at it to hurry, but the Werewolf continued in the same soothing tones.

"Come now, Duplin, don't you want to be warm? Don't you want your body? No one can hurt you there. Look at it."

The ghost finally saw its body and went to it, passing Japer, Boult and Liam without noticing them.

"That's me," it whispered, wonderingly. It crouched down by the bundled corpse and touched the cold forehead. "Is that really me?" he asked the Werewolf.

"It is," the live thief said. "Y'are dead."

"What's that on my mouth?"

"It's to protect you," the Werewolf lied, "from anyone who would harm you. Do you see?"

There was a long pause, while Duplin examined himself. "I see," he said at last. "I'm dead, then." He began to sob again, and covered his face with a glowing hand.

"It's all right," the Werewolf said, moving next to his friend. "We're going to make it all right. But there's someone here—someone who's helped you—who has some questions to ask you."

"Who's here?"

"He's a friend."

Mother Japh beckoned Liam forward.

"Hello, Duplin," he said.

The dead thief could not take his eyes off his own face.

"Duplin?" the Werewolf prodded. "This is a friend."

"What's he want? I'm dead."

"I want to know about the animals that were chasing you, Duplin."

The ghost looked at him then, raising its eyes from the body and staring directly into his. "The birds."

"Yes," Liam said gently. "The birds. You said they wanted you to help them, but you couldn't. What did they want you to do?"

"They were giant," Duplin said, and he sounded tired and frightened, and tired of being frightened. "Giant birds with long claws, and they wanted me to help them, but I couldn't."

"That's right. But what did they want you to do?"

Duplin bowed his head, as if trying to remember was difficult. "They wanted my help. They said they'd give me my body, but I didn't know where it was. And I didn't have a heart. How could I help them without a heart?"

"What did they want?" He knew—he was sure he knew—but he wanted the ghost to say it.

"I can't remember."

Forcing patience, Liam coaxed, "Did they want you to go to Temple Street?"

"Yes!" the ghost said eagerly. "That was it! They wanted me to go to Temple Street, and they said they would give me back my body to do it! But my body is here. How did it get here?"

"We brought it for you, Duplin. What did they want you to do in Temple Street?"

"They wanted me to steal a bird. A friend of theirs. But you can't steal anything when you have no heart."

"Your heart is here, Duplin."

Liam nodded to Mother Japh, who reached out and pulled the lead plate away.

Duplin resuming his crying, leaning forward across his body as if to embrace it. Mother Japh stood up and backed away, motioning for Liam and the Werewolf to do the same.

Stroking his body and weeping, Duplin's ghost faded slowly away, dissipating into the air until nothing was left but the corpse.

The ghost witch sighed. "Well and well. That's done. We can send him to Laomedon's temple tomorrow, to prepare him for burial." She looked at Liam. "What was that about Temple Street, eh?"

He let loose the breath he had been holding and shook his head. "I'm not sure. I have to figure it out." He looked at the Werewolf, who was studying his friend's body. His fists were clenched, and he stood rigidly upright.

"We'll take him. We'll bury him."

"As you will," Mother Japh said softly.

The princeps turned to Liam. "I suppose I should thank you, Quaestor."

Liam only half heard him; he was thinking about what Duplin had said, about the birds and the help they wanted in Temple Street. And another thought, an impossible thought.

"That's crazy!" Japer burst out. "I say it's crazy! He killed Duplin, I tell you, and this is a trap!"

"Shut it," the Werewolf ordered.

"No! He's a wizard! He's faked the whole thing!"

Liam looked up just in time to see Japer pull a dagger from his sleeve.

"Quaestor!" Boult shouted.

Fanuilh! Liam projected.

And then Japer stumbled, dropping heavily to the ground, his knife clattering into the trash on the floor. The Werewolf, too, suddenly slumped down, though far more gracefully than his underling. He folded, bending at the knees and then down onto his side.

There was silence for a long moment, and then Mother Japh spoke: "And y'are no wizard, eh, Liam Rhenford?"

They checked the sleeping thieves, to make sure they had not hurt themselves falling down. Japer had a few cuts on his face, but otherwise they were fine.

"We'll leave them here, with the body. When they wake up, they can take it with them," Liam said. The other two only nodded, very pointedly not saying a word. "Boult, will you see Mother Japh home?"

"Yes, Quaestor."

"And what'll you do?" the witch wanted to know.

"I am going to stay here for a moment. I have some things to think about."

"This is to do with that in Temples' Court, doesn't it? I was right, wasn't I?" There was an edge of worry to Mother Japh's voice.

"It does, yes," Liam answered. "But we haven't done anything wrong. Now, please, go home. They will wake up shortly, and I do not think they will be happy."

They left, Mother Japh shooting a glance over her shoulder as she went out the door. Liam did not notice. He was looking down at the Werewolf, thinking furiously.

Duplin's giant birds had to be stone gryphons, and they must have tried to enlist his help in freeing the one slated for sacrifice in Bellona's temple. It made sense; stone gryphons traveled the ethereal plane, and so did ghosts. If they wanted help, they would look there and find Duplin, who had died that night, before his house was robbed and before the break-in at the temple. They had offered him his body back so that he could help them and then, most probably, die properly, but he had refused, or been too deranged by his recent death to be of any use. So who had helped them?

He thought he knew, and the answer bothered him.

On the other hand, he had an idea of what he would do the next day. He mulled it over for a minute, then nodded to himself and started searching the Werewolf. When he did not find what he was looking for, he went through Japer's pockets, and came out with what he wanted: a small set of lock picks. He put a gold coin in Japer's pockets and the picks in his own purse, then left the wineshop and strode hurriedly through the dark streets to the stables.

Fanuilh joined him on the ride back to the beach, perching on the saddle in front of him.

"Does it make sense to you?" he asked.

It is possible.

"Yes, but does it make sense?"

No. Why would the stone gryphons need help? Why would he help them?

They reached the cliff path and started down. The stars were brilliant overhead, and the moon lit up a shining road across the sea.

"There is one way to check, you know."

How?

Liam did not answer at once. He let Diamond plod across the beach, to the door of his shed.

"His grave. We could dig up his grave."

He looked beyond the shed and the house, to the sheltered nook by the cliff base.

And what would you find?

"Nothing," Liam said at last, and then suddenly dismounted and threw open the door of the shed. "Nothing at all. I'm going to bed. Wake me an hour before dawn."

Apart from the message Fanuilh sent to wake him—the dancer from the distant port, banging a drum and shouting "Wake up!"—he had no dreams at all.

As he dragged himself out of bed and into the kitchen for hot water, he wondered if this was a good sign or not. Certainly it indicated how tired he had been, and the grit in his eyes and frequent yawns attested to how tired he still was. Washing and a hot cup of coffee woke him up but he was not happy with the hour, or with his sketchy notions of what he would do in Bellona's temple.

"It should be easy," he told Fanuilh over their coffee. "The cage has to have a door. They can't have built it around the damned thing."

What if it is locked?

"I doubt it is. Why put a lock on a cage for an animal? They don't have hands, after all. And if there is, I have Japer's picks." Over which, he noted with some satisfaction, he felt no guilt at all. The thief was mean, and he had left a coin. If they were difficult to replace—lock picks could not just be bought in the market—that was not his problem.

Yes, but why?

He had no answer for that, but he gave one anyway: "Because it feels right, familiar mine. I never liked the idea of a gryphon in a cage, and now that I know he has friends trying to get him out, I like the idea even less. Plus—and this is important—I can get away with it."

Are you sure?

"Quite sure. And if I cannot, then I won't try."

The dragon dropped its head to its bowl, taking in a deep whiff of coffee smell.

The chair was comfortable, and for a few minutes, Liam toyed with the idea of staying at the beach all day, avoiding Southwark entirely. When he had finished his coffee, however, he got up from the table and went out to the shed. Fanuilh padded after him.

Fresh, cold air drove the last of the sleep from his brain, and he stretched briefly on the stone patio, taking in the predawn blue of the sky, the rustle of waves on the sand. It was a good place to be, and again he wondered if he should go into town.

Diamond snorted in the shed, and he went to it reluctantly, carefully averting his gaze from the spot near the cliff where he had buried Tarquin.

There was a crowd gathering in Temple Street as dawn approached, a fearful group of almost fifty, huddled in the road and exchanging tense whispers. A Guard saw Liam and pointed to the cul-de-sac.

"The Aedile's attending you at the end, Quaestor."

Liam belatedly returned the man's salute and urged Diamond on. The horse pressed through the crowd, people standing aside quickly, as if they were afraid to touch it. He caught sight of Coeccias by the entrance to the cul-de-sac, pacing in front of a row of Guards, all armed and armored, each carrying a torch.

"Rhenford! Good morrow to you!" It was clear the Aedile saw nothing good in it, and he snapped at the Guard he had ordered to take Liam's horse for being to slow about it.

"I see everything is ready." Through the gates of Strife's compound, he could see acolytes in shining chain mail assembling. Bellona's men were massed in front of her temple, equally polished. Guiderius and Alastor stood by the fountain, conferring with an elderly man in a red silk coat with a wheel stitched in gold thread on the back. "This Quaestor business—people saluting, orderlies taking my horse—I must say, I could get used to it."

Coeccias turned from studying the conference by the fountain and offered him a appraising look. "It could be permanent, you know. We'll discuss it later. For now, you should get yourself into the temple. The duel will start any minute."

"I was joking."

"I was not."

He let it drop. "Who is the man in red?"

"The Hierarch of Fortune—note the wheel. He's agreed to officiate. There'll be prayers and the like before the duel itself, but the parties'll have to be here soon, so go to, get into the temple."

Shrugging, Liam started across, then stopped as he heard his name being called. When he turned, he saw Mopsa duck out of the crowd and run up to him.

"Morning, Uncle! What are you doing here?"

"I'm going to pray, and I'm in a hurry. What are you doing here?"

"Practice," the girl said, patting her pocket and grinning at the sound of coins clinking. "Crowd's been here most of an hour. I'll be able to retire soon."

"I'd retire now, pickit. One of those Guards is giving you a look. Now I have to go." He did not want to be rude; he was surprised she was talking to him at all.

"Can I come with you? I want to watch the duel, and I can't see it from here. I'm too short."

"I'll be inside the temple for the whole thing. I won't see it."

"Oh," she said, disappointed.

"Look"—he hesitated, "look, did the Werewolf say anything about last night?"

"About what you did for Duplin? Sure, and he did. That was good on you, Uncle. Everyone said so. Even if you are too close with the Addle."

Which meant neither the Werewolf nor Japer had said anything about being put to sleep. He could understand that; in an organization like a guild, prestige and face were important, but he could not understand why the girl would still associate with him.

"All right," he said hastily, "you can come along. But you'll have to wait outside while I talk to someone, and don't get in the way of the priests. And whatever you do, don't steal anything."

"I've had enough already," she said smugly, and followed closely behind him as he crossed the cul-de-sac, careful not to go too near the fountain, where the three priests were talking. He stopped by the steps of Bellona's temple, behind the silent ranks of Her acolytes, and turned to the girl.

"Wait over there, just around the corner. You should be able to see everything and be out of the way at the same time. If someone tells you to move, move. All right?"

"I'm not a fool, Uncle," she said.

"I have my doubts," he replied, and started up the steps before she could answer. He did indeed have his doubts. She did not seem to hate him, as she could have: he worked with the Aedile, and she was a thief. They should have been enemies. Apparently the Werewolf had spread the

word that he had done a good deed for the Guild by helping
Duplin.

Not that I didn't have my own reasons for doing it, he
thought, but that was beside the point. They had known all
along that he was friends with Coeccias, and the Werewolf
had brought guards to Narrow Lane, but now he was saying
Liam was all right, and had not warned Mopsa off. Did that
mean they would not bother him in the future?

No one stopped him until he was inside the doors, when
a single guard barred his path with a spear and demanded
his name.

"Liam Rhenford. I am here to see Scaevola."

The man's demeanor changed immediately; he was expected. "Hierarch Scaevola is back there." He stressed the
title, and pointed to the door by the altar.

Liam thanked him and headed for the door. The temple
was dark, lit by only a few candles around the altar. As he
crossed the floor he stole a glance up at the dome, where
the cage hung. He could just barely make out the stone
gryphon, lying listlessly against the bars.

Another guard waited behind the inner door, and when
he heard Liam's name he immediately led him down a narrow corridor toward the rear of the temple. They went down
a flight of steps and along another hall, past a row of cur-
tained-off cells to the last one, where the curtain was pulled
aside. The guard leaned in and gave Liam's name, then
went back upstairs.

Liam looked into the cell. Scaevola was standing in front
of a straw pallet, his arms raised, allowing an acolyte to
buckle on his sword belt. Cloten was leaning against one
wall, chewing angrily at his lower lip.

"Good morning, Liam Rhenford," Scaevola said, smiling tiredly.

"Good morning, Hierarch Scaevola. Hierarch Cloten."

He deliberately used both titles, and was pleased with Cloten's glower.

"Are they finished up there?"

"Who, Hierarch?" Liam inquired politely.

"Alastor and Fortune's idiot, who else?"

"They were still talking when I came in."

"I had better go and see what's keeping them," Cloten said, leaving the cell, only to stop by Liam and turn. He pointed a finger at Scaevola. "Remember, Hierarch—fight your best. The honor of our goddess is at stake."

Scaevola only nodded, and when Cloten was gone, he signaled for the acolyte to leave. When they were alone, he took off the sword belt and put it back on a different way, with the sword slung on his back, the hilt projecting over his shoulder.

"I am glad you could come," he said, his fingers nimbly adjusting the buckle.

Scaevola sounded as tired as Liam felt—more so, perhaps—and for a moment he searched the cracked skin under the new Hierarch's eyes for signs of shadows, and then remembered that the other man never slept.

"I got your note," he said, rather lamely.

"I wanted to thank you. You were right when you told me to pray. I did—and She answered me."

"You had a sign yesterday," Liam said.

"Yes. We were all in the main hall, at our prayers. I had prayed all night, but I prayed even more then." The sick man's voice grew soft, as if remembering something particularly beautiful. "And then we heard the host, thundering down Temple Street, and they came into the temple, and rode in a circle around me."

"You saw them? No one else saw them?"

"Oh, we saw them," Scaevola said, still awed by the experience, "and they formed a circle around me, and when they doffed their helms to me, they all had low-root. Can you imagine? An army of heroes, all with low-root, bowing to me."

It seemed a fairly unequivocal sign to Liam, but he was glad to hear an edge of humility in Scaevola's tone, as if he still found it hard to believe—not that the host had come, but that they had come for him. "Then why is Cloten still Hierarch? Why aren't you in charge? Why are you fighting this duel?"

Scaevola cocked his head, as if considering a strange idea. "Why shouldn't he be Hierarch? The visit means only that I am blessed by the Lady, not that Cloten has fallen from favor." Liam frowned his disagreement: the host bowing and removing their helms indicated to him that they recognized Scaevola's leadership—and if they did, so certainly should Bellona's mortal servants. But Scaevola was not paying attention, caught by his own thought. "Though he does seem to doubt the truth of what we all saw, which some are taking poorly . . . but as for the duel, it has been contracted in our Lady's name. It must be done."

No one will die today, Liam recalled, and he was trying to think of a way to tell Scaevola this when the other man continued.

"Did you know, Liam Rhenford, that duels such as these can end in draws? Keeper of Arms Alastor told me: if the fight goes on long enough, and neither man is killed or draws blood, honor can be satisfied." He smiled then, a wistful, mature smile that fit his ruined face very well. "I must go now. We will begin soon enough."

Liam followed him out of the cell and up the stairs, staring at his feet all the way.

Scaevola paused in the temple, kneeling at the altar and bowing his head for a moment, then rose in a fluid motion and headed for the door. He stopped when he saw that Liam was not with him.

"Are you not coming?"

"I'm going to stay here," Liam said, standing by the altar. "In case the thieves come back while everyone is outside."

Scaevola digested this, looking pensively into the fire pit. "Of course. Wish me luck, Liam Rhenford."

"Good luck."

The sick man looked up at the dome, then back at Liam. "And good luck to you."

He was not wearing armor, Liam saw, only a light robe of black cloth, which flared as he spun to the door and strode through it.

There was no sign of the guard at the door. *He must have gone out to watch*, Liam thought. *He's probably right there on the steps, just outside*. It would have been better if he was inside. Still, he was alone in the temple.

He jogged quickly to the outer doors just as horns blared in the cul-de-sac. They blew a fanfare, then another, then stopped. He cracked one of the doors just a little, just enough to see, and then Mopsa thrust her head in.

"Aren't you coming? They're starting!"

Liam jumped back, startled, one hand on his chest.

"Gods, girl, don't do that!"

"What? Aren't you going to watch?"

Outside, someone was speaking to the assembled temples. The Hierarch of Fortune, Liam guessed. He did not recognize the voice, and he could not make out the words. Mopsa stared at him.

"Well?"

"No," he said quickly, bending down to take her by the shoulders. 'I'm not going to watch. But you are. I want you to stay here by the door and watch everything. If the duel ends, or if anyone comes up those steps, I want you to whistle. Can you whistle?"

"Can I whistle, he says," she joked, as if he had asked

if she could walk. "Sure, and I can whistle. What are you going to do?"

"Don't worry about that. Just watch."

He left her by the door and ran back to the altar. He had counted on there being a guard, had prepared Fanuilh for it. The dragon could have taken care of it, and he would have felt safer. A guard would have been a certainty, something to get out of the way, clearing the room. Without one, he could not be sure that someone would not come back to check. He had no choice, though, the girl would have to do.

Fanuilh, he projected. *Where are you?*

On the roof, master. What happened to the Guard?

They didn't leave one. I want you to watch, in case someone comes back. What's happening out there?

Hierarch Cloten is making his accusation to the red priest.

Tell me what happens.

He examined the altar, the shelf behind—the treasury chest, the staple for the chain. He ran his eye along the chain, up the wall, across the ceiling to the dome. It would not be easy, but it would not be as hard as the wall outside.

Kicking off his boots, he climbed up onto the shelf and grabbed the chain. There was no slack, but the links were big enough for handholds. The metal was cold.

Hierarch Guiderius is replying.

Hand over hand; it was not so hard for the first stretch, his fingers fit in the wide links, his toes, too. *Like a lizard, a lizard, a lizard*, he repeated over and over, up the wall, the chain cold and dry, sweat already on his back.

The red priest is speaking, proclaiming the duel.

He reached the second staple and hung there for a moment, putting his weight on his feet and letting his arms rest. *Don't look down, whatever you do. How far is it? Far enough to splatter.*

The chain slanted away, into the dome. That would be the hardest part. He was breathing heavily, waiting too long, putting it off.

"Go," he told himself. "Go."

"Uncle?"

Mopsa called again. "Uncle?"

"Watch the door!" he hissed, looking over his shoulder. It was a mistake. She was standing by the fire pit, miles away. Far enough to splatter.

Another fanfare blew outside, and he shouted: "Watch the door!" He could see her look up in surprise, her jaw drop. Then she shut it and ran back to the door.

Liam grabbed hold of the chain where it angled away from the wall and pulled himself up, flinging his legs over it, clasping with his knees. He was no longer a lizard, but a monkey, clambering upside down along a branch. Sweat poured down his forehead, slicked his fingers, itched on his shins. The lock picks in his purse clanked, and for a sickening moment he was sure they were going to fall out. Had he tied the purse closed? He stopped moving, listening, his eyes shut . . . there was no clatter, the purse must have been closed.

Then he was a monkey again, holding the image in his head—*No monkey would be stupid enough to do this*, he thought, and shoved the thought away—going farther up the chain.

If he tilted his head far enough back he could see the front of the temple, the tops of the doors, the middle of the doors . . . he pulled his head back before he saw the floor; it made him dizzy.

And he was almost there, he was at the edge of the dome, and one hand slipped, reaching for a grip. It dropped down, as if there were a weight attached, and he stared at it, the floor beyond it, amazed by its treachery.

They are squaring off to fight. They are bowing to each other.

Liam grunted and swung his shoulder, forcing the recalcitrant hand back up to the chain, making it grab, pulling again. He passed the lip of the dome, hanging at an even level with the cage. There was a shelf there, where the windows were, within reach, but if he stopped he would never go on, so he kept climbing. The muscles in his arms and legs were quivering, and his thighs hurt from grasping the chain, but he was almost there.

He kept telling himself that—*Almost there, almost there, almost there*—forgetting the monkey, focusing on the length of chain from which the cage hung. He would not need to go all the way to the top—he could reach from the chain he was on to the other, it was not far.

It's not far, just high.

There was more light in the dome. The sun was rising from behind banks of gray clouds in the east.

He reached once and missed, swinging on the chain, but regained his balance and reached again. His fingers slipped through a link, got a firm grip, and then he jumped.

The chain moved just a little, but it set the cage swinging, and he embraced the chain like a lover.

It's not strong enough. It's not strong enough. Gods, let it be strong enough.

It was, but it swung for long seconds while he clung there, gentle arcs that made his stomach turn over. Then it was finished, and he looked down into the cage, into the eyes of the stone gryphon.

They are starting to fight.

The creature was staring at him, settled back on its haunches with its beak open.

"Hello," he said weakly. "I am here to rescue you."

The gryphon squawked curiously, cocking its head.

"Never mind," he said, and let himself down the chain

until he was standing on top of the cage. It swayed a little under his feet, but when he lay down, spread-eagled, it stopped. The gryphon imitated him, lying flat but following him with his eyes.

The bars were set close together; he hooked an arm through them and twisted his body around to the edge. The cage tilted, and he slid over the side, pushing his feet between the bars. It tilted more, but the gryphon pushed itself against the far side, trying to balance their weight.

"Thanks," he told it, though the cage was still leaning at an uncomfortable angle. He would be done soon.

There was a lock, and it was indeed locked, but it looked simple. With his free hand—the other was starting to protest its unnatural position—he fumbled open his purse, drew out the largest of the picks.

He took three deep breaths with his eyes closed, then he fit the pick into the lock, jiggled it once, and heard the tumbler click.

Scaevola does not seem to be trying to win.

Liam dropped the pick, ignoring the sound, a second later, of its hitting the floor, and pulled himself away from the door of the cage, letting it swing open. The gryphon tensed, sleek muscles bunching under its gray coat, but it waited.

"Did he tell you I was coming?" Liam asked wearily. He had half expected the creature to leap at the door, knocking him from the cage. "Did he tell you to be so cooperative?"

The creature's tongue, black basalt and thin like a stiletto, flickered over its beak.

Then Liam climbed back up onto the top of the cage and lay there prostrate, exhausted. It hurt to breathe—the cold air in the dome seared his throat—but the bars were cool on his burning face. He heard a noise from behind him, tried to raise his head.

Scaevola is only playing with Strife's champion. He is not fighting. Cloten is shouting.

The noise behind was a window opening in the dome. A gust of bitterly cold air washed over him.

"Well," said a familiar voice. "Thank you, Rhenford. You seem to have saved me a great deal of trouble."

Liam forced his head up, looked over his shoulder.

"Hello, Tarquin."

The wizard stood in the window, smiling a little and chewing on a corner of his mustache. A stone gryphon shoved its head past Tarquin's waist and squawked at the one in the cage.

CHAPTER 17

SITTING ON THE shelf by the altar, Liam pulled on his boots as quickly as he could.

"I really wish you had left the rug where you found it," Tarquin was saying. He had used it to bring them down from the cage, and was now seated on it cross-legged, hovering just in front of Liam. "I had to go all the way back to the house to get it."

Three gryphons sat on the edge of the fire pit, staring impatiently at Tarquin's back, occasionally flaring their wings. Mopsa hung by the side of the altar, her eyes round with wonder. Liam had tried to reassure her, but Tarquin claimed his attention, ignoring the gryphons and speaking quickly.

He could hardly believe the wizard's presence. He had guessed at it the night before, had even considered digging up the grave in which he himself had placed the wizard to confirm it. But it was still amazing.

"I'm sorry about that. I did not know it was you."

"And you threw out all of my things! Cleared the shelves completely! Do you know how expensive dragon's tears are?"

"I did not know you would be coming back for them," Liam said, a little peevishly. "How was I supposed to know? I'm no wizard."

Tarquin regarded him critically. He was wearing the

blue robe in which he had been killed, but the tear from the dagger that had killed him was gone.

"No, you are not—that much is certain. Still, I am glad you took care of that lock. There's not much in my spellbook for locks. I had prepared a few spells, but they would have taken far longer than just picking the fool thing. I had no idea you were such an accomplished thief."

"It was a simple lock," Liam said. There were things he wanted to ask, but the wizard was speaking again.

"How do you find the house?" he asked, combing his beard with his fingers.

"It's very comfortable."

"I did not leave it to you, you know. I left no will. Fanuilh faked it."

Liam's jaw dropped, and he stammered for a second.

"I don't object," Tarquin said, raising his hand for silence. "I am happy it has fallen into good hands, and that the little beast has a competent master. I only tell you this because there are some things in it that I wish to give to other people. One other person, really. You will know who I mean when she arrives. She is to have my spellbook, and whatever she likes from the trophy room. The house I bequeath to you."

Liam stammered a little more.

"Do not thank me," Tarquin said, and then hesitated. "It is the least I can do after you . . . avenged me." Gratitude did not become the old wizard; he sounded awkward, and cleared his throat loudly. "I will have to go soon. I have made a list here of apothecary shops, and the things I took from them. I would like you to see that they are paid. I believe that is fair—if you hadn't thrown out all my supplies, I would not have had to rob them. As it was, they had very little that was of any use. Most of my spells were useless. I tried to tell them that"—he gestured toward the stone gryphons, still waiting patiently by the fire pit—"but

there was no one else who could help them. That thief
would have been perfect, but he was not adjusting well.
They can do very few things in this plane, you know. For
all of their apparent solidity, they are helpless as babes here,
and the iron of that cage completely threw them—it's a
base element, after all. They knew me from before I died—
I'm sure Fanuilh has told you about my experience in the
ethereal plane? It was there I met them—and they were
sure I could help. What could I do but try?''

The voice was the same, as were the slightly pompous
turns of phrase, but Liam could only stare, slack jawed, at
the man who should have been dead.

''Of course, I did not think it would be so difficult. All
those guards, and no material components—and no experience as a rescuer of helpless ethereal creatures. I was quite
at a loss.''

One of the stone gryphons cawed, and Tarquin waved
at it.

''Yes, yes, just a moment. In any case, Rhenford, my
little adventure is over, and they have to return me to the
Gray Lands. I cannot say I have enjoyed my return to life
very much, but there you are. I must go, and you must, too.
This temple will not long be a place for mortals.''

He held out his hand and Liam took it, held it.

''Wait. There are things I want to ask you—''

''You do not want to know what it is like to be dead,
Rhenford,'' the wizard said, gently disengaging his hand.
''As for the rest, you can make it up. Aedile Coeccias will
believe you implicitly.''

He spoke a single, strange word, and the rug started to
rise, heading for the dome.

''Wait!''

''You do not want to know,'' Tarquin repeated, and then
the gryphons took flight, shooting up to the dome and out

the window. The wizard followed them, angling the rug, and then was gone.

Liam slipped off the shelf, and blew out a heavy breath. "Who cares what it's like to be dead?" The list of apothecaries lay on the altar, along with Tarquin's spellbook; he picked them up, folded the list, and stowed it in the book. A broken link of chain dangled from its spine. "I want to know what he meant about mortals in the temple."

Mopsa came out from behind the altar. "Uncle?"

Liam turned his head, smiled uncertainly. "Well, pickit, what do you think of that?"

She jerked her thumb at the treasury chest. "They say there's a fortune in there."

"There may be," he agreed, "but that wasn't the job. The job was up there"—he pointed to the empty cage—"and as lookout, you are entitled to a tenth of the split, by the Legium. Worse luck for you there is no split. But I will make it up to you. Now stop looking at that, and let's go."

He had to take her by the shoulder to get her away from the altar; as it was, she kept throwing longing glances over her shoulder as they went.

"Who was the old man?"

"A friend of mine," Liam said, and refrained from adding: *Who's been dead for two months.*

"Another wizard?" She did not seem bothered in the least by Tarquin's appearance, or that of the extra stone gryphons. He wondered at her imperturbability.

"No, not another wizard. A real one. I am not a wizard."

"Ha! Y'are not a wizard!"

They were throwing long shadows; they looked like human forms cut from black velvet, stark against the brilliant light emanating from the altar behind them.

Liam stopped, holding Mopsa by the shoulder. He heard a sudden uproar from outside.

"Where's the light—" she began, turning under his hand to look at the altar. "Oh."

Closing his eyes, Liam mouthed a prayer, turned, opened his eyes.

Bellona stood on her own altar.

She glowed, but it was not like Duplin. It was as if she were made of diamonds, and all the light of the sun played over her, sparking a thousand random points of golden fire.

He had to squint just to face her, and even then he could not see her face behind the nimbus that coruscated around her. Still, he thought she was smiling.

She stepped off the altar, in a smooth stride, though that should not have been possible. She seemed no taller than he, but as she walked toward them, she reached up and tore the empty cage from the dome. It dwindled in her hand, till it was no more than a bauble. Each step sent a shock through the temple—through Southwark—but Liam and Mopsa were rooted to the spot, frozen by her radiance.

Then she was before them, and Liam slipped to his knees, overcome with terror and awe. He had been in the presence of a god before, and the feeling was the same: shame and exaltation, a foul taste in his mouth for which he was inexplicably grateful. He hung his head before her.

"Liam Rhenford," she said, and it sounded as though a thousand voices were speaking, as echoes flew and broke all around the walls of the temple. "You have done me service. For cleaning my house, I give you this."

She took his hand—the touch burned, but only briefly—and pressed the now-tiny cage into it.

"We do not forget," a thousand voices said, and then she walked past them, each footstep a tremor, and flung open the doors of her home.

Liam turned his head, shading his eyes, and saw her

face the crowd in the cul-de-sac. The sky was black, but Bellona was a new sun, bathing the terrified faces in golden light. Her words were like thunder—no, he realized, there was thunder, blazing from the black clouds overhead, but her words rang over it, like the shouting of an army.

His mouth was dry; his hand, where she had touched it, was swollen and puffy, burned brick red.

Mopsa had fainted.

Gods, he thought, *don't let her stay long.*

Coeccias echoed almost the same sentiment eight hours later. They were sitting in the barracks, drinking from mugs of beer—Herlekin's was closed, everything was closed.

"It'd not like me to have a god walk Southwark every day," he said, without a trace of irony. "There was a riot in the Warren—did I tell you? A riot. A gang of roughs, sure the end of the world was on them, or at least the end of the Duke's law. And the fires as well, but you know of those, eh?"

Liam nodded. He was smudged from head to foot with ashes, his clothes torn. Both of his hands were burned and aching.

Out of the unnatural darkness that had heralded Bellona's arrival, lightning had flared, striking fire to four spots in Temples' Court. In the confusion after her departure, the fires had raged unchecked. He had spent most of his day helping to fight them, hauling buckets from wells, clearing the buildings nearby, tending the burned. Over fifty people had been seriously injured; miraculously, none had died.

"Miraculously," he muttered, and stifled a groan.

"Eh?"

"Nothing."

Mopsa came to a few moments before Bellona disappeared, and ran off at his instruction. Once during the course of the day he had seen Scaevola, carrying an un-

conscious woman away from a burning building. There had
been no time to speak, only to nod and hurry on.

"They are going, you know," Coeccias said.

"Who?"

"Bellona's men. Going north, back to Caernarvon. Not
all of them, though. Just that Scaevola, and Cloten, and a
small guard. They're leaving Alastor behind, and some
men. The damned place'll be a shrine before the month is
out."

"What happened?"

"Eh?" Coeccias peered owlishly at him, tired and confused. Then his eyes cleared. "Of course, you were not
there. That Scaevola, he was only teasing the other, drawing
him on, fighting but not, if you see. And still the grandest
display of swordplay I've ever seen. And then the sky went
black, and She came out of her temple." He paused, taking
a long draw from his mug. "I don't know what She said—
it was like a roaring wind, an avalanche, the sea in a frenzy
on the Teeth. I could not understand a word. But by the
end, Cloten was on his face, begging pardon, and the only
person left standing was Scaevola."

They sat silent for a long while, each nursing his own
hurts, sunk in a strange, anticlimactic gloom. Then Coeccias
chuckled and reached into his pocket, pulling out a crum-
pled piece of paper. He tossed it at Liam but it fell short,
landed on the floor.

"What is it?" He did not want to make the effort to
bend over and pick it up.

"Acrasius Saffian's response. The courier brought it
during the hurlyburly. It says there's no conceivable way
that theurgy could break a wizard's wards. Better late than
never, eh?"

The Aedile laughed weakly. Liam made the effort to
pick up the paper—and threw it in the fireplace.

"Better never," he said, but he smiled as he said it.

"It was Tarquin Tanaquil, eh? All to free that gryphon?"

Liam had explained as much as he knew already; he could not muster the strength to go over it again. "Yes."

Tarquin, the bearded man that Cloten had seen, who had cast a sleep spell on the Hierarch after a gryphon knocked him down. Tarquin who had broken into the apothecaries' shops, looking for the materials with which to cast the spells that would free the captive gryphon. Tarquin who had broken into Liam's house to steal his own belongings.

"And you were in the temple, weren't you? When She came?"

Liam looked up, met his friend's glance. He thought of the tiny cage in the pouch at his belt.

No, I left before she came. No, I was hiding. No, I fainted as soon as she appeared.

"Yes," he said at last.

"Someday," the Aedile said, standing and groaning as he did so, "someday I'll want the whole tale. All that of Tanaquil and the gryphons, and of what you saw when She came. But there is more to do for me this day, and you should to your bed. Not today, then, or tomorrow. Or the day after. But someday. Will you?"

"I will," Liam promised, and stood as well.

They shook hands on the steps of the barracks, and Coeccias headed off on some unspecified errand.

Diamond was waiting patiently under the eye of a weary Guard. Liam climbed slowly into the saddle and urged the horse toward Auric's Park. He did not want to leave Southwark by the city gate. It was too close to Temple Street.

It began to snow as he trotted onto the road that led to his house, and Fanuilh fluttered down between the flakes, taking up its usual position in front of him.

"Well," Liam said. "Look who's here. The master forger."

I am sorry.

"Sorry? Sorry you gave me a magic house?" He was not annoyed. The house was his now.

I thought you would be displeased. In the days after Master Tanaquil died, it seemed to make sense. Who else would have it?

"Don't worry about it, Fanuilh. I am not displeased. Who else would have it, indeed? And Tarquin did not contest the will. I am just curious how you did it."

A simple spell, an illusion. It made a different will, duly registered, look like one for Master Tanaquil.

"And you cast it?"

Yes. As I told you, it is a simple spell.

They had reached the cliff path.

"Hmm. You'll have to show me one day."

They did not communicate after that; Liam stabled Diamond and trudged into the house in silence. He had brought Tarquin's spellbook from his saddlebags; now he placed it back on the pedestal from which it had been taken.

I cannot say I have been bored, he thought as he took off his dirty clothes in the library. *I have reunited a ghost with its body, and made the acquaintance of a den of thieves. I have stolen a gryphon, met a dead friend, done a service for a goddess. I have tried to convince half a city that I am not a wizard, and ended up convincing the whole city that that is precisely what I am. And I have properly inherited a magical house and a tiny dragon from their previous owner.*

His sleep, when he claimed it, felt richly deserved.